SHADOW'S CHOSEN

DARK WORLD MATES

OLIVIA RILEY

BEFORE

The city below sparkled. Its blue and orange lights spread across the planet like an infectious growth across skin. A ship floated above it in space, its nose aimed straight at the land below as if ready to strike the atmosphere and plunge. Inside, from the pilot's cabin, a dark purple shadow in the shape of a man watched the city pass by.

"Vesra is ready," came a voice. The shadow moved. It left the cabin and headed down the passage. As a door slid open into a circular, windowless room, the shadow stepped inside and waited for the door to close before striding over to the central terminal. With swift fingers, it accepted the call. The lights in the room dimmed as a holographic display blinked to life. A man, as still as a corpse, sat in a room unseen. His black eyes stared down the length of his sharp nose to judge the shadow before him.

"You have found the humans then?" said the seated man in a low, grated voice.

The shadow slowly raised a hand to its head and tapped two fingers at its ear.

The man leaned back. "Good." He studied the shadow carefully. "You never disappoint, do you, Nezka?"

Nezka lowered his arm. "Not you. Someone else maybe."

The man smirked, but his eyes remained cold. He took up a cup at his side but did not drink. "How many?"

"The tracker reads maybe twenty, thirty tops."

"Any women?"

Nezka hardly moved. "It's uncertain. The city is not their own, we know that much. My guess is they are an expedition team new to the planet. They are trying to make ties with the people here."

The man tapped at his glass. Nezka waited a few seconds before saying, "Do you still wish them extracted despite the deal being lost?"

The man's hairless brow lifted. "So you have heard about the nillium prince."

Nezka crossed his arms. "He's dead. And the houses are fighting for power in Xolis."

"It's true." The man's eyes narrowed as he finally lifted his cup with a pale gray hand and took a drink. As he set the cup down, his eyes brightened. "But despite this rather surprising turn of events, the nillium are still desperate in their need for children. The fighting will end with death, and they will become more aggressive in their need to repopulate. The humans will be the nillium's most precious resource. And our greatest bargaining weapon. I want them." The man's face darkened, his mouth set in a hard frown. "Get them to me. Whatever it takes."

Nezka bowed his head and moved back from the terminal until only the orange glint of his eyes could be seen in the dark. "Whatever it takes."

CHAPTER ONE

Elise sat on the top of the terrace wall, one knee drawn up to her chest while the other dangled off the edge, looking down to the bottom of a rocky beach with crashing waves. Ahead, the sun's light was beginning to brighten the horizon, a pale white beam illuminating a sickly green sky. Elise sighed, fist under her chin, watching in disappointment at another dull sunrise. She knew what to expect, and yet every morning she came out like clockwork to watch. It was her one moment for peace, but she preferred a beautiful orange glow under a blue dome over what she saw now. Terraformed planets were never that impressive to begin with.

Elise closed her eyes as the light hit her (a cold light she noted), and a soft breeze touched against her hair. She imagined the sound of laughter and her sister's voice in the distance along with the crash of waves. A memory of her and her sister running with sand kicking up her legs floated into her mind. She inhaled and a salty, not so pleasant ocean scent filled her nostrils. The memory faded quickly.

"Didn't take you for much of a meditator, Stirling," came a familiar voice behind her.

Jerico.

Elise couldn't help smiling as she opened her eyes and turned her head to see her teammate walking toward her, a broad shouldered, dark-complected man with a grin plastered on his face in greeting. Elise brushed tendrils of brown strands out of her eyes and spat out the ones that got stuck to her mouth as the breeze whipped her hair into her face. "Just in the mornings," she replied. "And I'm not really good at it."

"Yeah, me neither," said Jerico, shrugging, his smile dropping slightly. "They are ready for us, just so you know."

Elise stood, not so gracefully, brushing away a small dusting of sand that had somehow managed to stick to her white shirt and leggings. "Think I got time to dress?"

"I wouldn't worry about it."

Elise looked over to see Jerico wearing his black pants and gray shirt, sweat forming on his collar. He'd clearly been out on a run when he'd been called in. If the others were waiting too, it meant they were wanted now, not later.

"Let's do this then," Elise said and moved to follow him. They made their way across the terrace and passed a clean-cut lawn where a large statue of a gray and silver star with a heart cut into its center stood on display, the words "Grayhart" written beneath it along with "Discover. Learn. Connect." in small letters below. The large glass-sided building towered just ahead, alone against the dull cast of light brightening the sky. They passed beneath a covered archway before entering through a set of doors into a large foyer with a security desk at its center. The guard nodded in greeting as they walked on to the elevators.

"You think it'll be a boundary mission?" Elise asked as they took the elevator up to thirty. They had only been on one of those before, but it had been a false lead. No outsiders or newcomers, just gyda exiles and runaways outside standard earth territories.

"Doubt it," Jerico said, looking straight ahead. "Probably a stranding."

"Another?" Elise said, looking at him and shaking her head. "I hope not. You think they would learn by now they need security on those ships."

"You know how it is." Jerico crossed his arms. "They want to keep peace and look unresisting, even if it means taking heavy risks."

Elise snorted. "Yeah, like getting stuck on some messed up world where giant crabs eat off your legs."

"They were giant centipedes I heard."

Elise grimaced. "Jesus."

Jerico shrugged. "That team knew what they were getting into. I think Grayhart is finally getting the message, though. They need soldiers on their ships. Too bad they still have bad beef with the military, ever since Lazris."

Elise frowned but had no good response. She didn't blame the research facility for breaking off from the military back when they were once part of a branch called "S. E. A. R." or for being weary of making ties after the Lazris incident. But it seemed lately they were calling for a lot of aid with more of their expedition teams exploring farther past human territory and getting themselves into worse danger.

Good thing there were teams of operatives like Elise's team that were willing to give a helping hand. For the right price, of course.

The doors opened, bringing them out to a central lobby where the rest of Elise's team now stood waiting. Elise locked eyes with Adrien first, their team's leader, the perfect example of a cover model for the American cowboy—bright blue eyes, clean cut hair, and a smile that got hearts racing. He gave her his usual side grin as they approached. Elise noticed most of the team still wore casual wear like her and Jerico; only Adrien wore his full military uniform.

"Was she out on the beach again?" Adrien asked Jerico.

"I wasn't on the beach," Elise answered.

Adrien smiled at her. "Your hair is a mess."

"Thanks," she replied not so nicely.

He tried to reach a hand out to her, but Elise backed off. His hand lowered but not his smile. "I told them we would have been better prepared if they hadn't rescheduled the meeting."

"Forget it. They don't need to see us in full gear to know what they are getting," said Bruce, the hulking , tattooed mass standing beside her wearing gym shorts and a tank.

"Something changed you think?" said Reese opposite her. "Calling us in early like this?"

"Possibly," said Adrien.

"Better late than early. I'm ready to get the hell out of here," Amy, the tall brunette on Elise's other side commented. "This place is too clean cut, and it smells like pine cleaner."

"We will be very happy to get you on to your destination as soon as possible, Ms. Hendriz," came a voice behind her. They each looked around and saw a sharply dressed woman standing just outside a set of doors, as if appearing from nowhere. Her red dress suit hugged her body nicely, a silver star pinned above her left breast. Glittering black eyes assessed them with a sort of sly expression, though she did not readily smile. "If you will join me inside, we can begin." She gestured to the doors. Adrien took the lead, nodding to her as he passed; the others followed.

Inside the windowless room was a long oval table with a screen stretching around the length of the wall. Displayed on the table was a holographic map of an unknown city. The team filed in and took seats while the woman in red took her position at the front.

"My name is Sia Gray, Cohead of Grayhart along with my sister, Dahlia. I brought you here because we are in desperate need of a team of operatives such as yourselves with your unique set of experiences." Sia looked to Adrien. "It is my understanding that you all have had experience with missions involving non-human individuals, namely the gyda, am I correct?"

"That's correct," Adrien answered.

"As you are all well aware, Grayhart seeks to explore the vast realms of space and to find intelligent and advanced life. Ever since our merge with the gyda...and the incident at Lazris...we have been dedicated to this one goal, sending out teams on dozens of expeditions." The screen along the wall changed suddenly to that of an image of a ship taking off into the sky. A Grayhart ship. "Of course," Sia continued, " exploring other worlds comes with its own set of risks."

Amy murmured something (Elise was sure she caught the word "centipede" somewhere), and Adrien gave her a stern look.

Sia too looked over but did not falter. "As much as we try our best to prepare all our teams for their journeys, there are always inevitable dangers they will face. Some we have anticipated. Others not so much." Sia leaned forward, placing her hands lightly on the table. "The mission I have for you is a first of its kind, and it very well may be the most...unique mission you will face. All information from here on out must be kept confidential." Sia gestured to the holographic city on the table. "The city you see before you, as you might have guessed, is not human made."

It was hard for Elise and the others to keep an indifferent expression. Some looked confused, others stunned. As they studied the city, Elise and Adrien leaned in to get a better look.

"This is a real city?" Adrien asked.

"Yes. It is called Tyrminis, on a planet named Irosa. It has been recently located by Grayhart 16. The drogin—Irosa's inhabitants—welcomed them happily. From the information they have gathered and sent back to us, we have learned a great deal." The image on the screen changed to that of a planet with a dark brown and blue surface covered by endless amounts of blue and orange lights on one large mass of land near its equator, stretching from coast to coast.

A few cursed. Elise stared at the glittering orb, speechless.

"We have learned that this very planet has served for some time as a sort of midway point for travel. The drogin many years ago had the same curiosity as us in finding intelligent life. Only, instead, they sent a signal for others to come to them. Grayhart 16 caught on to this signal and found Irosa. They have been on the planet for a couple months now, gathering as much information as they could, building connections, and learning." Sia straightened, taking out a remote pointer from her suit pocket. "All was going well until three days ago when team 16 went into the lower sectors of the city and ultimately vanished."

Elise shifted in her seat. Before she could open her mouth, Jerico said exactly what she was thinking, "And you want us to find them?"

Sia nodded her head once. "That's right.

The team glanced around, some locking eyes, others staring at the image of the city.

"Assuming they are still alive, what makes you think we could ever find them?" Adrien said after a short pause. "That city looks about twice the size of Texas alone, and when you say lower sector, that tells me there are levels to this city. They could be anywhere."

Sia tilted her head slightly back as she regarded him. "That is very true. And trust me when I say we have been diligently working with the drogin to locate them. I was prepared to tell you that I was merely hoping for your best efforts with what information we could find, even if all we had was whatever the drogin told us and our trust in their honesty. However," Sia pointed her remote toward the city, and a small beacon of light blinked upward from a location near its eastern half, "only less than twenty-four hours ago, this signal started going off. We traced it and found it to be one of our own. We think it is one of the crew members who must have started the S.O.S. using one of their own devices and sending it toward our location."

"Great, that at least gives us something," said Jerico.

"So we fly down and grab em' up, no sweat," said Bruce. "Load up a few of the big guns in case there's trouble."

"I'm afraid it will not be that simple," Sia stated. She clicked her remote again so that the city came into focus and actual buildings became recognizable. Below the blinking light, Elise could see a large circular complex poking out from a network of smaller buildings and streets.

"What's that?" Elise said, pointing.

"That," Sia answered, "is one of the city's energy deposits. The building feeds a certain area of the city its power using whatever means the drogin have learned to harness their energy." Sia zoomed out so that the wider area around the building could be seen. "It is, unfortunately, no longer in their grasp."

"What does that mean?" Adrien said.

"It means they no longer have control of it," Sia said.

"How so?"

"The deposit, and a vast amount of the area around it, has been taken over by an underground crime organization the drogin have been battling with for years. And it has been a struggle." Sia returned the city back to a high aerial view where, this time, they could see many miles in each direction and where a set of walls enclosed the energy deposit and spread outward, encasing the city in sections. "These," Sia highlighted the walls in red, "were gateways leading to the various sectors of the undercity, but now they are overrun by crime lords, anarchists, and those working within the organization the drogin call the 'Red Blades.' The city officials have been fighting to keep them back at all costs, but still, the Red Blades find ways to spread and take over new territory. Now they control a vast section of the undercity, and all the drogin can do is try to keep them from spreading into the higher sectors."

"Why not take them out from above then? Or send in armed forces?" asked Jerico.

"Trust me—they have tried. And still do on occasion. But the city's ships mysteriously stop working when they get too close to the bottom. Likely, the criminals are using some sort of advanced electro-magnetic shields to depower the ships. As for armed forces, they have sent some in on occasion, taking back some of the territory in the process, but it is slow going. Thankfully, with the disappearance of our crew, the drogin are taking the matter very seriously. You will not be going in alone."

Elise looked to Adrien who glanced her way then turned back to Sia. "How do we know we can trust them? The drogin. We are outsiders to their city—what gives them cause to want to help us at all?"

"Good question, Captain Hauk. I think someone with better convincing could answer that for you." Sia turned to the screen along the wall and an image of a man—no, not exactly a man, but close—appeared before them. Elise blinked several times as she looked into the eyes of the alien, whose large, almond shaped eyes regarded each of them in turn.

For a second, Elise thought he looked like a rather cranky looking dog (namely of the larger breed like a Doberman) but with no long snout, just a bump and two slits for a nose and dog-like cropped ears on each side of his hairless head. There were no whites to his eyes, just golden-brown pupils encased in a watery gray. The more she studied him, the more her mind tried to piece him into a human-like image, and he started to look a little like some kind of fantasy crea-ture, like those orcs or werewolves she'd seen in the videogames her brothers use to play.

The drogin sat at a terminal in a room not much different from their own. He bowed his head, and Sia did the same.

"This is Councilman Qorey," Sia said. "He has been helping us and working with their chief of enforcement to stifle the crime of the undercity."

The councilman began to speak in his foreign tongue, and the QS translator built into the call system kicked in.

"Pleased to meet you all." He looked to Adrien and said, "We completely understand your apprehension. We have been working to establish a connection with humans since the first team arrived. The drogin pride themselves on integration and melding of cultures from all across our known universe. There are many who have come from all over, and they have made a place in our great city. We had hoped the same could be said for those of Earth. We also have a common enemy, one whose power and influence we let spread too far. It was our own fault for we didn't take such a threat seriously until it was too late. But now we are ready to fight them and stop these criminals once and for all. We want to help our human friends. Teams of professionals such as yourselves will be at your side as you make your way into the undercity, and, with our elite tech, we are confident we can make the vermin scatter to all corners, bringing those responsible into our hands. And brought to justice."

Elise pursed her lips and stifled a laugh. Adrien gave her a warning glare, and she subtly placed a hand over her mouth. Whether by the translator's doing or just how the drogin talked, his words came out dramatic and over the top, as if the speech were rehearsed for a large crowd, not a handful of soldiers. The drogin even smacked his fist in the palm of his other hand, a clearly human gesture he was trying to use for their benefit. The effort wasn't lost on them, but it still looked extremely forced. A few cleared their throats, and Sia raised her brows at them. The drogin didn't seem to notice.

"If you come," the drogin continued, "we will equip you with our most advanced weaponry and armor along with all necessary supplies. You will not be alone in this fight."

"Thank you, Councilman Qorey," Sia replied when she was certain he was done speaking. "We will continue to stay in contact through this process."

"My pleasure." The councilman bowed his head again, and Sia returned the gesture before his image disappeared.

"That was...very convincing," Amy said, and a few burst out in a fit of quiet giggles.

Sia's mouth curved ever so slightly as she looked at each of them. "It's a dangerous mission I ask of you, but I don't ask it lightly. Grayhart cannot afford to see another team vanish and come back with so few or, worse, none at all."

Elise and the others turned quiet again.

"You mean like Grayhart 12?" Adrien said suddenly. They had heard about that team. Gone too far out of human territory only never to be heard from again.

"A strange coincidence...or perhaps a sign from a higher power one might say," Sia said in a sad tone. "Only a few days before team

16 vanished, we got a message from a crewmember that had been aboard Grayhart 12. Only three somehow made it back. They are returning here to give us a full report and will likely return to Earth or a civilian world after. Who knows what horrors they faced." Sia leaned against the table to look down at the city. "I would not see it happen again. For that, I am desperate. If you agree to go, to find this team and bring them back to us safely, I will pay you triple the usual price."

This got their full attention. No one said a word and waited instead on Adrien's order.

"We need a minute to discuss," he said after a moment.

Sia nodded. "Of course." She straightened and made for the door. "Take the time you need. I will be right outside."

As soon as the door closed, the whispers flew.

"Fuck me, that's forty million to the lot of us," Bruce said in a loud hiss.

"Yeah, except this feels a hell of a lot like a suicide mission," Amy said in turn.

"You heard the drogin, though. He said they would give us some of their weapons. I'd be down for a trade," Jerico added.

Elise looked to Adrien, who met her gaze. "That's a lot of money. Probably could live nicely on it if you don't go ham at the bar every week," she said honestly.

Adrien thought it over then raised his voice over the others. "We'll vote on it." Everyone quieted up and nodded in agreement to a vote. "All those in, raise your hand."

Bruce's and Jerico's went up immediately, followed by Reese, Helen, and Tom. Adrien raised his and looked to Elise. "One more mission," he said.

Elise knew she was going to raise her hand no matter what. But deep inside, she was hesitant. Amy—who hadn't raised her hand—wasn't completely wrong. It would be a difficult mission. But not impossible. If they made it back...

You saved us...our hero...thank you...

The memory of the little voice still rang true in her head, even when her heart jolted at the thought. It took effort not to think of the past—of the little voice laced with fear and the dark jungle where it had come from—as she raised her hand.

"Looks like a clear winner...send her back in," Adrien ordered Tom.

As Tom opened the door and Sia entered the room, Adrien stood and nodded his head. "We're in."

CHAPTER TWO

NEZKA SAT SILENTLY AT HIS PILOT SEAT IN THE DARK CABIN, watching the lights of the city pass by. A soft blue light blinked at him, but he ignored it, his eyes narrowing in on a map of the city displayed before him on the console.

Eight turns of the planet. Eight days since he had spoken to Vesra in the callroom. Eight days since he had prepared his team to gather the humans. And as soon as they were geared up to go, what should happen but for the humans to go missing somewhere in the lower levels of the city. Five days now passed since their disappearance, and there hadn't been a single sign. What should have been a simple extraction now was the very opposite.

Nezka's hand, which had been resting calmly on the arm of his seat, slowly tightened into a fist.

Fuck.

The blinking blue light continued to flash and, without looking down, Nezka tapped his finger on the pad to take the call.

"Ruumas is back," came a low voice, "with one of them."

Nezka ended the call and lurched out of his seat, making his way out of the cabin and straight down the hall to the end of the ship. The sounds of moans, muffled by the door, grew clearer as Nezka entered into the holding dock where a small pod-ship sat amongst crates of supplies. Ahead, a group dressed in silvery black armor suits similar to his own stood around a creature with its back turned, crouched on the floor with its head bowed. Its clothes were ripped, droplets of blood staining the collar. As Nezka approached, the group stepped back save for one who barely flinched as Nezka stepped close to meet him.

The skra, an amphibious looking male with dark green skin, blinked at him. "He's stable. Just a little roughed up."

Nezka didn't look away. "Did anyone see you?"

The skra lifted his webbed hand and shook it once. "No."

Nezka turned and looked down at the creature before him, one of the cityfolk—a drogin. He crouched down, and the drogin lifted his head enough to see him, letting out a pitiful hissing cry. He spoke in a stuttering, unrecognizable speech, shaking.

Nezka gestured to his team, and one of his men came around and took hold of the drogin's head, placing a voicer across the drogin's mouth—a simple mask with a vent at the front. It took a few moments until the drogin's speech became clear, translated through the voicer.

"Please...please..." came a grated, wheezing voice. A small earpiece was shoved into the drogin's ear, and Nezka waited a short moment longer before speaking.

"What do you know about the humans?"

The drogin looked at him, confused. His eyes shot all around, and Nezka took hold of his chin to bring him back to focus on him. "Where are the humans?"

"Hu...Humans...?"

"That's right. They came here not too long ago. The team that was new to the city."

The drogin looked away then back. "I don't know...where they are."

Nezka's hand tightened on the drogin's jaw. "I think you might. You're a watchman at one of the gates. You saw them go into the undercity." His head tilted as he examined the shaking creature before him. "What do you know?"

The creature whimpered and said nothing until Nezka shook him slightly, and he yelped. "They...they went in to gather information about those living below. They didn't come back." The drogin tried to shake his head away, but Nezka held him tight. "The undercity is filled with a foul breed. They were warned not to go."

"Who took them?" Nezka asked calmly.

"I don't know for sure... I don't, I swear!" The drogin panicked as a knife came into his periphery. "But it was likely them! The Red Blades! They control...the undercity. They know everything!"

"The Red Blades...?"

"The criminal underlords. Their leader...no one has seen. No one knows...where they hide."

The knife lowered, and the drogin's breathless pants quieted only slightly.

"What else?" Nezka said patiently.

"Wh—what else? I...don't know."

"Are they looking for them? Your people?"

The drogin seemed to think on this for a moment, and then his eyes brightened. "Yes. Yes, the city officials have been looking. And there is talk of a bounty."

"Bounty?"

"They are looking to put a huge sum on the heads of the leaders and criminals responsible. And on the heads of the Red Blades. You...can see for yourself with my Ulink."

Nezka rifled through the drogin's clothes until he found what he assumed the drogin was talking about. A thin, oval-shaped device with a simple interface. "This is tied to your network?" he asked.

The drogin nodded, and Nezka pressed against the device, lighting up its screen. "Ruumas, take this and download all information then link to their network." The skra took it as ordered and disappeared. Nezka grabbed hold of the drogin. He picked him up, forcing him to his feet.

"Please...please...don't kill me," he begged.

"I can dispose of him," said Silfres, the lygin watching nearby, a large feline with a scar across his nose and a dark mane.

It would be easier. But Nezka was just starting to get back into a good mood with this new set of information, and for that, he felt the drogin deserved to live. He let go of the creature, who stumbled back. "Wipe his brain. We will drop him somewhere."

Without question, the lygin took hold of the drogin and dragged him away. Nezka looked to the others who waited his command: Wruk, a grex with a wide lizard face and yellow eyes, Vijnn, a corax with a shark-mouthed grin, his back fins trembling in anticipation, and Jazlin, a nillium female with pale gold skin and crown-like points on either side of her head, adorned in a set of leathers. Some of Vesra's finest men and women at his beck and call.

"Make for the central callroom," he ordered. "I will meet you there."

The grex and the corax went as told. The nillium female didn't move. Nezka tilted his head at her, and she smiled.

"Leadership looks good on you, Nezka," Jazlin said as she leaned against an equipment box. "Surprising for one who only ever works alone. Always in Vesra's shadow."

Nezka stared her down then moved in, coming up close against her. "I know something else that looks good on me," he said low and watched as the nillium female tensed, her breath catching. She only faltered for a moment, her skin darkening slightly along her cheeks, but her composure returned quickly, and she lifted her leg up, encircling it around Nezka's lower waist.

"Oh, I remember," she said softly, almost purring. "And I wouldn't mind making you look good again."

Nezka was sorely tempted. And he certainly wasn't ashamed to do it here and now, whether anyone saw them or not.

A memory of a nillium's threat whispered in his mind, and he almost laughed.

That pompous ass of a prince really thought he had everything under control. The nillium men believed all their women were housed in their care, like pampered prisoners on their sacred planet. But many didn't care for that life, and more than a few slipped out any way they could. Even if it meant being in the care of a crime lord like Vesra.

Yes, the nillium prince really thought he had his women safe from others' prying, curious hands. He had threatened Nezka not long before his death to stay far away. Funny, since Nezka had already had a taste.

And it was good. Jazlin was lovely, there was no doubt. But as his hand touched against her thigh, trailing slowly upward, he had a vision of someone else in her stead.

No, not really someone else. Something else. Something new...something different...softer. But less tame.

The first time he laid eyes on a human woman, he had been curious to say the least. And he hadn't felt that level of curiosity in many years. The ones imprisoned on the nillium's home world were as strange as they were alluring, in the way one would feel discovering something fresh and unique and not entirely unpleasing to the eye. Though they had a build similar to a nillium woman, they looked less proud, less rigid, their skin not golden, nor scaled or rubbery, but soft. He'd only glimpsed the humans from a distance, save for one girl who he had a brief encounter with. He had been surprised and pleased to find a fiery spirit in her, small but promising. Had he wanted to take her to a room and see what that spirit could do? Yes. But only because she was new and intriguing. The feelings were no deeper than the many other times he had wanted (and had) a woman of a different kind.

He might have considered persuading her to a bed (but never to force—he hated the idea of a struggling, unpleased woman) because he could tell she was curious of him as well, though she hid it behind her fear and anger.

As soon as he smelled the nillium male on her like a bond mark and sensed that she was with child, he dissolved such a temptation. He didn't like playing with others' mates.

Still, the want was there. The human girl had tried to stop him from hunting for others of her kind, but, even if he wasn't under orders from his master, Vesra, or under a loose contract with the nillium prince, Korzien, he would have gone looking for them. For curiosity's sake. And by some strange pull he had yet to understand. A larger promise somewhere far away.

He gripped at Jazlin's upper thigh, bringing her closer, hearing her sharp intake of breath in his ear, and sighed. "Another day. As much as I'd like to, I worry we have little time. And we both know how impatient a man Vesra is." He drew himself away from her, gently pulling her leg from his waist and setting it down on the ground. "But you won't be far, and there will always be time enough after." He gave her one of his wicked smiles. Curved fangs grazed his lower lip as he touched the side of her face like a lover.

Her gaze turned on him in disappointment, but she did not press for him to stay, and he did not linger.

The temptation to draw her against him, to feel her smooth touch, was there still as he turned and went out of the room, but he pressed onward, ignoring his instinctual wants for more important matters. He walked down the passage, making a sharp left at a set of doors which slid open at his approach. Inside the small circular room, his team stood or sat around a large round slab in the center currently displaying a holographic image of the planet that slowly turned below them. Irosa.

Nezka approached the display and tapped on the planet so that it focused on a specific area of the city. The door behind him opened again, and Jazlin settled herself against one wall. Ruumas, who had been sitting at a console on the far side of the room, turned in his chair.

"The data is transferred, and we have access to their network," he stated. "I've looked into their outer transmissions and found several messages. One includes the bounty the drogin mentioned. They are seeking those even outside their system. Perhaps their own are inferior."

"Or they don't wish to risk their people's lives," hissed Vijnn. "Better to seek others to take the bait and see if any come out alive."

Nezka stood silently thinking as he stared down at the map before him. He tapped on it again, and the city focused in closer. "This is the gate through which the humans entered." He pointed to a city pass into the lower levels. "If there is any trail, it will start there."

"We could sneak in and use the pulse tracker to search around," said Wruk, eyeing the map as well. "Wouldn't be too hard to catch a trace."

"Except, according to the information in this Ulink, the gates between the upper and lower levels are being heavily watched and guarded," Ruumas replied. "They'll find us eventually and wonder what a bunch of outsiders are doing roaming the borders trying to get into the undercity."

Nezka stayed quiet again, thinking. His eyes narrowed as he studied the endless passageways and maze of roads through the undercity and the gates between them along with tunnels and bridges leading to different sectors. They couldn't fly over without being seen, and the city's security was likely advanced enough that they could override the ship's systems, forcing them to land. If they were to have any leeway into the lower sectors, they would have to put up a front.

"What else do they say about the bounty?" Nezka asked.

Ruumas swiveled back to his screen and searched the network. "They are looking for teams or individuals to send in. Currency seems like a good price...mainly for the heads of the leaders of gangs, including these Red Blades. There are only a few pictures and names but not much else."

Nezka crossed his arms. "We go in seeking this bounty. That will give us access to the undercity and gain trust with the city leaders. Let them think we are there to exterminate their enemies. But it will be the humans we are looking for."

The others seemed to grow excited by this prospect.

"A double mission?" said Vijnn, rubbing his scaly hands together. "I like it."

"Do we get to take the heads of the gang leaders if we like?" asked Jazlin from the back.

Nezka smiled. "If you want. But only if it doesn't deviate from our true goal. Understood?"

The others barked in agreement.

The door of the room slid open once more, and Silfres stepped inside. "You won't believe it," he said to Nezka. Then he looked over to the skra. "Ruumas, check the map on the pulse tracker, and bring it up on the main display."

Ruumas opened up the map as the lygin moved to Nezka's side. "I happened to catch the signal going off as I was checking the ship's radar," Silfres said. "The drogin's mind is clean by the way."

"The humans were found?" Nezka could feel his spines tingling in hopeful excitement.

"Not the ones we are looking for, unfortunately," the lygin said, and in that same moment, the map on the slab changed to that of Irosa, tiny but still visible. Not far from it, just outside its orbit, was a steady pulse slowly making its way closer. Silfres gestured toward the pulse. "But new ones just arrived."

The team went silent. They looked to Nezka, and his eyes flickered to each of them. He looked down at the small pulse for a long moment as if it were a signal calling to only him. He traced a finger along his neck, across the beaded necklace that hung close to his skin, and smiled. "Gear up. We are going down."

CHAPTER THREE

Elise's seat jolted and shook as her team's ship hit the atmosphere. A dull roar deafened her as they fell and the engines fired, tendrils of flickering sparks hitting the glass.

A nice way to wake from a nap.

The halo-shaped device that had rested firmly across her head lifted slowly, and she blinked several times, coming out of her sleep. The others sat in rows on each side of her, all facing the window that gave them a clear view of the vast city coming in fast before them. The ship began to slow, and, from the corner of her eye, Elise saw the ship's controls being taken over by an unknown pilot. Likely those at the city terminal making sure the ship landed safely at the docks. When they hit the ground, it was with a soft bump and nothing more. Smooth landing.

They waited for the ship to decompress and power down before unlocking from their seats. Though the flights were faster now than they had been some years ago, Elise still felt like she'd been sitting in the seat for months, even though it had only been a few days. She stretched her legs and unhooked from her seat then slowly rose, watching the others do the same.

A few groaned and cursed. Bruce immediately did a few leg lunges.

"I still hate flying," said Jerico, not far away. "My stomach feels inside out."

"I told you, you should have taken a pill, man," said Reese, groaning as he bent his back.

Helen came around and checked their vitals. "You all will live. As usual. Jerico, don't throw up in the empty storage again. Use a waste box." Helen aimed her little scanner device at Elise and nodded her head. "All clear."

The doors opened with a hiss, and they each took up their bags and gear and stumbled out onto the docks. The area was huge, larger than any of the docks at home, spanning several football fields in length. But surprisingly, Elise saw few other ships parked with theirs. Only one other was stationed close by. A large, black ship, sharp and ominous. As they gathered outside on the platform, Elise couldn't help stare at it curiously.

"Whoever owns that one must be a scary son of a bitch," said Tom, next to her.

Elise eyed the ship seriously for a second longer then shrugged. "Or they're just edgy," she said as she swung her bag over her shoulder.

From a doorway not far ahead of them came a set of drogin. They bowed their heads once as they approached, and Elise and her team did the same.

"Welcome to Tyrminis," one said, a tall drogin with pinkish brown skin, caramel colored eyes, and tufts of fur-like hair across her skull. By the slender build, Elise was certain it was a female. The woman greeted them slowly, but Elise and the others could understand perfectly well. Sia, with the help of the city official, Qorey, had linked their headsets to the drogin language program. While they traveled, they learned and memorized the drogin speech. The technology was advanced and brilliantly impressive. What would have taken a few months with Earth's tech took only a few days, preparing them to interact with the people of Irosa without issue.

"My name is Toni. Please follow us." As Toni turned back toward the door, the two other drogin at her side helped carry their bags.

They entered a large burgundy building made of a steel Elise could not identify but that reminded her of the chrome of a car. The doors slid open for them just like the ones at home, but the glass making up the windows and walls of the interior were of a darker shade. Some, Elise noticed, were darker or lighter depending on what rooms they were trying to hide. Everything seemed to be made of glass or metal, even the floor and ceiling. The lights which made up the frames of the ceiling and walls brightened as they walked by. When they came to a circular main foyer, Elise stretched her neck up and saw a kaleidoscope of colors and lights at the very top, basking the area in reds, blues, and purples.

"The energy they would need for all this has to be insane," whispered Amy, close by.

"And we thought our cities were wasting power," Elise mumbled. As her eyes studied the various levels above, shaping the interior in a cork-screw design, she noticed no plants or fountains which usually adorned human foyers. Just many lights and a few screens displaying neon-lit images advertising strange products.

"Your rooms are prepared." Toni gestured to the floors above. "My two assistants will guide you to them, and you can get settled in. When you are ready, please return to this floor. Come midday, the city officials will call a meeting with all active teams. There are others who will be joining you at this meeting, all whose mission involves the undercity."

Before any could question her about anything else, Toni left them, and her assistants beckoned them to follow.

* * *

Their rooms were far more luxurious than what was necessary for a team that was likely only spending one night in them. No one complained, of course, though Elise felt a little uncomfortable at the idea of sleeping in a bed that was twice her size and having what was equivalent to an apartment all to herself. As she cleaned up in the obnoxiously large bathroom then dressed out of her flight suit and into a simple pair of leggings, T-shirt, and slim jacket, she observed the cityscape outside her bedroom window. There was no doubt that it was breathtaking. And intimidating. The smallest buildings she could see were taller than the ones on earth. And the largest looked like they touched the sky, clouds sweeping past them indifferently. As Elise looked down, she saw a web of bridges and streets. Surprisingly, they were not bombarded by cars but what seemed to be trains. Overhead were several flying vehicles going in and out of the towering skyscrapers. It seemed their main sources of transport in the higher levels were trams or small ships. One railway was partially hidden by a series of tunnels, and when she saw the train speed by, she almost missed it. It flew by just as fast if not faster than the bullet trains on Earth. What cars did hug the roads were very small—most even looked like bikes. The streets and bridges were crammed otherwise with people. When Elise focused in on the cityfolk, she was shocked to find some were not drogin but other species, those from other far-off planets. A few looked like cats, others like lizards. All were colorful and unique in a sea of moving bodies, walking along a backdrop of neon lights and brightly colored words.

She stared down at the scene for a long time, thinking about the people below and those at home. How strange and vast the universe was. And how little she felt within it.

Her hand instinctively reached out beside her but caught at nothing. She turned her head and looked at the empty space with disappointment.

She wished her sister were there.

A knock came at her door. Taking a deep breath and putting on her tough girl face, Elise turned from the window and headed over to the door to let whoever was on the other side enter.

Jerico smiled back at her, his hand resting on the side of the door. "Adrien is calling us down." He entered the room and whistled. "Wow, you got a way better view than me. All I got was the side of the building over."

"It's crazy, isn't it?" Elise said, shaking her head as she peered back out the window. "It's so..."

"Overwhelming," Jerico answered. "Yeah. To think we will be down there by tomorrow morning. Well, okay, judging by the planet's rotation, about twenty-six hours give or take."

"You think we're ready?" Elise asked then looked over at him.

Jerico shrugged. "As ready as we'll ever be. Why? You having second thoughts?"

Elise's gaze fell back to the window. "I...no. I don't know. It's just...different."

"Well, we are about to get the full run down. And we won't be going in alone, remember."

Elise nodded but inside she was uncertain. She just had this strange feeling. Not awful. She wouldn't commit to that. But strange. She'd never felt it before on any mission, but maybe it was because in the past she knew what she was getting herself into. She knew this would be a challenging mission, and that in itself didn't bother her. She was always up for a challenge. Her father had raised her to be prepared for anything—attacks, strandings, storms...everything. And it wasn't like they hadn't been preparing. They had gone through the whole plan over and over while they readied to depart. They had learned the language, they had learned what they needed to about the planet and its people, and they were about to meet the other teams who would be joining them. Sure, there was always the risk of failure or death that put any soldier on edge. But this felt different. Something about the mission made her feel off.

But she'd never backed down before, and she wasn't about to now. She had her team with her. Together, they'd be unstoppable. So, with that thought, she brushed the feeling away like it was a pesky bug and smiled at Jerico.

"I know that smile. You're ready to kick ass." Jerico patted her back then drew her out of the room. "Let's do this."

She followed him across the hall to the elevator and took it down. Just like at the Grayhart facility, they reached the main foyer and found the team waiting for them.

They were not alone.

Elise felt the current of uneasiness in the air as soon as she stepped inside. There were drogin about now, who she could only guess were the city militia or law enforcement. They wore faded black and gray uniforms, the closest to casual wear that wasn't full on armor. They had white armbands with an insignia on each—a shield with a circle in its center. They stood nearby in their own groups, whispering or talking low, their faces turning as they peered over to the far wall.

Her team stood silent, rigid, their eyes drifting over to the same place the drogins' gaze wandered; over to a different group sitting by a thick glass wall, just below an ad for some kind of bubbly soft-drink, the glow basking them in red.

Elise felt herself stop short as she looked at them. They were definitely not from the city. She was certain. By their strange silvery black armor and the way the others seemed to distance themselves from them, she knew they must be outsiders. And boy, did they look like a gnarly, violent sort. Each one unique but also giving off a similarly wicked sort of vibe. Especially one in the middle to whom they seemed to gravitate closest. A scary son of a bitch if she ever saw one. With his dark purple skin painted or perhaps tattooed with white streaks across his arms and neck and along his face like a skull. Pointed ears, white hair, and—perhaps the most disturbing to her—large wolfish eyes, orange like fire. He studied her team with a sharp interest until Jerico called her name, and his gaze turned to her.

Their eyes locked, and Elise found herself frozen. Just like a deer in the presence of a wolf. He grew still too as he noticed her, and it seemed time stopped briefly as they stared at each other.

"Elise, come," called Adrien in his rough voice, one she knew he only used when he was agitated by something. The purple devil tilted his head, and Elise forced her eyes away, making her legs move till she found herself in the shelter of bodies that were her team. She could never remember freezing like that. But then she'd never encountered anyone who looked like death before either.

The team huddled closer than usual, and Elise could feel the tension in each of them. She felt it too, in herself.

"Who the fuck do you suppose those lot are?" said Reese in a low mutter.

"I don't know, but they don't look friendly," said Amy.

"They look like the type we should be fighting down in the gutter city below," Bruce commented.

"We shouldn't judge," Adrien said, quieting them. "Remember, we are outsiders here too." He didn't sound convincing.

The others didn't comment, and Elise had to keep herself from glancing back toward the far wall. A heat had begun to simmer at her back, along with that telltale uneasy feeling of being watched. When she dared peek back over, she saw the dark alien still watching her. She shuddered and quickly looked away.

From another doorway, Toni and her assistants entered. They went over to the group of armored aliens at the wall and bowed. She began to speak to them, and they seemed to understand. Elise noticed a light blinking in their ears as they turned their heads. Some kind of earpiece that she assumed was a sort of translator.

The group got up, and a set of doors opposite opened, revealing a short tunnelway to another section of the building. The drogin began to move toward it.

They followed inside, Elise keeping her eyes focused ahead instead of at the group of creepy aliens that lingered behind, knowing if she looked, she'd see Mr. Death watching her again. Her jaw clenched, and her fists tightened, but she refused to meet his glare as they walked past. It occurred to her as they made their way down the tunnel to the next door that the ship they had seen parked at the dock must have belonged to this dark group. What were they doing here? And why? Surely, it wasn't to aid them. They didn't even know who they were.

As the door at the end of the tunnel slid open, Elise and her team stepped into a dimly-lit, dome-shaped amphitheater with a circular dais at the very center. The team of drogin took their seats near the front, and Elise and her team took seats along the back wall, while the dark group of aliens took theirs by the door. As they each settled in, Toni and her assistants waited by one wall until a pair of drogin in formal uniforms similar to a military commander's entered and started for the central dais. One of them, Elise recognized.

"High day to you all," said Councilman Qorey, looking very much the same as he had when they last saw him. "I am Councilman and Official Qorey, and this is Official Oryn. We are city sector officers and heads of security and enforcement." He brought up his hand which was gloved in a sort of strange metal, and, with a quick wave of his fingers, a large holographic image of Irosa appeared above him. "You have all come or been brought here for different reasons, each one connected to a larger goal. Approximately twelve days ago, by Irosa's cycle, a group of explorers from the earthian territories called humans trekked into the lower sectors of the city and have hence disappeared. As most of you from Tyrminis know, for several years we have been battling the various gang lords and their breed, closing off gates, trying to fight their spread. It has been, as you know, a hard fight." Qorey gestured with his gloved hand, and the planet grew until the city came into view above them. "They have taken over nearly a quarter of the east and south sector of the undercity. It is time we took it back." The city came in even closer, focusing on the same section Elise and her team saw back at Grayhart, the area stretching from the first gate where the Grayhart team disappeared to the energy deposit many miles off and past several other gates, bridges, and tunnelways. "It is our hope to not only find the missing explorers but also to retake the undercity and take out the enemies who have stolen it from us. We still start at the edge of this sector." Qorey pointed to the gate. "This is where their territory begins. We will go in as one. Most of you have been hired to merely take out the threats." He looked over to the team of outsiders and bowed his head. "We thank those willing to aid us. You will be well compensated for each mark that you take out. As for the team from Earth, they are here to find and rescue their own. It is our job to help them as well." Qorey waved his hand again, and the gate zoomed in closer, followed by a blue line drawn across the map. From here, he explained their plan. They would go in through the tunneled gateway together and travel straight across, each team taking siege to the sector points and clearing a path for Elise's team. They would search each stronghold for signs of others until they came to the energy deposit, where hopefully, they would find the lost Grayhart team. It sounded simple enough, and Qorey seemed confident that only the gangs would cause trouble. Those living there should stay out of their way.

"We will depart tomorrow morning at dawn," concluded Qorey. "All groups should be ready and waiting at the east dock. Officer Oryn will be there to command you." Qorey waved his hand, and the map returned back to an image of Irosa. Before they rose from their seats, Toni stepped up to the dais, bowed, and spoke quickly to the officials. Qorey gestured with his hand, and Toni slipped away. "Yes, I forgot," he said. " To all who would like to prepare for their mission or who would like to test out our armory, training grounds have been situated on the mid-level common rooms. An assistant will show those who are unfamiliar with our weaponry how to use them properly. It is also a good place to interact and get to know each other before tomorrow. I highly recommend you all visit sometime today. If you have any more questions, you can contact us through your Ulink which can be found in your rooms. Thank you and good luck to you all." With that, Qorey stepped off the dais and headed out of the theater. The drogin began to disperse, a few eyeing them curiously, some nodding their heads.

Elise looked around and caught Toni once again speaking to the team of outsiders. Elise couldn't hear the female drogin, but she caught her gesturing to her ear and saw a small triangular device in her hand. The purple alien (their leader, Elise presumed) took it and replaced his earpiece with the device Toni had in hand. Each of her assistants offered up more of the ear devices, and the team took them. She said a few more words then bowed, and the team left.

"Hey, Elise, you coming or what?"

Elise looked up and saw her team already moving out of the theater and Jerico giving her a weird look as she sat alone. She leapt up and followed them out, only to stop at the door where Toni now stood.

"What did you give to them? That other team," she asked as Toni bobbed her head at her. When the drogin gave her a confused look, Elise pointed to her ear.

"Oh, those are our most latest and advanced translators," Toni explained. "They not only let the user understand the common tongue but also send transmitters to the brain to aid in memory and speech. Very similar to what was given to you and your team while you traveled here. In a couple days or less, depending on how fluent they are with language, the team will be able to understand and speak drogin."

"So, they really aren't from here?" Elise asked curiously.

"They are not. From what we gathered, they come from Xolis. Thankfully, we are quite familiar with those within that territory. Many immigrants and refugees from that empire have made a home here," Toni said.

Elise thought that over for a long second and became both fascinated and disturbed. *Empire.* Just when she thought it was shocking enough to learn about this advanced civilization, knowing that there were others was...intimidating to say the least. She wondered if the Grayhart team had known and how much the facility was keeping secret. Whatever it meant, Earth and its territories were in for a huge wake-up call. "So, they...have come all this way to help us?" Elise asked.

"For the bounty," Toni said. "Now, if you will pardon me, I must attend to other matters. Please enjoy your stay." With the room emptied, Toni let the door close shut then turned away. Elise stood there for a moment longer. *So they are bounty hunters*, she thought then slowly slipped back toward the elevators where her team waited.

"You going to the training room too?" Bruce asked as Elise came up beside him in front of the elevator doors.

"Is that where everyone else is going?" Elise asked.

"Not me," said Helen. "All the medical supplies will be available on site and a short video on how to use them. I'm sticking to my room and having a long bath."

"I'll pass too," said Tom. "I wanna know what kind of tech they got. And what their network is like. Supposedly these Ulinks they provide are like our ISpads, only smarter."

"So, you in?" Adrien asked her as the elevator door opened.

Elise stepped into the car alongside them. "I'd like to see what they got," she said. Judging by everything else she'd seen so far, the drogin's weapons were likely way better than her team's. And if they wanted to be on the same playing field as the others, they'd be wise to learn how to use them.

"I heard one of the drogin mention sparring pits," said Reese. "Wonder how well they fight."

"Better than you, I imagine," said Amy.

Reese muttered a couple of dirty words her way, and Amy laughed. Elise grinned too. "I'll take you on, Reese," she said. "Give them a good show."

"Yeah, right."

The elevator stopped at mid-level, and the doors opened to a long hallway beyond. Already, there were large groups of drogin practicing with weapons inside enclosed rooms on either side. Glass walls gave Elise a close view inside each one. As Helen and Tom took the elevator up, Elise and the rest of her team went down the passage until they came to an empty room with a drogin assistant at the doorway. By the door was a rack with a load of weapons in various shapes and sizes. The drogin bowed their head to them and explained each gun to the team—how they fired and the range and power of each. Some shot blue fire, others electric rounds. There were armor piercers, smoke poppers, rocket launchers, and guns that even shot poison. As they chose their weapons carefully, they each took their positions at various firing spots and fired several rounds at concrete thick poles situated at the far back wall of the room. Elise chose a small but—what the drogin called—easily accessible yet powerful shooter and took position. The handle of the gun was light, and she was pleased with the ease of grip. What was strange, however, was its shape. It had a look of a slingshot or a small crossbow only there was no string attaching the two bow ends. As she fired, bright yellow arrows shot from the top base. When she held the trigger, the gun seemed to power up, and when she released the trigger, the arrows shot brighter and went farther. It was strange as all hell, but she loved it and chose it as her main shooter. She also chose what was largely a sniper rifle that could be easily carried behind her back as her second.

Bruce, of course, chose the largest and most obnoxious weapon that shot heavy armor piercing rounds while Jerico and Reese chose guns that shot electric rounds. Amy went with poison shots and Adrien chose fire. Once they were satisfied with their weapons, they gave the guns up to the drogin who made a checklist of their gear for tomorrow. From there, they left the firing area and headed farther into the training quarters. The hall opened out into a wide space, leading them onto a transparent bridge that looked down into several walled off areas. One was clearly a glorified gym, with equipment that looked more like massive robotic machines than the simple weight lifts from Earth but which the drogin used easily. In the second room were simulators of some kind, with virtual headsets and game-grade guns (a glorified arcade, Elise thought), and at the far back, in the last section, the biggest by far, were the sparring pits where drogin wore padded armor and took to fighting in pairs or even groups. Beyond them was a separately closed off part of the building with a drogin guarding the door.

Elise was convinced to try the simulators first. They were astoundingly advanced, with realistic projections of the cityscape below. She practiced with aiming and maneuvering alleyways and streets but soon grew tired of it, uninterested in the virtual copy. She tried out the machines in the gym next, guided by an assistant on how to use them. Afterward, she knew she'd be more sore than she had been in a long time but was grateful for the burn. She was finishing her last set when a pair of drogin walked over to her and Amy, who sat nearby with a pair of weights.

"High day to you." One drogin bowed.

Elise could see by its bulkier frame that it was male, its slender face reminding her of a greyhound. Elise bowed her head in turn as she wiped the sweat from her neck with a towel.

"My name is Ronin," he said. "This is my brother, Bo." The other merely bobbed his head.

"Elise." Elise tapped at her chest. "And that is Amy." She pointed to the female behind her.

"Very nice to meet you." Ronin's eyes shifted between her and Amy. "We are scouts for this sector. We met some of those from the other team. Those who have gone missing. Terrible thing to have happened. I sincerely hope they can be found."

Elise smiled out of politeness. "I hope so too."

"We will be helping your team tomorrow to track a path to them."

"You've been down in the undercity before?" Elise asked.

"Yes, a few times for smaller missions."

"What is it like?"

Ronin tilted his head back, his honey-colored eyes looking up at the ceiling then back at her. "If I can be very honest...it is a dark place. Not for the weak willed. There, the immoral and tainted make their home. Perhaps I shouldn't be saying but...you deserve to be warned. It is a very dark place, not just physically."

Elise looked over to Amy, who merely shrugged. "Well, we wouldn't have expected a cheery wonderland."

"Of course. I wish there could be another way..."

Elise was about to ask him "another way for what?" when Jerico hollered for them at the stair.

"We got a situation at the pits," he called to them.

Elise forced herself not to roll her eyes. *I swear on my life if one of them started a fight already with these people, I'm going to clock them in the head myself.* She smiled again at Ronin. "Thanks for the heads up."

"Are you going to the sparring pits? May we join you?" he asked.

Elise couldn't see any reason why not. "Let's all see what kind of trouble we started."

Together they left the gym and headed on to the bridge. At the end of it was a small double stair leading down into a large open area set up with enclosed pits in rows of four. One could walk a path past each and look down into them. At one in particular near the back, a large group was huddled tightly together. Through the many drogin that were barking and growling, Elise saw Adrien yelling while holding Reese back from jumping down into the pit. Elise shot down the stairs along with Jerico and Amy. They pushed their way to the front once they reached the pit, and Elise looked down to see Bruce on the ground with one of the alien bounty hunters on top of him, a nasty shark-like male with rows of sharp teeth and black eyes like a doll. The shark was whaling on Bruce, who covered his face with his arms. Elise was struck speechless as she watched, the drogin and her team wild with excitement and fury all around her. When she looked over to the other side of the pit, she found the hunter's deathly leader staring back at her across the way, his eyes bright with wicked amusement. The rest of his team beside him jittered and laughed. She froze again as she stared at him, and his mouth widened into a grin that showed her a set of curved fangs, a long pair then a shorter pair beside them. A real shit-eating grin if she ever saw one.

She responded with a tight-jawed frown, hands clenched into

fists. Though her heart started hammering at the sight of him, she didn't dare look away. Oh, how she wanted to smack that grin right off his gruesome face.

A pair of drogin in uniform jumped down into the pit and finally separated the two. The shark leapt out with ease while Bruce had to clamber out with the help of the drogin.

"You fight as dirty as you look," Reese snarled, with Adrien still holding him back. "I'll kick your ass right here, right now, shark boy."

The shark hissed something back, and the others of his group laughed once more.

"Enough!" called one uniformed drogin as they exited the pit. "We aren't here to fight like this. These rings are meant for light practice only!"

The group of hunters didn't seem to listen or care. They jeered away until Reese pulled out of Adrien's grip and dropped into the pit. The group's leader nodded to one of his own, and an amphibious looking alien joined Reese in the pit. The uniformed drogin were pushed back as the crowd huddled in closer to watch. Elise stepped to the edge to jump in and separate them but was caught at the arm by Jerico, who shook his head.

The pair circled each other several times, the amphibian crouching low. Reese struck first but wasn't quick enough, his opponent dodging easily around him. He tried to strike again, punching left then right, but missed every time, the hunter clearly toying with him. When Reese went for a loose roundhouse kick, the alien dodged that too then hit Reese right across his neck and shoulder, taking him to his knees. Reese fumbled back up only to be hit once more across the stomach and face until he was backed into the wall. He kicked his leg out to stop the hunter from coming, but the alien didn't falter. He jumped up and slammed his feet into Reese's chest, taking him out once more. Reese buckled and fell, but the alien kept on hitting.

"Stop," Elise shouted. "He's out! Stop!" She wrenched her arm out of Jerico's grip and dropped into the pit. As the alien was about to kick Reese in the stomach, Elise got between them and blocked the blow. She hissed at the sharpness of his powerful kick but didn't fumble back. The alien stopped and backed off but only for a second, only to assess her. Elise put up her arms and took a fighting position. Behind her, Reese stirred, and Adrien and Jerico climbed down to aid him. Elise didn't relax her stance, but the alien didn't come at her. Instead, he looked to his leader, who made a quick gesture, and the amphibian stepped back.

Elise kept her position for a moment longer then dropped her arms. "You think it's fun to beat a man when he's down? You're sick," she called up to the head hunter.

The crowd of drogin quieted as the leader crouched down, his elbows on his knees. He tilted his head at her, his eyes traveling down her body, and Elise felt herself flush. He said something she didn't understand and remembered he couldn't yet fully speak drogin.

"What did he say?" she asked the drogin around her. They looked at each other, and Ronin stepped to the edge.

"I can understand Xolien," he said. "He says that he thinks it is necessary for those to learn how to fight every way possible. That the enemy will fight dirty, so shall they."

The head hunter said more, and his team snickered behind him.

Ronin looked to Elise apologetically. "He also says 'yes, it is fun.'"

The leader grinned again at her, and Elise was very close to rushing over and pulling him down so that she could show him just how fun it really was. Then she realized how stupid that would be. She hated to admit it, but he could likely overpower her, and her team had been laughed at enough already.

"Well, I bet it won't be so fun when you get your ass beat." She scowled. The alien huffed as if the mere thought that he could be defeated was entertaining at most. He talked at her again, and Ronin repeated.

"What? By you? I could lose both my legs and one arm, and I'd still have the upper hand." He laughed.

"Is that a challenge?" Elise asked.

"Elise, don't," Adrien said.

"No. It's a warning. You don't want to fight me." His gaze fell across her once more. "I wouldn't want to put a mark on that pretty little face anyway. Though" —at this, Ronin hesitated and grimaced— "the thought of you beneath me is a tempting prospect."

Elise felt sick. She was beyond words at first, trying to process what he said. That she had just been so very insulted and so shockingly hit on by this savage looking monstrosity shook her. She fumbled with her words then started for him when one of the uniformed drogin pushed his way back to the front.

"If you truly wish to fight each other without severely injuring someone, take it to the mission arena." The drogin pointed to the door at the far back of the sparring pits where a metal door remained closed and a drogin continued to guard it. "There, we shall see which team has a real advantage. What do you say?"

Elise and her team eyed the other but said nothing.

"Not a bad idea," said Ronin. "The mission center is a great way to prepare too. Would also be a good way to let off steam."

Elise looked over to Adrien, who glared up at the head hunter then back at her. "Do we really want to get into this before tomorrow?"

"It's either that or risk a fight later on," said Jerico. "I say we end it here, and whoever wins wins, and let it be."

Elise looked back to the head hunter whose eyes narrowed on her. Hers narrowed back at him. "I'm in."

CHAPTER FOUR

"How the hell did this fight start anyway?" Amy asked as Elise and the others suited up in padded armor in a changing room situated to one side of the sparring area. "And don't say it was because one of them looked at you wrong."

Bruce, now taped up on parts of his face, tugged on a padded armband. "Shark boy was beating up on one of the drogin. Felt I needed to step in."

"And you honestly thought that was a good idea?" Elise asked as she flipped up her hair and tied it into a high ponytail.

Bruce shrugged. "He was being a cocky little shit about it. I figured I'd teach him a lesson."

"Yeah, well, lesson learned," Adrien said, adjusting a pad on his leg. "Now I have two beat up team members and possibly a couple more after this...whatever the hell this is that we are about to fight them in. You're lucky the drogin have amazing medical tools, or you'd be toast tomorrow. And for fuck's sake, don't let Helen see you tonight. She will lose it."

"Got it," Reese muttered as he shoved on his padded boots. "Let's just kick their ass in this one match—"

"—and be done with it," Jerico countered, eyeing him and Bruce. "Seriously, we don't need more enemies, especially ones we have to work with. Are we good?"

The others nodded, though they might not have been so happy about it. Even Elise was wary of the thought that, come tomorrow, they would be working together with this team of hunters. Side by side with *him*. It left a sour taste in her mouth, but she kept her lips shut. Better to get all her anger out in this little game. Then maybe she'd wipe that nasty grin off his face.

Once the team was geared up, they headed out of the changing room and toward the far side of the sparring room where the large metal door stood. Several drogin in uniform were talking amongst themselves, and the team of hunters were there waiting.

"All right, here is how the mission arena works," said a drogin with cropped ears and slicked black hair. "Once each team enters the arena, the simulation will start. Inside, you will need to traverse the obstacle course laid out for your particular match. You will also choose one prop weapon to fight the various enemies you will face. Your goal is to get to the end of the course and take into your possession the key then activate it without taking too many hits. It must be activated before the time marker runs out. If you take too many hits, your armor will glow red, and you're done. Understood?"

"Seems simple enough," said Jerico. The others nodded in agreement. Elise caught eyes with the lead hunter again, who gave her one of his devious smiles. Another alien, one with golden skin and a body that Elise could clearly identify as female, sauntered over and pressed close to him, giving Elise a fiery glare before reaching up and biting playfully at the hunter's neck. The hunter hissed then grinned, wrapping an arm around her waist to pull her in closer. The alien female whispered something in his ear, and they each laughed. Elise's jaw clenched as she felt her face heat, but she dared not turn away.

"System ready," came a woman's voice over some unseen intercom. The door finally slid open, and they each entered.

It was immensely dark at first. Then a few lights flickered on, and

Elise caught a quick glimpse of a vast arena where the floor and inner walls moved and changed. Then the lights went out, and a wave of blue washed over everything, turning the arena into a simulated copy of the city, with buildings and alleyways, roads and walls. A maze cut from a small portion of what they would find outside the training hall. When the exterior of the simulation was complete, placing them in what looked to be a central square, Elise's eyes shot around and spotted several silhouettes along walls and around buildings holding weapons, aimed and ready. A set of racks rose from the floor displaying several shooters and blades. Elise approached and took up the gun she had chosen earlier in the shooting range. Her team chose theirs as well, and when she looked over, she saw the group of aliens picking theirs. Elise noted what they took. The large lion-looking one took a heavy-duty gun like Bruce had, while the shark and amphibious one took long range weapons; the golden woman took a set of blades, and the lizard took twin handguns. Their leader, Elise observed suspiciously, took nothing.

Cocky bastard, Elise thought. But she would show him. She'd been trained at an early age to shoot and fight by her father. The alien might look intimidating and powerful, but Elise wasn't afraid. Nothing scared her, and this guy wasn't about to change that.

"You will have thirty minutes to secure and activate the key," the woman's voice said, echoing over the city. "Ready positions."

"We got this," Jerico whispered to Elise as they separated themselves from the other group to stand just before a set of alleyways. "You're probably the fastest out of all of us, so just run for it, and I will cover you."

Elise said nothing as she took a position beside him. She kept her eyes straight ahead, gun in hand, and didn't stir, even when she thought she heard a low laugh from the other end. A loud bell sounded, and they were off.

Elise didn't hesitate. She made straight down one alleyway and immediately heard gunshots and saw the sparks of their light go off behind her. She saw one simulated drogin on the top of the wall at the end of the passage and took aim as she ran. The drogin saw her, but he wasn't quick enough, and she took him out before he could even aim his gun her way, hitting him with bright yellow light in the chest and head. His image crumbled into a thousand pieces and disappeared. Elise pushed herself into a sprint and leapt at the wall, digging her foot into its side and using the leverage to reach the top, grabbing hold of the ledge with one hand and lifting herself over. She rolled then fell to the other side. There, she was met with two more drogin, a roughed-up pair in patched clothing. She took them both out as they charged her, and she dashed past without even looking back.

When she came to the end of the alley, she had the option to go left or right. She started for the left when she saw something leap over the building from above, making her stop.

Smart.

Thinking quickly, she looked around and saw a rusted ladder to one side of the building in front of her. Putting the handle of the gun between her teeth, she started up the ladder. When she stepped over onto the roof, another rogue drogin was waiting for her.

Too close to shoot him, Elise took the gun out of her mouth and struck him with it instead. The drogin's head knocked back, and Elise kicked his legs out under him before hitting him again on the head as his back hit the ground.

Two things happened as the simulated drogin turned to dust. One: she heard someone shout in the distance and two: she caught a shadow leaping over her.

Elise rolled to the side just as a blade came down where she had been standing. The golden woman bared her teeth in a cat-like snarl as Elise shot to her feet to meet her. The alien lunged forward, and Elise just barely dodged in time, missing a cut to her stomach. The woman hissed and struck fast, but Elise kept her distance each time. She blocked a few of her blows and got out of the way of others, but Elise could tell the woman was well-trained, and her chances of taking her down were slim. She couldn't play defense forever, and time was running out.

As she leapt away once more, Elise caught sight of another drogin across the other building with his back turned. He had yet to notice them. Elise glanced at him then to the woman. She took up her gun and shot over the alien's shoulder as she leapt at Elise once more. Elise took a strike to the chest, which knocked her on her ass. Her armor pulsated, and the mark of the hit lay across her chest in a glowing red slash. The woman stood above her, smiling.

"Not bad for..." something, something, the woman said, but Elise couldn't understand. She lifted her blade to strike Elise square in the stomach, only to be knocked forward as several blasts of white light hit her back. Elise rolled to the side as the woman went down, and she saw the drogin blasting away in their direction. Elise took the chance and skirted out of his line of sight before dropping down to the roof of a smaller building. She ran across it, parallel to two other buildings until she clambered down to the street below with gun still in hand.

She ran on again, feeling a slight burn in her arms and legs and lungs, but that didn't stop her. As she ran along the street, she heard another shout from far away followed by the sounds of gunfire everywhere. She still didn't dare stop. Even as a bomb went off close by and—though it didn't scorch her or truly harm her—knocked her off her feet momentarily, she was up again and sprinting down another road.

She leapt and rolled over another wall and skirted around a set of blown-out buildings, only slowing for a moment to sneak around a gang of drogin hanging around nearby. As she came to a bridge, she hesitated. She looked around and saw another bridge down a ways along the same river-crossing not far from her own. No one was there that she could tell, so she started forward.

Midway across, she felt something whoosh over her head. She ducked down and pushed her legs to move faster as she looked over in time to see a flash of blue and green light strike the pavement right in front of her. Cursing, she slid to a halt and hunkered down against the bridge wall as more and more shots flew inches past her. She crouched and waited until, eventually, they stopped, and she slowly crawled her way across. She heard shots go off again, but this time, she saw no sparks of green and blue stopping her. Elise dared to peek over the wall and saw from the other bridge Bruce running across, his armor already hit several times along his back and front. He roared as he ran, his face going beet red as he shot aimlessly up toward the buildings above him. But as he came near to the end of the bridge, the blue and green lights hit him in the back, and he went down, his armor now glowing bright red.

He was out. And judging by the shouts she had heard, so were a couple others already. She cursed again and made a break for the end of the bridge. Shots fired her way, one catching at her leg. She barked out another curse but didn't falter. She leapt for the nearest building and made it just inside, blocking the fire that rained in on her. Elise slunk down for a mere second to catch her breath. She didn't know how many more strikes she could take before she was out, but judging by how many she saw on Bruce, she liked to think she could take a few more before she was done. She forced herself back up and made her way out the other side of the building and onto the next street.

She took out two more drogin and went over one more wall until she found herself within a large open square. Only a fountain took up the center, dried up and crumbled. At the back was a wide building with thick rows of pillars. Leading to the building was a set of steps where a pedestal sat. On top of the pedestal was a glowing red ball.

Elise could only assume the ball was the key.

She took one step and then instantly jumped back as gunshots rang out close by. Jerico came into the square and hunkered down near the fountain. He had a few marks on him, but he was still going. The lion-like alien came into view and began shooting his way in, firing endlessly, lighting up the square. Elise watched as the fountain became rubble, and Jerico was forced out from behind it. He fired back and hit the lion once but not before taking several hits himself.

His armor went red, and he went down. He wasn't dead, Elise knew, only what looked to be knocked out. The drogin wanted to make sure no one cheated and kept going even after they lost.

The lion pushed Jerico's body out of the way and went for the steps, only to take fire at his back. He, too, went down, and Adrien came into view, taking his place. He was breathless and sweating and looked to be only one mark away from knockout, but he went for the ball without glancing back and didn't see the shark-like alien hunkering down on top of a wall. Elise took aim and fired, hitting the shark across the chest. He went down, dropping on the other side of the wall. Adrien swerved around as she stepped into the square with him.

"Stirling, you made it," he panted.

Elise's eyebrows rose. "You're surprised?"

He laughed softly through his breaths then gestured for her to stand by him and watch the buildings. "They're good. Not that that's a surprise. One took Reese out almost right away. Amy not long after." He pointed to her chest. "Who got you?"

"Goldie. She almost got me on one of the roofs, but I outsmarted her."

"Really?"

Elise shrugged.

"Pretty sure it's just you and me now," Adrien said, backing up. Elise did with him. They each eyed the square with guns raised. "But there's at least two of them. Go for the key. I'll cover you."

Elise lowered her gun an inch as she did as commanded and creeped over to the pedestal. Carefully, she reached out for the key and took it up in one hand. No trap sprung, no hoards of drogin came. She eyed Adrien, who merely nodded. With her gun still raised in one hand, she crept back down the steps and stood with Adrien in the square.

"Guess the others were too slow." He smiled and put out his hand. Elise placed the key in his palm. He gripped it tight. "Better luck next—"

He went down. The ball dropped from his hand and rolled out into the middle of the square, hitting the pile of rubble that had been a fountain. Elise blinked, confused.

"What...?"

"Better luck next time."

Elise swerved around and saw the lead hunter standing above her on the steps. She let out a hiss of breath and took a step back. Slowly, he made his way down, watching her before eyeing Adrien on the ground. The alien nudged him roughly with his boot and made a clicking sound with his tongue. Elise backed away as he stepped over Adrien and stood before her. He tilted his head, studying her closely. She didn't care for the heat in his eyes. Nor did she like how they sparked with amusement.

She noticed he had no hits to his armor. In fact, he looked the same as he had at the start of the match. He hadn't even broken a sweat, if he even sweat at all. She looked down at her fallen teammate with a deep frown. She hadn't even seen him get hit, nor was there any weapon in the alien's hands to blame.

The alien moved closer, and Elise felt her muscles tighten, ready to flee or fight. She heard movement behind her and turned to see the green amphibian pointing his gun straight at her. Elise raised hers when she heard a raspy sort of snicker behind her.

Damn it.

She looked back, and sure enough, the lead hunter was laughing. He gestured quickly to his teammate, who lowered his gun and backed away.

Ah, so he wants to play.

"Just you and me, huh?" Elise said in her own tongue. She chucked her gun aside then raised her hands into fists, planting her feet firmly. The leader stopped laughing, but his smile never faded.

"You're bold for a soft-skin. I like that," he said. Or something along those lines. Some of the words were off, but his drogin was improving already. He took a stance if not in a mocking sort of way, and they each stood their ground. Elise knew he was waiting for her to strike first. She took a deep breath then moved.

Not toward him but away. Dashing toward the crumbled fountain, reaching for the key.

She was only a few steps away from grabbing it when she was promptly pulled backward and dropped to the ground, landing square on her back. The alien leader stood above her like a tall, ominous shadow. Elise rolled back onto her feet as he circled her. He laughed again.

"Clever little thing too. I like that."

Elise growled and moved again, this time toward him. She swung out one fist then the other, but he blocked both with ease. He was shockingly quick, dodging her strikes with little effort. Elise had always prided herself on her swiftness, but he was undoubtedly faster, more agile. Frustration rose in her, and she pushed herself, attempting to land a punch or kick any way she could but was unsuccessful. And all he did was laugh.

Crying out in anger, Elise swung her leg up high, hoping to catch him in the head. Not only did he block that too, he also caught her leg and swung her around. Elise went flying, yelping in surprise as she fell on her hands and knees. She fumbled back onto her feet, and he was right on her. Only by sheer luck did she block his first blow but not the second which caught her in the stomach. Even with the pads, it knocked the wind out of her. She stumbled back as she choked for air and tried to take a defensive stance, backing away quickly from his attacks. She swiped at him like a damn cat as he came at her, and in turn, he caught her wrist, swinging her around until her back was against his chest.

Elise felt her heart jolt as his arm came around her in a steel grip, crushing her close to him.

"You're fun to fight, I'll give you that." His other hand came around and gripped her hip. "Though you could learn a thing or two."

Elise clawed at his arm, but he didn't budge. "Screw you," she hissed.

She felt his breath on her neck and could practically hear him grin. "That can be arranged," he said, gripping her harder, making her gasp. A sharpness, like a blade, grazed her ear, and Elise panicked. She simultaneously dropped her weight and elbowed him hard in the lower stomach. He let her go, causing her to nearly fall forward. She swerved on him, fists at the ready, when she felt something wet trickle down her ear. She touched at the spot and found blood on her fingers. The bastard had bitten her.

"You are a fucking fiend," she spat.

The alien eyed the blood on her fingers. He took a step toward her, and she instantly stepped back. The amusement in him was gone now. His eyes darkened, and he came at her once more.

Elise tried to back up, but he seemed finished with this game. When she thought for sure he was going to knock her out and end it, he went around her instead and picked up the key.

"I'm not finished," Elise said as he gripped the ball tight. "Hey! Do you hear me?"

He began to press a button along the ball's top, but before he could activate it completely and end the match, Elise lunged forward and gripped his arm. She swung a leg at him again, and he took her blow. The spot where she hit his armor glowed red. With the key still in hand, he turned on her and this time blocked her punch. His eyes glowed bright with fire, but Elise refused to be burned.

A few more blows were thrown until she was once again swept onto her back. She started to get back up when he pushed her down and started to straddle her. Elise cried out in surprise as she struggled to get out from under him, but he pinned her hard and fast.

"Stubborn too." He glared down at her, and she thought he looked rather pissed off. Until his lips curled ever so slightly. "I like that." His fist came down, and Elise felt the strike to her chest, not as hard as the last but hard enough to make her armor glow red and make everything go dark.

THE LAST OF THE SUN'S LIGHT FELL OVER THE CITY. NEZKA watched the night come, slowly but surely, swallowing everything into darkness. The city's lights glowed ever more bright, in all manner of colors. He watched them with ease as he sat along the top of a twisted statue, made to look like an odd growth, like some tree carved out of metal. The garden was empty now and quiet save for the trickle of water nearby. The plants glowed too with a yellow light. It was beautiful in its way. At least to those who could appreciate its beauty. But Nezka did not look to them, only to the city beyond the garden's balcony and what waited below.

He would see little rest tonight. He rarely slept before a mission. Most would say that was foolish but not to him. It morphed him somehow, made him sharper, more in tune. More aggressive. And that, in turn, made him more prepared.

Not that he felt he needed much prepping. The mission was simple, more so than many of the missions Vesra had put him on in the past. There would be a few deaths, he was sure of that. Maybe even one of his own. But that was always the risk—the price sometimes to be paid—and he wasn't worried for them. They would either hold their own or perish. This was the law of all hunters.

Yes, with so many aiding him, the mission would be small compared to others. And when it was done, he would succeed as he always did. Dozens of worlds, unforgiving in both their nature and people, had yet to ever stop him. To see him fail. And few ever surprised him. This city was no different. Its people, as new as they were, did not impress him. As advanced as they were, they were docile, submissive. Weak. They occupied little of his thoughts, and come tomorrow, he would feel very little when he was forced to take out those who stood in his way.

The humans, on the other hand...

They stirred in his mind if not for the fact that they were his target. One, in particular, stirred more than the rest, and if he had any thought to notice or wonder about it, he remained unconcerned. They still had their orders. A brief meeting not even an hour ago reaffirmed to his team what they were set out to do; no matter if some had a new urge to take a few of the humans out just for challenging them. The humans were not to be harmed. When the first initial group was found, he would set into motion their capture along with the human soldiers. They would be his. Until given to Vesra.

And perhaps as a reward his master would allow him to keep one...one with a fiery spirit brighter than all the rest. With lovely dark eyes and long silky hair.

Nezka closed his eyes. He still could taste the blood on his tongue from where he had bitten her. An accident, really. He had only meant to graze. Not to break skin. Only to see what she would do. Well, she certainly hadn't disappointed. Though her little freak out had caused the bite in the end.

He laughed softly at the thought. Ah, but she had been such a joy to watch. He had followed her through the arena, if only for the mere entertainment of seeing her in action. She was certainly a spry little thing. A passionate fighter. But with an embarrassing disregard for her surroundings. Several times, he could have knocked her out easily. Especially when she thought it wise to pause for a quick rest in one of the buildings and didn't so much as look around to see him crouching right nearby. Perhaps it was a human trait, a lack of awareness.

But she had been entertaining, nonetheless. It was really too bad...

Nezka frowned. He opened his eyes to see the city once again below him.

It was really too bad he would have to take her to Vesra.

He sat for a long while just looking at the city when he heard the soft patter of feet nearby. Someone had come into the garden. He did not move nor make a sound as the person in question walked close to where he sat, and when he saw who it was, he became even more still.

As if summoned by his thoughts, the human woman he had played with in the arena came into view just below where he sat atop the statue. She was alone and considerably more calm as she walked a lighted path over to the front of the balcony only a few paces away.

He watched her for a long moment, just taking her in. Watching the breeze catch in her hair, watching the lights shine on her skin. She wore simple clothing, but it hugged her figure nicely. When he felt he'd studied her enough, he deliberately made a sound to get her attention. It didn't take much for her to turn around suddenly and see him.

"You," she said with extra disdain after a brief moment of staring up at him in surprise. "Why are you following me?"

Nezka smirked. "I wasn't. I was here first."

That answer didn't seem to please her any more than if he had confessed he'd actually been following her. She turned away from him to look at the city. The breeze picked up, brushing her hair back, and Nezka caught a glimpse of a small band of white around her outer ear where he had bitten her. Besides that one small detail, one wouldn't have thought she had been in a fight. Though he had given her a fair match, he had made sure not to hit as hard as he could. Even with the padded armor, he could have damaged her severely if he had wanted to, but he wanted her breathing.

"Why are you here anyway?" she asked, looking back at him angrily.

"I could ask you the same."

She grimaced and turned once more away. "I wanted to see green before all I saw was steel and concrete."

Nezka thought that over for a moment then dropped from the statue. He moved to the balcony and stood only a few feet away from her to lean against the rail. Though he was learning drogin quickly thanks to the translator, he was having a hard time finding words in their tongue that he wanted to say back to her, so he instead remained silent.

"I hope you're happy then," she said after a pause. "You won your fight. I'm sure you feel real superior. Not like beating on a bunch of people would have made that any different."

Nezka drummed his fingers along the rail. "True." From the corner of his eye, he saw her frown and cross her arms. "Not that it was much of a fight."

Her lips thinned as she looked over at him. "Oh? If I count right, there were only two of you left at the end. I'd say we held our own pretty well."

Nezka shrugged. "Two. Five. One. The victor remains." He looked over at her and smiled. "But if you want a rematch, I wouldn't mind seeing you on your back again."

That thoroughly annoyed her, and all he could do was laugh. Her reactions were the funniest damn thing he'd seen in a long while. Her attempts to hide her shocked anger were useless with such an expressive face.

"You really are an asshole," she muttered. "And I don't think I have met someone I hated so much in such a short amount of time."

Again, he had no drogin words yet equivalent to what he wanted to say, so he said in his own tongue, "Most do when first encountering me. But that's because I'm usually about to kill them."

She looked at him, confused. "What?"

He took a step toward her. "Or they are very afraid. But you're not very afraid, are you? Or at least you hide it well with your anger."

"What the hell are you saying?"

As he continued to approach her, he could tell she wanted to back away. Only her stubbornness kept her locked in place. Her hands turned to fists at her side, and she grew very still, but she did not flinch as he got as close as possible without touching her. He tilted his head and closed his eyes, waiting until he heard the soft thumping of her heart, a steady yet fast rhythm, though not as fast as he would have thought. He felt the heat of her, could taste her scent on his tongue, like the smell of a storm or of an ocean, the slightest hint of salt and the very small yet still detectable metallic scent of fear. He could see the energy radiating from her through the small sensors along his brow and the colors she portrayed were colors of rain and lightning and a sun at dusk. When he opened his eyes and gazed down at her, he saw her watching him with growing suspicion.

As if possessed, his arm rose up without thought and reached for her, needing to collect the final sense of her. He went to touch her bare arm when she immediately slapped it away, breaking the moment.

"Don't touch me again," she hissed. "Come tomorrow, we will have to go down together, we might have to work together, but I don't ever want to talk to you again. I don't ever want to see you looking my way. You stick to your job, and I'll stick to mine, and when it's over, we will return home, me to my world and you to whatever nightmare hellhole you likely come from, and that will be it." She pushed off from the rail and walked away then stopped mid stride and turned back. "And if you get in my way tomorrow, I won't hesitate to take you out."

Nezka watched her go, fierce little thing that she was. Her threats brushed off him like a speck of dust on the wind, but the disappointment he felt could not be so easily swiped away. His eyes narrowed on her as she slipped out of the garden and disappeared. Too bad. She thought she hated him now? She was in for a rude surprise.

CHAPTER SIX

As dawn came, Elise and her team assembled down at the east docks, not meant for ships but for other methods of transport, mainly the trams that would take them over to the gate leading to the undercity. From there, they were told, special armored vehicles would take them through and across the lower sector. Though most of the higher city's transport was by train and ship, the drogin had built special cars to traverse the city below, capable of taking heavy fire and powerful enough to plow through walls if need be. The trams of the lower city were either destroyed or overrun, and since ships were unable to land in fear of electric strikes, shields, and outage barriers, they needed another way to get to their mark which, by their calculation, was located a little over eighteen miles out from the nearest gate not yet taken over by gangs. Theoretically, if they drove straight through without a single incident, it would take anywhere between a half hour and an hour at most. Since they knew that was unlikely in every possible way, it would take them most of the day, possibly into the night depending on what they encountered.

The drogin soldiers waited near the tracks, geared up and ready to go, wearing armor and carrying shields. Elise knew they would mainly be used as a distraction, taking out the smaller groups and lower-tier thugs guarding their strongholds, blowing out buildings if they had to. Elise and her team were to take one of the middle cars and aid when possible until the area was cleared and they could make a quick sweep, making sure no humans might be hidden somewhere they shouldn't. The hunters would go in with them initially but would then separate throughout the process to slip inside the more heavily fortified sections to take out the leaders of gangs. Once they made it to the energy deposit, they would go in again while everyone else attacked from the outside. Once the place was cleared from the exterior point, Elise and her team would go in, take out any remaining baddies, and find the missing team. It was going to be a long day, but by the end, Elise was confident they would find the Grayhart team and get back home, still ignoring the odd feeling that clawed at her even if it seemed now they were more prepared than ever.

Elise fixed on the last of the armor atop her suit and clipped her chosen handgun to the holster at her hip followed by the sniper at her back. The drogin's tactical uniforms were much more...flashy than any of the military's back home. Usually her team wore the same gear consisting of blue or black camo pants and long shirts with vests and pads. The drogin had given them suits equivalent to what they had similarly worn in the arena yesterday only with much more heavy-duty armor and in various colors. Bruce and Reese wore dark blue, Adrien and Jerico wore red, and Tom wore a deep green; Amy and Helen wore steel-gray, and Elise somehow got stuck with white. When they activated the chargers and lights along their suits, each one lit up with a different color ranging from yellow to orange to purple. Elise's lit up...pink.

She wished she could ask for another, but it was too late for that, so, as she adjusted the suit and armor one last time, she grimaced but resigned to bear it. She'd only have to wear it for today.

So, suck it up and get serious, Elise. Who cares about the stupid color? Let's just get this over with.

The rest of her team tested their suits carefully, making sure they could move and walk properly, that nothing snagged or pinched.

Reese looked down at his and laughed. "We look like...shit, what's that old cheesy kids' show? Power Knights? Power Police?"

"Power Squad," Amy said bitterly.

"Why the fuck did we get saddled with this while the rest are all wearing one color?" Bruce said, eyeing the drogin.

"Probably so we stood out for them to see," Adrien answered. "It's not a big deal. They seem...sturdy enough."

They all looked unconvinced, but before they could comment more about it, the drogin officials were calling everyone over to a dais set up by the tracks. As Elise and her team made their way over, Elise spotted a group not far ahead of them wearing silvery-black armor. The hunters. Their armor looked a hundred times cooler and more versatile. The lead hunter turned his head, and Elise immediately looked away with a scowl.

"All right everyone, you know your place in this. Let's have a smooth ride," Qorey said, gazing around at them. "Everyone is equipped with their new Ulink which are each connected to a map and local tracker. You will also be able to contact anyone from this mission through it." He lifted up his own, an oval shaped device similar to if a bit smaller than the ISpads or smartphones back home, and pressed down on his, making it light up. "If you press and hold on each of yours, they will be activated."

The drogin soldiers did as told and unlatched their Ulinks from the clip on their arm or at their waist. Elise had hers on her upper arm. She held it down and watched it light. As she happened to look over, she noticed the team of hunters didn't move to activate theirs. In fact, they didn't seem to have one at all. Instead, Elise saw a thick band on each of their wrists equipped with a small screen. She eyed them suspiciously when the tram came into the dock.

Everyone shuffled around and lined up as the tram halted and the doors slid open. There was soft ping as lights lit up the edges of the dock. Elise followed her team inside, huddling close as they packed the tram to its limit. The section they stood inside smelled like a fresh pair of shoes as air blew down on their heads. Once everyone was inside, the doors shut, and the lights dimmed. Elise took hold of a bar along the roof to steady herself, but as the tram shot away from the dock, she was pleased to find that, as fast as it moved, it did not jostle her in any way. And boy, did it move. The scene from the windows turned into an unrecognizable blur of light and color. Few spoke around them save in soft whispers and occasional growls that the drogin made. Elise looked around and caught Adrien staring at her. He winked and nodded, his way of saying everything was going to work out, something he always did right before a mission started. Elise smiled and nodded back at him in return, her way of saying she was ready.

The tram slowed to a stop, and the doors opened. The drogin spilled out, leaving Elise and her team last to exit. Beyond the green-lit station lay a road, its lines glowing yellow across the pavement. Parked along it were large tank-like vehicles with tires nearly as tall as Elise and an exterior covered in blue-gray steel. Their backsides were encased in a sort of metal cage with thick glass windows that had small circular openings, enough to put a gun through. Drogin were already piling inside as drivers opened up the doors.

"Earth team, follow me," shouted a drogin officer. They did as ordered. Elise stretched her head up to the massive buildings above and couldn't see the end. The shadow of these titan skyscrapers cast over them, dimming the sunlight, bathing the area in a chill gray. A light mist had fallen, and Elise wondered if it came from actual clouds or was just the dew falling off the tops of the towers above.

They came to their vehicle and hopped into the back, taking seats on either side. From the windows, Elise could see out every angle, even to the front when standing. There, she could see, some distance away, the gate—a wall cutting off another section of the city with a large tunnel leading down into the dark. Elise eyed it with growing anticipation as she felt a tap on her hip.

"You good, Stirling?" Jerico said, smiling up at her from where he sat, his gun resting on his lap.

Elise nodded quietly then took her seat next to him. The drogin took theirs, and all was silent save for the hiss of air blowing out from the vents at their feet. Elise's heart began to thump noticeably in her chest. She told herself it was just excitement or adrenaline. She watched from the window as drogin emptied the street save for those guarding the station and seeing them off. She saw Qorey outside talking with the other officials, their eyes aiming down to the tunnel. Some moved away from the group to talk to the drivers, others spoke low to each other, making gestures to the street and the cars. Qorey's gaze fell on their car, and as he and Elise locked eyes, she bowed her head to him. He did not move, only seemed to stare at her as if she were a stranger. He walked off with the other officers back to the station without another glance, and Elise thought maybe he hadn't seen her through the misted glass.

The vehicles roared to life, and the lights along the floor flickered. Elise was jostled slightly as the tank-car jerked forward and began to roll its way toward the tunnel. Elise gazed above, past the buildings to the misty sky above, until the mouth of the tunnel came into view, swallowing them.

Dimmed lights bathed the tunnel from every side, washing them in a sickly orange glow. The car slowed as it made its descent. Elise noticed several open doorways along the tunnelway, what she gathered to be stairways or passages in and out of the tunnel by foot. The tunnel began to open up the farther down they went until they came to a midpoint where a heavy metal door stood ahead of them and a stationway sat to the left side. The vehicle stopped, and Elise looked out to see several cars ahead, one of the drogin officers getting out to talk to the guards. There seemed to be an argument taking place, but of course, Elise couldn't hear it.

"Looks like they forgot we were coming," Jerico said then laughed. Amy cursed under her breath as the others watched with interest. Another pair of drogin came out from one of the vehicles, as did another guard. The team waited, watching and fidgeting in their seats.

"What's taking them so long?" Reese said, craning his neck around.

"Must just be a miscommunication," Adrien said. "Just give it a minute. Settle down. Bruce, sit down."

As soon as Bruce sat back, the metal door ahead began to open, and their vehicle moved. The first car ahead started forward, passing through the door. As it drove on to the other side, it simultaneously lit up in a flash of red, bursting into flames and sending a torrent of smoke billowing down the tunnelway.

The car shook, as did the tunnel, and the roar hit Elise with a deafening blast. Elise covered her face from the heat and blinding light and heard through the ringing in her ears the screams and shouts of those around her. Drogin scrambled out of their cars, and Elise heard the pops and zaps and saw the bright bursts of gunfire. One drogin dropped to his knees before he could even raise his weapon, blood gushing from his head onto the pavement.

It happened so quickly, but Elise didn't hesitate. She leapt up, trying to steady herself. Adrien shouted at them, and Elise saw the others moving. She shook her head clear, unholstered her gun, and went to follow them out of the car. Reese and Bruce jumped out first, but as Tom went to drop down, the car suddenly jerked forward, sending him tumbling out to hit his face on the concrete. Adrien jumped after him followed by Helen and Amy. Elise jumped then rolled, landing on her knees. Something whooshed past her ear, and she immediately pushed herself up and ran for the others. They dragged Tom to his feet and hurried behind one of the now unmoving vehicles as bullets pelleted the metal and rang against the tunnel walls, bursting in sparks of light.

"Where are they coming from?" Reese shouted.

Jerico went around the back of the car as Helen placed Tom against the tire to better examine his face. Elise followed Jerico to the back, and there, they crouched down and saw by the stationway a narrow passage where masked men spilled out. Back along the tunnelway where they had come from, flames licked the walls and shots of lightning struck cars and people.

"They are trapping us in," Elise said. The smoke was beginning to grow worse, making it hard to see, hard to make out who was friend or foe.

"Let's just light this place up!" Bruce shouted.

Adrien peeked around then pointed to the stationway. "There!"

They took aim and fired toward the station where several masked assailants in heavy black gear shot at them. Bullets flew. Some caught, others didn't. Their armor took a few of the hits, but Elise knew they wouldn't last with such heavy and relentless firepower.

The masked men backed off when a flash of silvery-black armor dropped down over them and started taking each of them out one by one, their barks of pain echoing, their guns firing chaotically all around. Elise couldn't identify which of the hunters it was, but they distracted the men long enough for her to look around for an exit. Unfortunately, all the passageways she could make out were blocked by the masked men or encased in flames. She coughed then crouched over Adrien, who huddled by the front tire.

"We need to get out of this. The fire..."

Adrien nodded, looking around for any way out. A few of the drogin had joined them behind the car, one badly wounded with a missing ear. "Hey! Can one of you drive this?" He pointed up at the car.

One of the drogin looked at him and then the car. "I can, but I don't know if we can get past the door."

"It's worth a try. Team ready up, let's move." Adrien shot up and started firing, flames licking at the station walls. Bruce started firing with him. Elise and the others, while keeping low, used their cover to dart to the next set of cars. Elise saw drogin everywhere—some still shooting, others sitting slumped over in their own blood. There were bodies everywhere, but Elise didn't stop to look at them. One of the hunters, the golden woman, leapt off one of the vehicles as a group of masked men started on a pair of defenseless drogin. The woman's face was cut up, but she didn't let that stop her. With an angry yowl, she disappeared just as quickly as she came, back into the fray of gunfire. Elise looked for the others but couldn't identify who was who. Everywhere and everything was chaos and confusion.

They made it to the nearest car from the door—which, surprisingly, hadn't yet been fully engulfed in flames—and jumped inside. The drogin, covering himself, leapt into the driver seat. As he shut the doors, air blew quickly out of the vents, evaporating the smoke, allowing them to breath. The vehicle rocked as the tunnel shook once more. Bullets pelleted the glass of their cage but didn't penetrate. Through the small openings, they fired their guns to try to stifle their attackers as their driver started the car and stepped on the gas.

The car sped through the door and hit the flaming mass that had been another vehicle, shoving it to the side of the tunnel. Metal ground on metal as the car pushed its way past. The fire licked at the glass, making the heat unbearable for a mere second before the tank finally freed itself. They drove on, bullets still hitting the glass as they neared the end of the tunnel. Elise could see the exit. Though it was very dark, she could make out the sliver of a street beyond.

The car sped for the opening. Elise looked to the others, who seemed fine save for Tom's cut up face and the ash staining their skin and armor. She glanced at Adrien and reached out, placing a hand on his shoulder.

"It's all right," he said, placing his hand on her upper arm, bringing her close so that their foreheads almost touched. "We're good. Everything is—"

Another flash of red blinded them, and the car jumped.

Elise went flying. She hit the side of one wall, neck bending back, face scraping the glass. Something hit her other side and knocked her shoulder. She went tumbling with the others as the car's back hit the ceiling of the tunnel in a blast of fire then dropped to the ground where Elise hit her head on the landing, and everything went black.

* * *

"Emergency...vehicle compromised...please exit the vehicle."

A red light blinked slowly off and on. Elise came to as the light stung her eyes and the robotic voice pierced her skull, making her head throb. She groaned and tried to sit up only to fall right back down. Her vision swam, but she didn't let that stop her from trying to sit back up. Shards of glass and debris fell from her suit, and she rolled slowly to her side then stomach. She blinked several times but couldn't seem to see. She dragged herself along and fell out from what she assumed was the car's back side. She moaned as every part of her felt pain. Her fingers tingled as she scraped and grabbed at the ground. She heard a scuffling sound nearby and another groan. She blinked and squeezed her eyes shut until her vision finally began to clear. Jerico dropped from the car onto his back beside her than slowly rolled onto his knees. He turned to her and grasped her arm with a shaking hand.

"Stirling. You okay?"

She nodded, but it seemed too slow. She seemed too slow, like she was waking from a long sleep.

"The others?" she slurred.

Jerico shook his head. "I'm not sure. I'm going to go investigate." Slowly, he lifted himself up, and the ground shook once more. Bits of dust and rock fell from the roof.

The tunnel. Oh, god, the tunnel is...

Elise pulled herself around. "Jerico," she called out in a weak voice. "Jercio...the tunnel."

He didn't seem to hear her. The end of the tunnel was close—she could feel the breeze. If they just got up and walked a few paces more...

Elise tried once more to force herself up but was only able to make it to her knees. She crawled as the ground continued to shake. Shouts and sirens could be heard farther back in the tunnel, but the gunfire had all but ceased.

Get up, you idiot. Get up, they need you.

With all her strength, Elise pushed herself up and stood on shaking legs. She turned to the car and saw Jerico pulling a member out but couldn't yet see who it was with his back blocking her view. She took a step to help him, and a terrible tremor forced her back down. She went to her knees again and was about to push herself back up when something jabbed the back of her head.

"Don't move."

Elise knew from her training what a gun felt like to the back of the head. She went still as the gun moved across her skull, and the owner stepped into her line of sight.

It was one of the masked men, his face fully covered with a ventilator where his mouth was and silver goggles where his eyes would be. His head was covered by a hood and across his chest was a large red X. He looked down at her and made a gesture with his hand. Several more men came into view, each wearing the same uniform as the one standing before her, with guns raised. From the corner of her eye, she could see one of them forcing Jerico and whoever he was helping, out of the vehicle.

"Make sure to get the others," said the man without looking away from her.

Elise wanted to scream, to fight, anything, but with several guns on her and her suit tarnished and body feeling like it had just hit a steel wall, she had no chance of beating them. Even if she could get to her gun, which miraculously had somehow been thrown out of the vehicle and now lay a few yards away, she'd be dead before she could fire.

The masked man released the gun from her head and gestured at her with it. "Get up."

Elise took a few deep breaths before trying to stand once more. As she slowly stood and raised her hands, thinking this was it, that she would rather die than be taken by them and so decided she was going to try for her gun after all, something hit the back of the man's head and he went crashing down in front of her. Dead.

Confused, Elise backed up as the other men shouted, aiming their guns at her.

"I didn't do—" she began to say when something flashed past her, and another man went down.

They started firing. Elise dropped back down as bullets flew, covering her head. She looked around and saw only feet scattering around her. Then her gaze found her gun once more, and she dropped her hands. Quickly, she crawled forward. As she reached for it and snatched it up, she rolled onto her back to take aim.

The last man dropped. The only one standing was death himself. Or what she thought was death until she took in his silvery-black armor and realized it was the lead hunter standing above her.

They locked eyes, and she opened her mouth to say something when a car sped its way down the tunnel. The hunter jumped out of the way as it approached, and Elise rolled to the tunnel wall. The car slammed right into the side of the tunnel and from there, the doors opened, and more masked men jumped out. Elise fired at them as they fired at the hunter who lunged at the men without pause. Their car hitting the tunnel was the last straw, and large chunks began to rain down. Elise stumbled to her feet and started for the car where her team still lay injured and where Jerico now sat against the back with Adrien unconscious beside him. As she crouched down and holstered her gun, Elise saw the blood on his legs where he'd been hit.

"Don't think I can walk," he said. "Adrien is still out. I don't know about the others."

"I'm here. Someone will come to help," she said quickly, her head finally beginning to clear, her senses once again becoming more alert. "We'll get everyone out. We'll get—"

More rocks fell, and the tunnel around them began to collapse. A cloud of dust swept in with the smoke, coming at them like a wave.

Elise shouted, covering her and Jerico from the rubble. She could no longer see, but she felt herself being shoved away as more of the tunnel roof fell. She heard shouts and saw flashes of light but nothing else as the dust grew thick.

"Go!" she heard someone yell.

Jerico.

She called for him when something grabbed her hard and pulled her around. A rock hit the side of her head, and everything clouded in her mind again. A cloud of black swam over her vision, and she felt herself falling. But instead of feeling the ground beneath her, all she could feel was her body being swept up against something solid and the wind rushing around her as she heard the sounds of the tunnel breaking.

CHAPTER SEVEN

THE FIRST FEELING THAT CAME BACK TO HER WAS THE SENSE that she was breathing. All else seemed to be darkness for a time and the odd feeling of being everywhere and nowhere at once, as if she were racing through endless moments or visions—some blurred, others vivid but seemingly infinite—and always there was a sense of danger, that she needed to wake, needed to focus, but every time she came to that edge of clarity, she was pulled back, like a wave ripping her from the earth, forcing her back into the dark.

Many times in that darkness she saw her sister, other times her team, and sometimes death dressed in black armor with eyes like fire.

When a light passed over her once then again several moments later, she held onto it until it brought her back fully to the edge, to where she could feel more than just her breath, where the radius of her senses grew. She heard distant noises like a roaring, heard water falling, smelled the sting of copper, felt the cold. She moaned as she awakened, or perhaps she had always been awake but could now fully clear her head, could really see. Her eyes were heavy, but she forced them open and blinked several times. It was dark still, but she knew now it was not from inside her mind but instead from the actual place where she found herself, wherever that was. The only light seemed to come from overhead, passing by every couple of minutes, a bright beam from above.

Elise turned her head and felt something soft underneath her cheek, covering whatever hard, sharp surface lay underneath. She tried to see more around her, but all that came into focus whenever the light passed were the rows of metal and broken piles of rubble and concrete. She blinked some more and saw that the metal rows were pillars holding up a building. A broken building with several holes in its high ceiling where the light shined through.

Elise moaned again as her head throbbed. Her shoulder ached something awful when she flung her arm out to plant her hand on the dust-filled floor. Slowly, she pushed herself up and let out a low hissing cry as the pain seared down her back. Her suit creaked as she rose into a sitting position, and when she looked down at her shoulder, she saw the large crack in the armor. Cursing, she touched at it with her good arm then looked around her. She couldn't identify what sort of building she was in, only that it was abandoned and in disrepair. As she carefully looked across and behind her, she noticed a large pit in the center where the skeletal remains of a ship had been left behind. She could gather from the damage above and below that it had fallen. Glass and metal parts had been flung across the whole surface, and scorch marks seared the side of the metal rows. Elise stared at it all in a moment of confusion that quickly began to clear as her memory fixed itself back together.

She attempted to rise when a noise close by made her stop and glance over.

"I wouldn't try that yet if I were you..."

Elise froze for perhaps a half a second before pulling her gun from her hip and aiming it at the shadows of a broken pillar ahead of her. There was a moment of silence before the alien laughed low. The light above swept over the rows of metal, and Elise got a better look at him as he sat watching her.

His eyes lit up as the beam hit him, just like a cat's or a wolf's, with the shine making Elise shiver.

"What are you doing here?" she said in a hoarse murmur. Her throat and mouth were awfully dry as she tried to swallow.

The alien hunter tilted his head. He had one knee raised where he rested his elbow. The other hand seemed to be grabbing at something by his thigh. He stared at her for a long moment, never even once glancing at the gun aimed at him, as if it were of little concern. "You don't remember?" he said finally.

"Remember what?"

"What happened."

Elise's gun dropped an inch. "The gate...we were attacked and the tunnel..." Elise's grip tightened. "What did you do?" she snapped.

The alien's pupils widened. He said something in his language then laughed again. "You think...I had anything to do with that? Truly? That I would be...here right now if I did?"

Elise opened her mouth then closed it. She remembered now seeing him attacking the masked men and the golden woman fighting them off as well. She lowered her gun some more but not fully. "The tunnel...oh, god. I have to get back. The others need me—" she tried to get up again but found her head swimming when she shot up too quickly. She fell back with a groan, her gun slipping from her grasp as she covered her eyes.

"There's no point," the alien said.

Elise dropped her hand to look at him with a frown. "They are not dead."

"I didn't say they were. But the exit is gone. The tunnel collapsed."

"Which implies you think they are dead."

He thought for a moment. "It may have only collapsed...some."

"Some?"

His eyes narrowed. "Not..." He was trying to find the right word. "Not...fully."

"Then I need to get back. I need to help."

He laughed again in that low husky growl, and her frown deepened. "You don't listen well, do you?" he said slowly, still trying to make the right words. "There is no way to get back. The tunnel exit is rubble. It is gone."

"Then there must be another way to—what?"

"We can't go back."

Elise stared at him then glanced up as the light passed by and shook her head. "Why?"

"You know why. They are looking for you."

She remembered what the masked gunman had said back in the tunnel.

Make sure to get the others.

Elise closed her eyes, not wanting to believe it. "Why?" she whispered, more to herself than him. "It doesn't make sense." She shook her head again then rubbed at her still throbbing head. "I don't understand."

"The mission was compromised. Someone planned the attack. And others on the inside were in on it." He too glanced up at the open roof then turned back to her. "If you go back, they may still be waiting. They will take you."

Elise rubbed at her temples as the throbbing turned into a dull headache. She wanted to scream, to curse at anything and everything, most of all at him for some reason. Even though it wasn't his fault technically, it was still him she was angry at. It made little sense at first, until she started to really make herself question why and found her answer when she remembered the last moment before the tunnel broke.

She stopped rubbing to glare over at him. He had been the one to pull her out. It had been him who had saved her from getting crushed, who had brought her here. Perhaps she should be grateful, but she wasn't. If anything, it only made her grow ever more suspicious of his motives.

Then she realized something he had said only a few minutes ago.

"You said 'we' not 'I.' What did you mean?" she asked.

The alien tapped at his thigh. "I don't follow."

"You said 'we can't go back.' And you brought me here. You could have killed me while I laid here or left me to die or to be taken by those thugs."

The dark beads along his brow, which Elise hadn't caught before, rose slightly. "You think I wanted to...kill you?"

"I don't know," she said low, watching him carefully. "But you said 'we' as in together. Why?"

He didn't speak for a long moment. The light passed over several times and Elise was close to losing her patience and forcing him to talk when he said, "Your Ulink is broken."

Shocked, Elise looked down at her arm and saw it was gone. When she looked back up, it was in the alien's hand. She opened her mouth to order him to give it to her when he threw it over, and she caught it, only for it to crumble in her hands.

"Did you do this?" she asked.

"No. But I was planning to."

She glanced back at him, wide-eyed. "What the hell for? I could have called for help if it worked! I could have—"

"It was being tracked. All of them were."

She gave him her best 'yeah, right' face. "And how the hell would you know that, exactly?"

"The woman drogin, the one who gave me this." He pointed to the translator in his ear.

"Toni," Elise said.

"She mentioned all Ulinks are connected to the city mapping system," he continued. "If the drogin officials had access, so did the attackers."

"So, what about yours?"

"I didn't take one."

"Why?" Elise said.

He tilted his head back, his mouth curving to one side. Elise took a deep breath, understanding.

"Because you knew that the Ulinks followed people, and you

didn't want to be tracked," she said softly, combing a hand through her hair. The headache was growing worse. She brought her legs up to her chest and covered her face in her hands. The alien said something in his language that she didn't follow, but she glanced back at him anyway and saw the glare of a screen from his wrist.

"Your band," Elise said. "They aren't tracking that?"

He turned his wrist to look down at it. "No," he said.

"So, you could call your team, have them come get us."

"Not that simple." Before she could say, "Why?" he put up his hand. "They could be dead. Or imprisoned. Or hiding. I have sent a message out but will only receive word if...if they are in a safe place to do so. Even then..." He said more in his language that she didn't catch then tried once more to say it slower in drogin. "Even then...they can't help us, and we can't help them."

Elise swallowed hard and felt a sickly, empty feeling in the pit of her stomach. She rested her head on her knees. "I can't stay here. I have to get back. I have to go..."

"You won't survive," he said in a matter-of-fact way, not just as an opinion. "You have no communication, no food or water, and only one weapon."

She lifted her head to say she had two weapons, but when she looked over her shoulder, she saw her sniper was gone, likely tossed off at some point when the bomb ignited under the car.

"You are alone. Against an uncertain number of people looking to find you."

Elise didn't want to be told the facts nor hear it from the likes of him. "I've survived just fine on my own. I've been trained since a little girl on how to survive in harsh elements. I can find food and water. I can find another weapon, and I can hide."

He snorted, and she wanted to slap him.

"And I can fight," she continued in a voice that grew louder and, to her relief, didn't shake. "And if I can get back to the higher sectors and get help, then more soldiers can come."

"And how do you plan to get back, exactly? The one gate left on this side is gone. If you go to other gates, more of those men will be waiting for you."

"A ship then."

His eyes brightened as they looked on her sharply. "That you yourself will drive? Assuming you can. Assuming you will even find one that works." He gestured to the pit behind her where the remains of one ship rested. "And without a map to guide you."

Elise gritted her teeth. "I'll figure it out. I'll find a way." She tried to shift her legs up so that she could stand once more. She was done talking with him, arguing and wasting time. Her team needed her, and she needed to find them.

"No."

"What?" she said, still struggling to rise.

"You won't figure it out. Not on your own," he said.

She stopped. "I don't need you to tell me—"

"You're weak."

She glared back at him, struck speechless.

"You're weak," he repeated unapologetically. "You won't last a day on your own in the state you are in. You hit your head, you are without water, and come night, someone or something may come that you can't win against. I have scouted the buildings close by, and most are abandoned, but they are also broken and give little shelter."

Elise's jaw clenched, and her hands tightened to fists. "I'm not weak."

He stood up and, before Elise could move, was standing right by her. "If you wish to leave then go. Try so now."

Elise glared up at him a second longer then started again to rise. Slowly, she got to her feet and steadied herself. The dizziness had lessened this time, though her balance was a little off. That didn't stop her from trying to walk. She started forward, making her way over to what she assumed was an exit, when the hunter appeared from nowhere and got in her way. She frowned and tried to move around him, but he blocked her.

"Get out of my way," she snapped.

"Make me."

Stunned at first, Elise could see he was serious. No smile played on his lips, no amusement sparked in his eyes, and his expression only darkened. Frustrated, Elise tried to push through him and found herself gripped by the collar of her suit and flung away. She fell to her knees and looked back at him with shocked fury.

"You can't force me to stay!"

"I can't?" he said. Then he came at her. Elise barely had time to swing herself around before he stood above her and pushed her down as she tried to stand. Elise scrambled back, trying to distance herself from him, yet, still, he followed her.

"I'm one of them. One of those masked men. Or just a stranger. I've found you resting in some building all alone." He picked up her gun which she had left carelessly on the ground like a damn fool, thinking only of her need to get away from him. "I've found you defenseless, your gun,"—he raised it then tossed it aside out of reach —"useless. You are weak from the attack and have no way to fight me." He leapt at her, catching her leg and dragging her toward him. Elise shouted and kicked but it did nothing. "I'm either going to kill you or take you. And you can't stop me." He tried to pin her, and Elise struck out, wrenching herself out of his grip only for him to take hold of her again. "Which will it be?"

She cried out with rage, her headache worsening, her body growing heavy. She hated him for stopping her and for fighting her, but most of all, she hated how right he was, even if she didn't want to admit it.

"Well?" he said, keeping her in place.

"Get off me," Elise whispered.

He studied her for a long moment and must have seen the defeat in her eyes because he released her quickly and let her sit up. He walked off without looking at her. "I'm glad you could finally come to your senses."

"Asshole," Elise cursed under her breath. But in the end, she was ashamed of only herself. She should be smarter than this. Better than this. Not acting on her emotions. It must have been that hit to the head but also the deep anger she felt at her predicament, of the fear she had for her team, if they were even still alive.

I should have known something was wrong.

She had felt that odd feeling, but because she couldn't explain it nor had any evidence at the time for its cause, she had decided to let it go, knowing it would have done nothing good for her team to mention it and they wouldn't have believed her anyway. Now she was alone in the undercity with the last person she would have chosen to be with.

Elise looked over at the hunter as his back was turned then over to her gun and knew she should just be grateful he hadn't been one of the ones to betray them because she'd most certainly be dead.

"If you want to survive...we will need to join together." He turned back to her. "I have a working map and information on how the city is run. You want out and a chance to find your team, you'll have to come with me."

Elise didn't respond, and he started to walk away.

"I'm going out," he said. "If you wish to try to leave again, I won't stop you. But it would be...good for you to stay. When I return, we'll talk over a plan."

"Why are you helping me?" Elise asked before he slipped out of sight.

The alien stopped and looked back. "Because you're going to help me finish my mission."

CHAPTER EIGHT

It didn't take Nezka long to find others. The small gang sitting out in one of the abandoned buildings nearby didn't notice his presence nor did they notice him take a few of their provisions, namely a pair of metal canteens and two bags which he stuffed with packaged food and a ragged set of clothes. They were clearly a harmless lot, possibly a lowly band of thugs or thieves. They were not like the masked men who had attacked them. Those men he was sure were part of a much larger, more complex gang, maybe even the one he had been tasked to hunt—the Red Blades. They hadn't fought with blades, but he had a feeling they were them.

They hadn't put up much of a fight but likely they didn't expect someone like him to be teamed up with the city officials. Likely, there were many more skilled in combat within their stronghold. Their attack had been well coordinated but that was because they had had a lot of time to plan, meaning someone knew many days before about the mission.

If he was pissed about it, he didn't show it. Was it a major inconvenience? Yes. But it wasn't going to stop him. There was still the possibility that the team of human soldiers might have survived. The tunnel had collapsed right at the exit, true, but the car built like a tank might have sheltered them. It was a low chance but a chance all the same. Even if they were dead, there was still the original team of humans still being held somewhere within the undercity.

And even if they were also found eliminated, there was still her...

Yes, he had saved the human woman from being crushed and was keeping her close now for the very purpose of his mission, or so he told himself. But he hadn't lied about needing her help. Assuming the other humans still lived, she could be useful in finding and getting his way to them...if he played this right, and if she behaved.

He smiled at the thought. No, she likely wouldn't.

But she would need his help, and he knew now it wouldn't be hard to convince her to follow him. Getting her to do what he wanted might be another issue, but if she was adamant about surviving, she would need to trust him.

His smile faded. Of course, once they got out, he would have to take her back to Xolis, back to Vesra. She would trust him only because he could get her out of the city, and he would betray that trust to take her to another, all so she could be sold off to the nillium—the rulers of Xolis—to be nothing but a breeder. If she was all that survived...

He would find the other humans, even if he had to do it all alone now that his team was separated. Where they were, he didn't wonder nor care at the moment. If they survived, they would contact him in time, and they would continue on as usual. He was confident some of them must have gotten out some other way, and he would know of it soon enough.

The gang of drogin laughed loudly as they sat around talking, breaking his thoughts. Nezka thanked them for it by stealing one of their guns. He took the holster for it too and clipped it to his waist, then he shouldered the bags and snuck out the back.

Before he returned to the place where the girl waited, Nezka climbed up the side of another building until he reached its top. The buildings beneath the higher city were wider and older, built with a sort of concrete and old metal unlike the massive chrome and glass towers from above whose bases could be seen at various points like giant legs planted in the middle of this lower part of the city. Bridges and tramways several hundred feet above his head connected together like a web along the sky, blocking out a lot of the natural light to which there was already very little thanks to the thick cloud cover miles above. There were, however, artificial lights seen all across the city from top to bottom, though they were much more sporadic in the lower sector. Still, he could see the neon colors and see the glow of larger buildings in the distance to one side, some domed, some tall enough that they even hit the top of bridges, seeming to keep it in place. There were even those few places where no bridges or trams went across and where the space was open to the sky.

Looking in the direction to which he would need to follow based off the map, Nezka saw not too far ahead, the next gate, a large, lengthy wall, with buildings placed above it, that served as a gateway for those to cross the next section of the undercity and for those to enter the lower or higher sectors. Of course, the tunnels and stairways had been closed off and blockaded to keep the gangs from spreading, but if one only needed to get to the other side of the wall, they could pass through a smaller gate or so he was told. This assumed, of course, that they weren't being guarded. But Nezka knew they would be. So, getting past those who controlled it now that he didn't have a whole slew of drogin soldiers at his back would be difficult.

He'd think about it later. For now, he needed to get back. He climbed down and stopped on the street when he caught something passing by. Or several large somethings. Some sort of stray beasts by the look of them were chewing up scraps of another animal nearby. Nezka watched them for a moment, taking note to avoid them before slipping away.

* * *

"You can't honestly be serious about this," the human said as she looked over the holographic map lit up before them by Nezka's techband which was laid flat on the ground so that they both could see it properly.

Nezka thought that an odd statement. Of course he was serious. "Why would I not be serious?" Nezka said plainly.

The human sighed, rubbing her head again. He wasn't sure yet if it was because her head still hurt or if it was a normal human sign of frustration. "We can't finish the mission," she said. "We are the only ones left. The plan should be to get *out* of the undercity, *not* go farther in. We might as well let ourselves get caught."

"We won't get caught."

The girl shook her head. "This is insane. No, actually, it's suicide. I won't go."

Nezka rubbed the side of his neck. "I have to finish the mission. If you won't come..."

She sighed again then took another sip from the canteen he had stolen. She grimaced as she swallowed, though he had made sure the container had been filled with water and not something poisonous or undrinkable by her kind's standards. Clearly, water didn't suit them either. Or she was just being fussy about it. "Why, though? Why go? Why not wait for more to come?"

"No one is going to come. There's no point waiting for help," he explained.

"The drogin will surely bring more forces," she said before taking another sip.

"You think so? Do you have that much faith in them? You think they will sacrifice more of their own just to save a small group of humans?"

She frowned, saying nothing.

"Besides, I know a better reason for you to go." He tapped at the map, bringing the energy deposit where the humans were said to be into focus. "If some of your team lived then they were likely taken by the attackers. I believe those same attackers are the ones who took the other group of humans."

Her eyes widened. "So you think they would be together?"

He tapped his ear, and she looked at him, confused. "Yes," he said.

Her eyes shifted over the map, her expression growing troubled. "If they are, then...I guess we have to go." She gazed up at him. "But how exactly are we supposed to get out after?"

"That...you will have to leave up to me." In other words, he didn't know yet. "But I can say the likelihood of them having ships is high."

"But I thought ships couldn't get down here."

"Only if there are outage barriers or shields in place," he stated. "But if they needed to leave or escape for whatever reason I'm willing to bet they have a way to shut it off."

"That's only a prediction. You can't possibly know."

"True," he said. "But the only way to know is to go and see for ourselves. Other forms of escape might present themselves in time, and who knows...by then, the drogin might actually come to our aid."

She didn't look entirely convinced, but he knew she wasn't about to say no if it meant getting back to her people.

"All right. Say they do have my team and that there is a clear way to escape once we save everyone. How the hell are we going to get there without, I don't know, being seen? Or caught?" She threw out her arm for some reason, and he watched her hand curiously as she pointed at nothing. "Obviously, I know there are other species walking the city besides drogin, I've seen them. They might think you're just another odd immigrant. But we don't know who is friend or foe, who might be working with who. And if those men are looking for me for whatever reason, if the wrong kind of person sees me, they might go running to those responsible for the attack."

"You're not wrong. And I have...ideas."

"Like?"

Nezka tilted back his head and smirked. "Besides just throwing down anyone who looked at you wrong or taking out every single person who got in my way? A disguise, if that's even possible. Or,"—

he tapped the map again, bringing up the wider area and highlighting a route.

Her brows lowered. "What path is that?"

"It's an old tram system. One which traveled underground."

Her brows rose. "You want to walk the abandoned tram tunnels?"

"That's the idea."

She shook her head, and he took that to mean she didn't entirely like the idea. "That could be the very path the gangs are using to get around."

"Maybe," he said. "Maybe not. And even if they are, there's several paths to use. Unless they are squatting in there, which I doubt."

She laughed softly. "And even if they are, you'll pummel them all, right?"

"Exactly."

She rubbed her head again. He wondered if she'd got hit there worse than he thought.

"I guess...it'll have to work for now." She got up slowly, and he watched her pick up her gun, holster it, then go for the bag he'd brought her.

"Where are you going?" he asked.

"If we leave now, we can get to the first station by the next gate before it gets dark."

Now it was his turn to laugh. He closed his eyes and rubbed the bridge of his nose. "Woman, you are entertaining at the worst and best of times."

She threw out her arms again. Strange. "Are you...serious? There's still plenty of daylight left. We should make headway now, while we can."

He tried to give her a stern gaze, but he couldn't help smiling, which didn't help. "As much as I feel your urgency to go, you are in no position to do anything, at least today. You'll need your strength if you want to keep up with me"—she murmured something in her language and he could guess what it was—"and I'd rather not have you slow me down. Or do we need another lesson on how you're not in a weakened state?"

She clenched her jaw then turned from him, dropping her bag to the farther end of the room and hunkering down against a pillar. "Tomorrow then."

"We will see."

She reclined against her bag and closed her eyes then, after a moment, opened them again. "I'm not 'woman,' by the way."

"How's that?" he asked.

"I have a name."

"Oh?"

She wrapped her arms about her and turned her head to look out over the darkened room. "You should probably know since...it's Elise."

"Elise?"

She nodded, and he took that to mean yes. "That is all?" he said.

She looked at him oddly. "Elise Stirling...not that you need to know my last name," she murmured

"Sorry, did you say Starling?" He really wasn't sure he heard her correctly with her human accent.

"*Stirling.*"

Hm. Pity. He liked Starling much better. "Nezka," he said, placing a hand against his chest.

"Is that all?" she said in a strange tone. Sarcasm?

He smiled. "Nezka...Voidstorm."

She snorted. But then seemed to look guilty for laughing. "It suits you."

He took that as a compliment. "Eat. Rest. If you can walk tomorrow without stumbling over yourself, then we will go."

She gave him a dirty look and closed her eyes. Then, after a pause, she unclipped her gun and rested it on her lap, gripping it tight, eyeing him again with clear distrust. "Just in case," she said and closed her eyes once more, pretending to sleep.

CHAPTER NINE

T̲H̲E̲ ̲R̲E̲S̲T̲ ̲O̲F̲ ̲T̲H̲E̲ ̲D̲A̲Y̲ ̲H̲A̲D̲ ̲P̲A̲S̲S̲E̲D̲ ̲B̲Y̲ ̲S̲L̲O̲W̲L̲Y̲ ̲A̲N̲D̲ ̲T̲H̲E̲ ̲N̲I̲G̲H̲T̲ had been excruciatingly long. Elise fell in and out of sleep several times, waking up periodically to eat one of the tasteless bars from her bag or to find another part of the building to use as a bathroom before once more trying to fall back asleep. Sometimes the hunter Nezka was there when she woke up, sometimes he wasn't. Every time she awakened, her heart would jump in her chest and her gun would instinctively rise, but when she found him nowhere near her, she calmed considerably. She knew she was going to have to learn to trust him. She knew she didn't have much of a choice. Still, she eyed him every so often in the dark, pretending to be asleep, watching as his back was turned, as he looked over something on his wrist band or while he inspected the gun he had likely stolen along with all the other items. She should probably be upset by that fact. Soldiers didn't steal from citizens. But in this instance, she couldn't bring herself to worry or care. There were more important things to think about.

At one point, she caught him with a pair of blades she had yet to see on his person, hidden in some pocket of his armored suit. He trained with them, using one of the broken pillars to spar with. The blades sliced through the metal and concrete like butter, and Elise found herself shivering at the thought of him using them on someone, cutting through muscle and bone like it was nothing. She noted how swift and agile he moved, how his limbs shot out and struck as quick as a viper, how he stepped and circled with ease. When he seemed bored of that, he started through the blades, aiming at random targets, making his mark every time without fail. He was good, she couldn't deny that. She wondered in one of her half-sleep states who had trained him, where he was from. Eventually, she fell asleep again, the sounds of his blades drumming in her head as she fell from reality and into nothingness. Then the dreams came—the crashing of waves, her sister smiling, a drogin dead on the ground, twin fires blazing in the dark, a blade cutting her open—and she'd wake again with a start, her gun aimed at nothing.

When dawn finally came, Elise was up and feeling groggy but still much better than the day before. The headache had subsided, and she didn't get dizzy when she stood or walked. She was no longer dehydrated or in need of food for energy and was deeply confident she was better and ready to move on.

"What the hell do you mean one more day?" Elise said as Nezka seemingly ignored her while reorganizing the things in his bag. "I said I'm fine."

He looked up and studied her from where he crouched and didn't appear convinced. "Just because you can stand and walk without issue doesn't mean you are better."

"Let's have a test then." She holstered her gun and walked several feet away before stopping and turning back. "Come at me, and you will see."

The alien stared at her then turned away to let out a low hiss of laughter.

"I'm serious!"

He stopped laughing then slowly stood and twisted around. "All right. Follow me."

She did so hesitantly. They made their way out of the building to another right across. Elise gazed above at the bridges and towers overhead as they walked, noticing bits of debris and garbage falling every so often, smashing down on the streets below. Disgusted, she followed Nezka into the next building that stretched long like a warehouse. Near its center was a wall half broken at the top. Nezka stopped just at the entrance and tapped something into the screen of his wrist band. "You've got thirty seconds. Run across, climb over the wall, and return in that time and we will go."

Elise opened her mouth then closed it. Arguing seemed pointless. Thirty seconds was a short amount of time and certainly didn't seem like enough to make it to the end and back. She was about to say how unfair that was when suddenly she thought of her father. "Don't whine at me. Just do it," he would say. And if she ever complained, he only made the training harder until she completed it. This was no different.

"Fine." Elise took position.

"When the timer goes, begin. Ready?" He lifted his band, and Elise bent her knees, her eyes zoning in on the broken wall.

As soon as she heard the sharp ring from his band, Elise kicked off with all her strength and sprinted like her life was at stake. No, not her life, her team's. She made it to the wall and dashed up it, climbing over then jumping down the other side. She rushed for the end then, pushing off the wall to give her momentum, she quickly turned and made for the other side. She climbed up the broken wall, hopped down and charged forward without slowing, sliding only as she came to the entrance.

She hadn't heard the timer go off, so she looked to the hunter for clarification as she huffed, leaning against the wall. "Well?"

He looked down at her, studying her carefully. "You seem greatly out of breath."

"Did I make it or not?"

Nezka watched her a moment longer then tapped once at his band. "You succeeded."

Elise smiled as she wiped sweat from her brow. She was a little lightheaded, but she wasn't about to tell him that. "There then," she said, still breathless. "Let's get going." She saw his mouth curve ever so slightly before she left and made her way back to their building to start packing their things. That run, she knew, had made her sweat under her armor and suit, but she didn't have time to think of a bath. She just wanted to get out of this place and closer to where her people were waiting.

They readied their bags and checked their gear. Elise noticed with disappointment that her gun's charge was already less than half full, and she had one charging clip left, the others lost to her in the attack. She would have to make do until she could find another gun. They had enough provisions to last them at least a couple days but who knew how long it may take them to reach the energy deposit at this point. Now that they had no vehicle to take them and were forced on foot, what should have only taken a day would now possibly take days maybe even a week, and that was only if they weren't stopped several times along the way. Elise knew better than to think they wouldn't run into trouble. She was expecting it. Even if the tram tunnels were unoccupied, at some point they would have to leave them. And then there was getting into the stronghold of this gang they called the Red Blades. Planning that could take time. Elise was just thankful they were finally setting out. Every day they wasted was a day that could be her team's last.

Elise secured her bag over her shoulder and kept her gun on ready-fire. She looked to Nezka, who waited close by with his bag across his back and gun at his side, watching her for any sign of weakness. When he didn't seem to find any in her (or decided now was too late to question her about it), he moved across the room and headed for the exit. "Stay close and do as I say. If I tell you to run, run. If I say hide, hide. Don't try to be a hero and shoot every threat you see. Think you can do that?" he said.

"Yes, I can follow orders. I was trained for that, you know," she said from behind him, glaring at his back.

"We'll see." She didn't see his face but knew he was probably smirking or something. He stopped just before the doorway to look around. When he deemed the area clear, he stepped out and moved quickly across the road with Elise following close by his side.

* * *

They ran into a small gang of drogin not long after they left. Thankfully, Nezka had noticed the group in time before being seen, and they hid themselves in another building nearby as the drogin ran around, barking and hollering and shooting their guns off for no particular reason. They seemed to be getting around on some kind of vehicle made out of used parts. It reminded Elise of the dune buggies her family had out at their second home in the desert, only this one was much more misshapen and had lights underneath for whatever reason, maybe just for show. It also had writing on its side, but she couldn't make out the words. Perhaps the name of their gang. They disappeared as quickly as they came, but Elise knew they were only the beginning.

The closer they got to the station that led to the tramway, the more drogin and otherkin they saw. Every time they encountered someone, they hid and waited till they passed, watching them carefully, hands at their weapons. Most seemed harmless if a bit unhinged. It was later that Elise realized that they were mostly just bums, scrapping around for parts to sell. One lone man looked like a mangy cat, his fur all knotted, some even missing. He looked like the same species as one of the hunters on Nezka's team. Nezka told her he was called a lygin.

"They're from your world?" she asked as the lygin moved away.

"Same worlds," he said, looking at her. "They come from the same territory."

Elise remembered what Toni said. She had said it was an empire. They had called it Xolis. Elise was curious about it, but now was not the time to ask.

They moved on, weaving through buildings and climbing over a few walls until they reached a path that took them to the entrance to the tram station. The entrance was nothing more than a tunnel that led down into the earth below. Above the entrance was a statue of a tram carved out of metal and a sign that must have lit up at one time but had long since been shut off. Blocking the tunnel was another sign. One clearly meant as a warning to not enter as it had a huge X at the top. Below the text were more words, drawn rather crudely, but Elise couldn't identify them.

"What do you suppose that means?" Elise asked after a moment of staring at the sign with uncertainty.

Nezka studied the sign for a second longer then started forward.

"Hold on." Elise caught at his arm and immediately let go as he looked at her. "Ah, maybe we should rethink this?"

Nezka tilted his head. He looked back at the tunnel then back at her. "You're afraid?"

"I didn't say that." Elise glanced at the tunnel. A breeze came up to meet them, bringing with it a musty, foul smell.

"You think it too dangerous then? If so, there is still the gate, but it will take more time to find a way through, and the likelihood of running into the Red Blades who now guard it..."

"I get that." Elise eyed the sign and the tunnel beyond.

"We face something either way. Maybe in there"—he gestured to the tunnel—"we can avoid whatever that something is."

"You sound very sure," Elise said.

"I'm not entirely. But the options are before us and we have little time."

At that, the roar of a loud engine could be heard close by. The drogin were approaching in their vehicle. Nezka didn't move, only looked to her for a decision. Elise knew she could tell him right then that they should try for the gate and he wouldn't hesitate. But he was right, the chance of them having to go against men that had weapons and had the advantage of higher, more secure ground was a problem. It likely meant another whole day of planning just to find a way through—something she couldn't afford. Whatever lay in the dark, she had to hope they could get past without issue.

And who knows, maybe it was harmless, right?

The sound of the car was growing louder. Nezka waited.

"All right." Elise stepped away and turned for the tunnel. "All right, let's go for it."

Nezka started again for the entrance, and Elise reluctantly followed. The breeze picked up, flinging strands of hair in her face. Elise brushed it away then readjusted her hair into a ponytail to keep it out of her eyes. The smell was unpleasant to say the least, like something that had badly spoiled. As they took the stairs down, the air began to warm up, not cool down like she expected. As the light from above faded, Elise turned on the lights on her suit and unholstered her gun. Nezka took up his gun as well, using the light on his scope to see.

The station was a mess, not that that was any surprise. The walls and floors were corroding, garbage and pieces of roofing scattered all over. Water trickled from broken vents above, pooling on the ground, turning piles of whatever debris had fallen into sludge. It really looked no different than some of the abandoned subway systems she'd seen back home. The only difference was the graffiti. Unlike the kind found back on Earth's cities, the tags or 'art' along the walls of this station glowed in the dark, as if backlit by some unseen light. It reminded her of those buildings where raves were held, where everything glowed in neon colors, the black lights giving them their shine.

There were no lights here though, so she was curious how they glowed so brightly on their own. The glow of them even lit up the station to a degree. Enough for them to see the railway and the two tunnels going off in separate directions.

Nezka checked the map. "The left goes toward the gate, and from there, a connected route passes below to the other side. We could take the trail as far as possible till we can't go any farther, bypassing several miles without being seen."

"I'm not so sure I want to be down here that long," Elise said, observing the many miles of tunnels before them.

"We'll go as far as we can. We can make some distance, at least, before sundown."

Elise agreed to that, and Nezka closed out the map. He stepped over to the platform and jumped down with ease. Elise did the same, though with not as much grace. She was noisier than him, her boots scraping against the ground, kicking into random junk while he didn't seem to make a sound as he made his way cautiously down the railway tunnel.

Guess I need to work on that, Elise thought and tried her best to step over rocks and garbage like he did while still trying to keep up.

The farther in they went, the less graffiti they saw and the less garbage they found. Some sections were crumbling away while others were slick with putrid water from rusted pipes. Elise saw what looked like the city's equivalent to rats skirting around her boots. Only they had longer tails and ears. There was no sign of anything else lurking, but she continued to keep her gun at the ready. The breeze seemed to warm up the deeper in they went, and the smell strengthened. This didn't slow the hunter, though Elise couldn't help feeling concerned about what might be waiting ahead.

At one point, they found a service tunnel, a slight short-cut to a connecting railway. From there, they began to hear voices and knew they were approaching the under part of the gate. The closer they got, the clearer the voices became.

"Boda, for fuck's sake, it's dead already. Just let it be."

A dull bang rang out, like something hitting the ground. "Hate when they come out of the dark like that, gives me the creeps."

"Just be glad it was one of the kids." Someone laughed.

Nezka paused at the end of the passage to look out. Elise couldn't see much with his back in the way, but she did make out the flicker of a light and a pair of shadows moving along the far wall of the tunnel.

"I'm sick of this shit, for real. There's no point being down here, Kodi. No one's gonna walk this."

"Lady Moth said to be on the lookout for those that might try coming along."

"Then why is it just the two of us patrolling? Rio, that ass, should have sent more of us down."

"You think we can't handle a couple of soldiers? Assuming any of them actually made it out when the gate got seized and the tunnel broke."

"I heard some got out. You never know."

Nezka put up his hand for her to wait. Then, slowly, he clicked off the light on his gun and snuck out of the passage, disappearing into the dark corners of the railway tunnel. Elise looked out from the end of the passage and saw, not far down the way, two drogin men wearing the same gear as those who had attacked them at the first gate, the large X's across their chests glowed red. Funny, despite their namesake, they didn't wield blades or knives of any sort. They instead had their guns drawn, not bothering to keep a close watch of their surroundings; talking with their backs turned as they stood on the edge of a platform.

"I think we should just go," one said. "Nothing is gonna come this way. And if they do, Moki will probably be awake. I don't wanna stick around if he is."

Nezka snuck onto the platform with a blade now in hand and was on them before they could even so much as shout or aim their guns. With lightning quick movement, he cut them down. One from the back then the other in the same fashion. They went down before their faces could even portray shock. Nezka didn't hesitate. He kicked the guns onto the tracks and began rifling through their pockets.

Elise, feeling it was probably safe for her to approach, did so. As she came to the platform, she eyed the guns at her feet. They were too big, unfortunately, to fit in their bags, and carrying them would be a pain as they required both hands to hold them properly. She picked one up and found them to be rather heavy as well. When she held one up and aimed, she found the trigger was locked.

"They won't work for us. They've been programmed to be only of use to those to which they were assigned. A security measure. I've seen it before," Nezka explained.

"Great." Elise dropped the gun back on the ground. "Find anything useful?"

"No." He stood straight but continued to eye them curiously. Then he placed his bag down and started pulling out a few scraps of clothing and flinging them to the side. "Actually, these masks could be useful."

By masks he meant the ventilators she'd seen the men wearing at the attack to keep smoke and ash out of their lungs. Probably used when they set off smoke bombs and the like. They were large and covered the whole lower half of their faces. Nezka stuffed the pair into his bag then threw it back over his shoulder. As he dropped down, Elise started forward to join him when she felt something squishy under her foot. She looked down and saw a tentacle. As her eyes followed it, she found it attached to a squid-like creature with several eyes. She cursed and jumped back, but the creature didn't move. It was clearly dead.

"Gross," she said, shaking the slime off her boot. Nezka came over and studied it, moving the creature with his foot. "What is it?" Elise asked, as if he would know.

Nezka didn't speak, only stared down at it. He closed his eyes and rubbed a hand along his forehead then looked back at her. "Let's keeping moving."

Confused, Elise gave the creature one last glance-over before following Nezka into the next tunnelway.

They passed the gate now, at least. But what little excitement she felt in that was overpowered by the growing sense of urgency to get out of the tunnels. Though she found it hard to know what Nezka was truly thinking or feeling, something in his walk and the way he stopped every so often to look around or to perhaps listen put her on edge. She found herself looking over her shoulder more than once and pointing her gun at everything that made the smallest bit of noise.

Despite her tension, nothing met them in the darkness, and after nearly a mile and a half of walking, she started to ease up, thinking maybe they wouldn't see anything after all, that they would pass through undetected.

But the smell didn't fade, and soon they were seeing signs of animal markings, or at least Nezka identified them as such. Slick black marks along the walls and cracks in the roof were clearly made by something Elise had no desire to meet. A really big something. But she knew they were too far deep now to turn back. She could only hope the hunter would steer them away.

Eventually, they came to their first dead end—a caved-in tunnel—and Elise could see the hunter was debating what to do.

"We could turn back and just find another route," Elise said after a moment. "I'm sure one would take us close, in the direction we need to go." Nezka pulled up the map. Elise drew up beside him to look over his arm. "Ah, see there,"—Elise pointed to another tunnel close by, only a little out of their way— "we take the service tunnel from there and head toward the central hub."

Nezka didn't say anything as he closed out the map. He turned and moved out of the now blocked tunnel, walking back the way they came. "We head south," he said.

Elise stopped. "South?" She hurried to catch up with him. "But that's way out of our path."

"It will be better."

"How?"

"Trust me."

Glaring at his back, she kept quiet, telling herself it was better not to argue, that he knew something she didn't, though she would've liked to have been in the know also. They picked up speed to gain back the time they had lost, but once they traveled down the service tunnel and came to a fork, Nezka stopped, and Elise thought she heard him murmur something low in his own tongue. Before she could even ask, she heard the voices and saw lights flickering around the curve of the south tunnel.

"Looks like they found their buddies," Elise said. "Guess we're headed to the central hub after all." She started for the north tunnel but Nezka didn't move. "Are you coming or not?"

Nezka looked back at her, the fires of his eyes bright against the dark. He started down the tunnel leading to the hub, and Elise followed him.

The musty smell strengthened, and murky water began to rise around their boots. An inky black that absorbed the shine of their lights.

"Hold." Nezka stopped. His eyes flickered down to study the water when the shouts of men grew closer, lights aiming in their direction. A few stray bullets flew by, bouncing off the walls.

"We need to go!" Elise nearly shouted as the noise rang down the tunnel. Nezka tugged on her arm once, pulling her to move faster.

They ran until the tunnel curved around slightly and opened into a long, vast chamber. As they paused by the edge of the tunnel, Elise could see that the central hub was made up of several railways with platforms between them and tunnels along opposite ends going in different directions. The tracks they currently ran on traveled across the second level of the hub with a platform to one side and stairs leading down to the other railways. From below, the trams sat at their platforms, now abandoned, and the tracks on the first level were completely flooded. Elise could see all this by the light that spilled from above, seeping through the holes and cracks in the ceiling. It made the place look ominous.

"When I say, make for the other side and don't stop," said Nezka.

Elise looked at him, confused. "What about you?"

The sounds of the men behind them were drawing closer. Nezka turned back toward the tunnel. "I'll be right behind you."

Not in the least convinced, Elise tried to make him look at her, but his focus was on the tunnel. Shaking her head and cursing under her breath, she readied her gun and looked down the tracks to the other end. One part was crumbling away, but besides that, it was a straight shot to the other side.

The lights were nearing, and the hollering of men grew louder. "Go," Nezka ordered. He looked back at her when she didn't move. "Now."

Elise, this time, didn't hesitate. Quickly glancing down at the level below, she rushed down the tracks with gun tight in hand. The first set of shots went off, and Elise couldn't help turning her head back to see. Behind her, the hunter was shooting into the tunnel, toward the men coming at him. Flashes of light burst from the tunnel-way, bullets ricocheting off his armor. Elise made it to the other side then slowed and stopped. Nezka shot back at the group of men while receding slowly down the tracks toward her. The men began to spill from the tunnel, and as they did, Elise caught the glint of Nezka's blade as it appeared in his hand. He shot the last of his bullets, making two men drop cold on the tracks, then threw the gun down into the abyss below. The water began to move under them, frothing and bubbling. Elise aimed her gun, ready to fire at the group, when a massive tentacle shot out and grabbed onto the tracks.

A creature much like a squid with several eyes rose up out of the inky black and started climbing onto the railway. The men screamed, and Elise lost sight of Nezka in the flurry of tentacled arms flailing everywhere. She knew she should be running away, but she couldn't seem to make herself leave. Instead, she fired at the beast, aiming for its head and eyes.

Her focus was so sharp on the monster, Elise didn't see the second squid, much smaller than the first, come up and reach out for her. It went for her feet, and Elise only noticed in time to jump back out of its reach but not before another of its tentacles swept her off her feet. She kept hold of her gun but fell back, her legs tossing above her. She rolled away as another limb came down then crawled closer to the tunnel, shooting at its head where she could see it rising onto the tracks. Just as the creature retreated back, Elise spotted Nezka in the fray of tentacles, dodging then slicing them in half. She got to her feet and started forward when one of the last men standing outside the tunnel shot a round of firebombs across the tracks. They went off in a blaze of red flames and hot white mist. Elise was thrown back as the tracks blew apart in several small sections and the monster reared up with a loud groan as fire seared its many arms. She covered her head and twisted her back as spray hit her, making her armor sizzle. The mist dissolved, and she peered back, only to see the smaller squid coming up for her again. She skidded to her feet as she fired, slowing it only momentarily as she forced her legs to move, pushing herself into a sprint down the opposite tunnelway. She didn't stop, knowing the creature was still behind her, chasing her as it slithered and squeezed its way through the tunnel for her. She didn't know how long she ran, but when she finally came to another small station, she let out a small cry of relief. She forced herself up the platform and pushed herself up the stairs until she saw the dim light of day. When she made it out onto a road, she fell to her knees, her breath like fire in her lungs.

She was so dazed at first she didn't register that it was raining lightly. She also hadn't noticed the pack of aliens standing close by. She lifted her head and, when she finally saw them, lifted her gun, only for it to be knocked out of her hand. She lunged for it but one of the aliens—a very large lizard—kicked it out of her reach and pointed a knife at her face.

"You look lost," it hissed in drogin. It gave her a grotesque, venom-dripping smile. "What a pity."

CHAPTER TEN

Elise sat curled up against the back of the car, hands and feet tied together with a metal coil. The vehicle jerked and shook along as it sped down the road, engine roaring loud in her ears. Above the noise, music blasted, similar to techno, and the aliens spoke and laughed, though she couldn't hear what they said. Four of them together, one driving, two sitting up front, and another clinging to the back. Two were drogin, one was that cat species—lygin—and the other was the lizard who was similar to another one of the hunters in Nezka's group. Elise assumed they all came from Xolis and had somehow found their way here of all places. They were a grody, rough-looking group, with dirty, padded clothes and makeshift armor. Even the drogin pair were different from the more docile looking kind seen above. If the drogin of the high city were like the fancier looking dog breeds, the drogin of the under city were the mutts and the wolves. They were bigger, meaner looking, like some deranged werewolf with hair unclean and wild, teeth crooked or chipped. They smiled at her with their wolfish grins, one now sporting her gun, the other rifling through her pack, throwing items onto the road. Elise would have spit at them if not for the gag in her mouth.

She didn't know where exactly they were taking her, only that they were going way south, far out from where she needed to go. Between where they were taking her and what they planned to do with her, Elise thought about Nezka and if he was even still alive. She'd seen one of the bombs go off near him just before she herself had been thrown back. That kind of fire would have seared the skin at that range, melted it. Coupled with the tracks breaking apart and the squid monsters waiting below, she couldn't possibly fathom that he had survived. What she felt in that regard, she couldn't really decide. She wasn't relieved or happy, that was certain, and she told herself it was because she had lost her one chance to get to the energy deposit. She had no map now, no weapon, no way to fight them on her own. They weren't taking her to where her people were held, so she could only imagine what they were going to do.

As a soldier, she'd been trained for torture, so that didn't scare her. If just a mere captive, she knew she could endure. But if they made her a slave...

A vision of walking out from the jungle flooded her mind. She could still smell the smoke, still see the fires, hear the cries.

Laughter cut away the memory, and the car veered around a corner, swerving across the pavement. The car picked up speed, flying toward what looked to be a large metal gate. Past it, Elise could make out several wide buildings. More cars came into view, some like that strange dune buggy she'd seen before, others more like racers with low ceilings; a couple were even sleek like the luxury cars back home. All had lights on their frames and underbellies and chrome sidings. It looked like a lot of the parts were stolen; she suspected the nicer cars had been too.

As they came to the gate, the car halted to an abrupt stop. Guards on the roof noticed them, and one waved as the gate slid open. They flew on through, passing a courtyard with more cars and some motorcycles, into a wide-open garage with, yes, even more cars. People gathered everywhere, more than she had yet to encounter in the undercity. Their clothes were dark, some wearing a rough hide, like leather, others metal plates. A select few wore an emblem on the backs of their jackets—a large thorny plant with jagged teeth for petals and claws for leaves. The drogin howled and barked as they passed, the car making its way to the other end of the garage where a wide door slid open as the car came to a final halt. The four aliens jumped out, and the lizard pulled her from the back, swinging her over his shoulder.

They swept past the garage door into an equally large building that, from what Elise could tell, had once been a ship hangar. They went around to a long passage on the side of the building, past a pit at the center where ships must have once been stored but was now empty, and then over to the back. The area was dimly lit save for the bright colors of tags and mutant designs covering the walls and floors, the glow assaulting her senses. Elise jerked and squirmed over the lizard's shoulder, and he promptly smacked her ass and thighs hard to make her quit. Elise hollered through her gag, but it came out as nothing more than a strangled, muffled noise. When the lizard finally stopped walking, he dropped her like a sack of clothes, and she hit the ground with a dull thud. When Elise twisted around and peered over, the first thing she saw were two small ships, broken apart and dismantled. Below them, several aliens of various kinds stood around. Between them sat a drogin, probably the ugliest drogin she'd ever seen.

"What is that?" he sneered, drool clinging to the outer corners of his mouth. He looked like a gnarly bulldog with sagging skin and matted tufts of hair along his skull, his fangs poking out from his bottom lip.

"Found it crawling out from Moki's tunnels," the lizard said, tapping her side with his boot. "I think it's one of those humans. Heard about em' on the main feeds. Pretty sure it's a female."

"Pretty sure?" the ugly drogin growled.

The lizard tilted its head in a shrug. "A hunch."

The ugly drogin, which Elise took for the leader of this large pack, eyed Elise with watery gray eyes. "The Red Blades are looking for these from what I'm told." He leaned forward and bared his teeth in an awful grin. "You did good bringing her to us, Ruzi. This is our turf, but those ass-kissing scum-crawlers have acted like the undercity belongs to them. Well, we keep her, and they'll come looking. If they want to buy, they'll have to pay in blood." He gestured for Ruzi to bring her closer. The lizard grabbed Elise's arm and dragged her forward. Elise grimaced through her gag as the drogin's disgusting face came inches to her own, his breath like spoiled meat, making her feel sick. "Besides, I owe the others a little fun." He swiped the gag from her mouth. "You understand me, human?"

Elise spit the saliva that had built up in her mouth on the ground. "Yes," she said through gritted teeth. "I understand you. Now get your gross face away from mine."

The drogin looked stunned for a mere second then laughed, his drool spraying on her suit. "Ah, this one has a tough side." His eyes traveled over her body. "She looks like a fighter. You a fighter, human?"

"I'm a soldier," Elise corrected. "First division. If you let me go now, you won't face repercussions. But if you keep me, I swear to you, other soldiers will come and they will kick the shit out of every single one of you." A small lie—she didn't know if any would come, but she hoped it made him at least marginally concerned.

The drogin scratched his jaw. "That so?" He looked back at the lizard and his small group. "I want to see her fight. It's been a while since we've had any good fights in the pit, eh?"

"I'd put in good credits," the lizard replied.

This was not the reaction she was hoping for.

"She's not drogin but..." He grabbed her chin and turned her head one way then the other. "She's not hard on the eyes for an outer species." Elise pulled away in disgust, and he dropped his hand. "Tell you what, girl. You make good in a fight, and you can be one of my prized fighters, make me some decent money. If not, well...you'll just become a prize for those looking for a different sort of fun, eh?" He smiled.

"Fuck you," Elise whispered in her own tongue.

"Sounds good." He waved his hand, and Elise felt hands drag her up. She fought them, even getting a punch into one drogin's neck and a kick into a lygin's stomach, but there were too many. They secured her arms quickly, though she continued to struggle. The lizard, Ruzi, circled to her front and kicked her hard in the stomach to make her stop. Elise's legs buckled as she gasped for air.

"Now, Ruzi, that wasn't necessary," said the lead drogin. "She won't be any good in a fight if she can't stand."

"Sorry, boss."

The drogin sighed. "Give her a minute then drop her in. Get the others."

An alarm went off, and the aliens began to disperse, shouting and howling, "Fight! Fight!"

People swarmed into the building, taking up every space along the rails looking down into the pit at the center. They clanged their metal arm plates against the metal bars and growled and hissed in excitement. Elise was dragged over to the pit and dropped to her knees at its edge. She looked down and saw the floors were stained with old dried-up blood and possibly piss.

As she was gaining back her breath, the crowd parted, and a lone female dropped into the pit. A drogin female with spiked, red-tipped hair and a face like a hyena. The woman snarled up at Elise as she flexed her muscular arms.

Shit.

At any other time, Elise would have been glad for the challenge. But she had just come out of a terrifying ordeal in the tram tunnels and then been roughed up by these foul low lifes, so she wasn't exactly feeling a hundred percent. But clearly, she had no choice in the matter unless she wanted the alternative of watching someone else fight to have her on her back. And no way was she having that. So, it was to fight and hope she could somehow pull through.

Elise struggled to her feet and straightened. She took two deep breaths before carefully jumping down into the pit. The crowd jeered and shouted as she placed her back against the pit wall, watching the woman drogin pace before her. Several screens turned on all along the building, bringing up some kind of ranking system and chart. People took out their Ulinks, and the credits rolled in on the screen as they placed their bets. Two words also popped up bigger than the rest: A name—Shodi—followed underneath by the word human.

Elise stared up at the screens then, with jaw clenched, turned her eyes back to the drogin. Her hands turned to fists, and she slowly raised them, taking position.

Just remember your training. They might not be human, but that doesn't mean you can't take them, Elise.

A buzzer went off, and the drogin female charged her. Elise leaped out of the way just in time for the woman's fist to smash into the wall where she had stood only a mere second before. Elise swerved around and kicked for the woman's head. The drogin blocked her foot with the side of her arm. She struck for Elise again, and Elise ducked. There was a lot of blocking and dodging, Elise focusing on what she felt were the drogin's weak points—their face, neck, and back of legs. The crowd's roar rang in her ears as she jumped away from the woman's strike to land a kick to her chest. The drogin jolted back and bared her teeth in a growl. The hit barely knocked her off balance. Elise could tell she was all brawny strength but not as quick. She charged her blows, hoping one would land and take Elise out. All Elise had to do was make sure they didn't land. She circled the woman, jumping back every time she kicked or jabbed, waiting for another opening. Judging by her mass, Elise could gather she was a heavy gal. And the heavier they were, the harder they fell.

The drogin swung at her, barely missing her, and Elise took that chance to drop to one knee and kick out the female's legs. The woman landed hard on her back, and in that stunned moment, Elise took her chance and leapt on the woman, catching her in the throat and face. The drogin snapped at her then shoved her off. Elise rolled back and, as the drogin leapt up to charge her, swung out her leg in a high kick, hitting the drogin right in the head. The drogin's legs buckled, and she went down on her face in a clear knockout.

Elise barely heard the howls of the crowd. She looked up at the screen and saw the woman's name disappear. She smiled and turned her head toward the direction of the pack leader, who sat watching by the edge of the pit. He clapped his hands then made a cutting gesture to the crowd, who turned quiet.

"Not bad, human," he called down to her. "You managed to take out one of our best trainees."

Elise frowned. "Trainees?"

"Unfortunately for you, that was Obel's little sister."

Elise twisted around and saw, while the drogin she had just won against was being carried out of the pit, another was taking her place. A much bigger, more vicious looking female with two scars across her cheek. She looked pretty pissed.

"Obel is one of my best fighters," the pack leader continued. "And she'll want you to pay for what you just did. Good luck."

A buzzer sounded, and Obel snarled. Elise stumbled back as the giant woman came at her with a long stride. Elise dodged her first blow, rolling away, but the woman was on her quick. Elise blocked a heavy swipe and was knocked back against the wall, Obel's arm coming down like a hammer, shaking Elise to her bones. Elise ducked one blow and swerved under to catch her twice in the stomach, but it hardly seemed to faze her. Obel swung out her arm and caught Elise by the shoulder, throwing her across the pit. Elise fell, rolling till she hit the side of the wall with a sharp bang. She rose onto her knees only to be once again picked up and thrown across the other way. This time, Elise dropped on her back, sliding across the ground. Before she could even sit up, the female was on her. She blocked Elise's kicks and pinned her down before swinging out one great hand and smacking Elise right across the face. Elise's lip split and her face went numb as she saw stars. She put up her arms to block her face, and Obel responded by biting. She went for her forearm first, tearing at her suit and cracking her armor. Elise jabbed at her face, cuffing her ears then ramming her knuckles into the drogin's cheekbone. The drogin yelped then turned her head and snapped at Elise's hand. A fang ripped through Elise's glove into the skin, and Elise shouted as the searing pain went down her arm. She clocked Obel hard in the nose to make her back off, and when the female lifted her body, Elise lunged forward and wrapped her arms around the female's throat. Obel bucked, but Elise kept a firm hold. When she thought she might finally have her, the drogin lurched back and crushed Elise against the wall. Elise's grip loosened enough that the drogin twisted out of it then bit Elise on the shoulder, cracking the armor completely and burying her teeth down into Elise's skin. Elise screamed in pain while smashing her palm against Obel's head. Obel backed off and let Elise slide to the ground. Through the pain, she still willed herself to fight. But as Elise threw out her leg to keep the woman away, Obel caught it and tore the armor plate off her thigh, digging her nails deep past the suit into skin then pulling Elise off the ground and swinging her around.

Obel let go, and Elise went flying. This time, when she hit the wall, she didn't get up.

* * *

"Well, you gave a good show at least," the pack leader said, his face grinning down at her where she lay. Someone had dragged her out of the pit and dropped her next to the drogin's feet.

Elise groaned in response, her whole body feeling like it had been smashed and ripped to pieces. Blood trickled down her lip just as it seeped out from her suit where she'd been bitten and scratched. She could feel her cheek beginning to swell and her back ached something awful. She lifted her head for only a moment before dropping it back.

This was it. She'd fought her best, but she'd lost. She would be a prisoner of this gang until they decided to kill her or sell her to those willing to pay. She'd never find her team. They would be lost and so would the others they had come so far to save. Elise felt no tears coming, but she felt her heart sink into her stomach. She watched the others laughing, the crowd now fixated on a different fight down in the pit below. She closed her eyes and slipped away for what she thought was only a few seconds until she opened her eyes and found the crowd dispersing and heard the roars of engines starting. Night was in full swing, and the pack was off in their cars to cause more havoc on the city streets.

A boot nudged at her back. "Take her into one of the empty rooms."

Elise was pulled up and carried off, first out of the building to the one across from it then into a dark corridor of rooms (offices probably at one point) and dropped into an empty one where the door slammed shut, locking her in darkness.

She lay there in the now quiet, her ears ringing, mouth dry save for the taste of blood. She really needed to check her wounds and stop the bleeding, but she couldn't bring herself to rise. She closed her eyes instead, letting herself fall asleep.

She was woken up by a pair of hands grabbing at her and the sound of quiet hissing voices. She didn't open her eyes despite how rough the hands moved her. She felt her suit being unclasped from the back and pulled off her shoulders. Cold water cut into her skin as someone wiped at her wound. They muttered something, and she felt a dabbing cold at her thigh. They were treating her wounds only so that she didn't die from them but nothing more. They splashed water on her face then closed the door behind them. Elise licked the drops of water from her lips then laid back down and somehow managed to fall back asleep.

Light spilled from the door, this time waking her up with a start, her eyes shooting open, her hands grabbing for a weapon that wasn't there.

"Rise and shine," came a familiar voice. Ruzi.

She was pulled up, forced to her feet as the lizard dragged her from the room and down the corridor. As they went back across to the building where she'd gotten her ass handed to her, Elise lifted her head and saw the light above was dim, what she presumed to be early morning.

The building was empty as Ruzi tied Elise to one of the rails along the edge of the pit then left her. She didn't know how long she sat there, maybe hours. At one point, he returned to let her go to the bathroom then allowed her a sip of water before tying her back up. She tried to work at the bindings, but they were metal coil cinched tight against her skin. She started to shout then to scream for someone to come, to give her some more water if not maybe even food, but no one came. She heard the cars coming and going throughout the day, heard people, but no one entered the building to check on her. She spent most of the day staring at the ships at the back of the room, wishing they weren't stripped of parts, wishing they worked.

When night finally came, the pack leader returned with his group. She was untied from the rail and placed next to him as his people gathered once more into the building.

"Since this human has proven unworthy in the pit, maybe she will be worthy in someone's bunk," he said to the crowd. They laughed, and Elise caught more than a few eyes looking her way, looking a little too hungry for her liking. "All bets are off," the leader announced. "The prize is before me. The match will be a free for all. All those wishing to participate, enter the pit now."

Elise watched with sickening despair as several men and a few women (including Obel, to her surprise) dropped down into the pit. Most were drogin with a smattering of lizards and lygin, all huge and bulky in size, even the women.

There was only one she didn't recognize species-wise, and that was because he was wearing a mask and hood. In fact, as she got a better look at him, she realized with horrified fury that it was one of the Red Blades. The pack leader seemed to notice him too and cut at the air with his hand to order silence.

"How the hell did you get in here, Red Blade?" The drogin's eyes darted around the entrances of the building as he frantically waved at his men to check for other intruders. "Have you come with others seeking this human? Because she won't be given over easily."

The masked man turned his head toward Elise then back to the pack leader. "It is only me who comes for her." His voice was low and grated from the voice box attached to the mask.

The pack leader looked down at him with a frown, clearly suspicious. "Just you, eh? Why would the great Lady Moth send only one of you to fight all of us?"

The Red Blade lowered his head. "I'm not here to fight you. I'm here to win her." He pointed to Elise.

The drogin's frown deepened. "Fine. Why has your mistress sent only one of you to win her?"

"Because I am the best fighter."

The pack leader snorted. "That so? Well, if true, I will allow you to participate. But the prize is only for a night if you come out the last one standing."

"No. I win, she comes with me."

The leader bared his teeth and put up a hand to keep his men back. "I think not. Maybe you didn't hear me, but I said she wouldn't be given over easily."

"I did hear," the lone Red Blade said. "I want to make a bet."

The leader's eyes widened. "A bet?"

"All of your best fighters versus myself. I win, and I take her."

This got everyone's attention, including the leader. Some laughed, others called him crazy. The leader threw up his hand for silence.

"That's a death wish, my friend," he said. But Elise could see he was thinking it over seriously. He looked to those around him, then he smiled. "All right. You take out all my best fighters, and she's yours. It'll be entertaining to see what happens. When you're beaten dead, we will send your body back to your mistress, eh?"

"Once I win, you will not stop me. I want her bag and weapon too, and I want a vehicle."

"Arrogant ass—" Ruvi began to hiss when his boss growled at him to be quiet.

"Fine. Since I honestly think you're bluffing and know the Red Blades aren't known for their brawling skills, I'll give you this." The drogin leaned forward in his chair. "A bet is a bet, and I don't need others thinking me a sore loser, so you have my word. If you somehow manage to win, you will have your prize, and I'll let you walk out of here without a problem. Deal?"

"Deal," said the Red Blade. Elise wanted to hurl, she was so angry, but she didn't think he could possibly beat them.

"We will even make it easier on you and have no time limit." The drogin reclined back in his chair. "I'll let you keep on your gear too, since it won't be a fair match anyway." He grinned. "Good luck."

At that, the other fighters turned away from one another and instead set their sights on the lone man. Elise sat up straighter so she could watch, uncertain who to root for. The rest of the crowd leaned in close to the rail in anticipation. They stood at the ready as the buzzer went off and the fighters moved.

Elise had seen her share of brawls. Bar brawls, base brawls. She'd even been a part of a few herself. She was used to the sight of men and women fighting; of them wailing on each other, pushing and shoving. She was used to seeing *human* men and women. But the ones in the pit were not human. And they *did not* fight like them. What she saw was so savage, so violent, it actually stunned her. She couldn't remember the last time something shocked her to this extent. And much of it came from the lone Red Blade. He was utterly ruthless. In a mere instant, one fighter jumped on him and was on the ground before Elise could blink, their jaw broken in. He was so fast, he moved through the fray of fighters, cracking ribs and jaws, breaking arms and shattering knees. Several fighters went down in only mere minutes. The others backed off to assess the masked man. Two tried to gang up on him, but, once again, he outpaced them. Blood gushed from the mouth and nose of one drogin as he fell, a lygin swiped from the back, only to have his hand blocked and twisted backwards then kicked so hard in the stomach he soiled himself.

Elise stared in bewilderment at the scene, not noticing at first that she had her hand covering her mouth. She dropped it but couldn't peel her eyes away. As terrifying as the Red Blade fought, she also couldn't help being a little inspired. He blocked so effortlessly and moved so gracefully nothing seemed to hit him. He knew where to hit and how hard to do the most damage. His strikes were as quick as a snake...

The more she watched him, the more his movement seemed oddly familiar. She swore she'd seen that sort of fighting style before, only less extreme. As the bodies racked up and only a few fighters remained, she knew something was up.

The Red Blade took out one of the lizards by kicking its head into the wall, leaving only two remaining: a large drogin male, perhaps the biggest she'd yet seen, and another smaller drogin with quick reflexes. They came at the Red Blade as a pair which turned quickly into one remaining as the smaller drogin went down on its back with its nose smashed in.

The large wolfish drogin turned to the Red Blade and snarled, baring his teeth. He struck out his long arm, cracking the stone wall of the pit beside him. He charged the masked man, jaws open, ready to bite, and the Red Blade merely ducked, uppercutting the drogin in the jaw, snapping his mouth shut. The large drogin shook off the blow and lunged, swinging his fist down which the Red Blade blocked then grabbed his wrist in one smooth movement, pulling him down and clocking the drogin in the head with his elbow. As the drogin fell forward and came crashing to the ground, the man swung around onto his back and hit him a few times more on the skull until he lay limp on the ground.

The crowd did not make a sound as the Red Blade rose amidst the sprawled out bodies. They eyed their leader, who hadn't moved, nervously.

Ruzi stepped forward and was quickly stopped by the pack leader's hand. "Don't even think about it," he hissed.

"I win," said the Red Blade. "Now I will take her and go."

"You...are truly skilled, Red Blade." The pack leader stood. "I...don't suppose I could offer you a chance to stay with us? I could use a fighter like you. And you could still have the girl all to yourself—"

"No." The Red Blade gestured to Elise. "We leave. Me and the girl."

The drogin grimaced. "Get her bag and weapon," he ordered his men. "I'm a man of my word. You may leave this place unharmed," he said to the Red Blade.

Elise didn't believe that for a second, but the men brought her things and forced her to her feet.

The drogin put up his hand for them to wait. "I would ask you to remove your mask first. A courtesy to those still living who'd like to know such a glorious opponent."

"No," said the Red Blade.

"I must insist," the pack leader growled. "Otherwise, I can't properly hand her over."

The Red Blade's hands clenched into tight fists then loosened. He lifted his hands, removing the mask and throwing back his hood.

Elise felt her body turn to ice and her breath catch in her throat. A few in the crowd hissed, some cursed and looked away.

"You...are not what I expected," the pack leader said after a pause. "But then, one who fights like you would have to look the part."

Nezka rolled his shoulders in a shrug. "It has its advantages. But I didn't want to scare your fighters away so quickly. Fair match and all." He gestured again to Elise without looking at her. "Now, we will be going."

Someone pushed at Elise's back, but she found she couldn't move. The alien before her was indeed Nezka the hunter in the flesh. Only, half his face was missing. The skin was gone, seared away, showing bits of muscles and bone, exposing his cheek bone, sharp teeth, and jaw. Flesh was burned on the outer edges, darkened to a near black. His left eye was partially blackened as well, leaving the coloring around the pupil to look red. If he looked like death before, now he absolutely was.

Someone shoved her forward, and she stumbled to the edge of the pit. Nezka looked up at her, taking her in as much as she did him. Her bag was kicked to her feet and her gun tossed on top of it. Elise hesitated, tearing her eyes away from Nezka to pick up her things. As she pulled her bag over her shoulder and holstered her gun, Nezka climbed out from the pit to stand beside her, ignoring those men who glared at him with vengeful intent. Elise, so stunned by the sight of him and what she had just witnessed, let him take her arm and pull her away.

The crowd parted as they worked their way out of the building, and Elise turned her head to look back at the pack leader, who watched them go, his men close, whispering in his ear.

As they made their way out to the garage, they found several cars of their choosing, but the one Nezka decided on was some kind of motorcycle with thick wheels, encased in a blue-black steel. No one stopped him as he hopped on the bike and started it. Red lights lit up its sides and across its wheels, and the engine purred to life. Elise looked around and saw people watching...waiting.

"They aren't going to just let us leave like this," Elise whispered as Nezka messed with the touchscreen on the cycle's dash and tested the controls. He revved the engine and adjusted himself on the seat so that Elise could sit comfortably behind him.

"They will. But only until we leave their keep," Nezka said in a low voice. "Then they are going to chase us. Get on."

Elise did as ordered and got on, pressing herself close to Nezka's back, hand clutching his waist. She might have been appalled at having to be so close to him before, but in this moment, she didn't trouble herself over it. She just wanted to get as far away as possible from this place.

"How good is your aim while moving?" Nezka asked as he backed the motorcycle several feet, positioning it out of the garage.

Elise gazed at the back of his head with a frown. "Accurate enough, depending on speed and how far away the target is. Why?"

"Have your gun ready. You're going to need to watch our back." The bike began to pick up speed as Nezka drove out of the garage toward the gate.

CHAPTER ELEVEN

Nezka knew they would come for them. He'd been around enough criminals and conmen to know every word of a deal could be twisted to work for their benefit. The leader of this pack of car thieves would let him leave their compound, but once he was outside it, they would follow.

Maybe if he was alone and had no time to lose, he would fight them, take them down slowly, one by one. He was tempted after seeing what they had done to Elise. But he knew now fighting them was a fool's idea. So, he would run until they could follow no farther. Which, by what he gathered after tracking them, was about a mile out to the north end till they hit a dried-out chasm that had once been a river. From there, judging by their route, the gang's territory ended. All he had to do was cross over into what was supposedly another's territory, and they would be safe. For a little while, at least.

Nezka built up speed as he skidded around a corner and took off down the road. It wasn't long till they heard the roar of other vehicles behind them. Elise clung to him tightly with one arm as she took up her gun in the other.

"Aim for their tires," Nezka said as he turned quickly down

another road. Taking the bike was a risky choice, making Elise vulnerable at her back, but it could get them through areas the cars might not be able to go. If he could lose them in time, it would be worth the exposure.

They flew down one street after the other, the screen on the dash helping Nezka navigate the maze of roads, looking for alternative routes. The gang knew the streets better and likely knew all the secret passages, but it was all he could do to try to lose them.

Nezka drove straight on, swerving past abandoned vehicles and other obstacles along the road. Something bright zapped by and crackled beside him. Another zap, and Nezka saw the sparks of electricity dance across the road. Elise let off a few rounds in response, and Nezka knew the pack was close behind them. "Hold on," he called and felt her grip tighten around his waist as he took a sudden sharp turn down an alleyway, too narrow for the cars to follow.

He exited off onto a different road parallel to the one before and continued on to the river-chasm. From the dashboard rear-view screen, he saw a pair of two-wheelers like his own shoot through the alley and race toward them. Elise shot at them, hitting the front tire of one two-wheeler, making it skid off the road and into a nearby building. The second didn't halt but sped up, closing in. It fell beside them, swerving closer, trying to hit them. Elise shot at the driver, but the sparks of yellow light did nothing to his armor. She went for the wheels instead, only for the driver to put on his brakes, causing her to miss. He drove beside them and tried to hit them again, but Nezka was prepared this time. He waited for another blockade in the road then kicked his leg out and pushed the other two-wheeler away, causing it to smash right into a large sign made of a slab of metal.

At the end of the road, Nezka could see the river-chasm and a bridge. He could also see several vehicles already there, waiting to block his way. Baring his teeth in a low growl, he quickly turned down another road before the bridge, racing east till the road connected to another, bringing them alongside the chasm. Vehicles followed behind, and more bullets and bursts of electricity whirled past to try and stop him. As another bridge came into view ahead, Nezka could see it was empty of vehicles but that a portion of it was broken off. Missing.

It would have to do.

At the crossroad, Nezka turned tightly onto the bridge just as a group of cars met him down one street. He straightened out then picked up speed, forcing the two-wheeler to its limit. Ahead, he saw the broken section, but he didn't stop. He thought he heard his name being called, but he refused to look back or to slow. He heard more shots pop off and the sounds of vehicles screeching to a halt as he jumped the bridge.

He felt Elise's arms wrap around his midsection in a tight grip as they fell. Her shout of surprise cut in his ear. The two-wheeler landed and hopped, jolting them across the other side. As soon as the wheels touched firmly on the ground, Nezka hit on the brakes, skidding the two-wheeler around into a half circle, blowing up dust and smoke from the tires. As the air cleared, Nezka got a good look at the other side and smiled. The cars had stopped, and the pack spilled out onto the bridge to howl with rage. A few shot off a couple rounds which didn't quite reach, but Nezka wasn't taking any chances. He turned around and drove off, putting distance between him and the chasm.

Elise, though still pressed closely against him, loosened her grip, her gun still firm in her hand, waiting, perhaps, for more danger to come. Nezka didn't stop until he felt her tap his side, wanting off. He searched around for a safe place, turning down a narrow road, through a low tunnel.

Out the other side, a large, nearly windowless building came into view, its sides made of some smooth stone with several levels of glass at the top. Nezka slowed considerably as he drove around a circular courtyard with a twisted statue at the center then up a wide ramp to the blown out doors of the building. He slipped inside, into considerable darkness, into a wide foyer with a high open doorway. Past that was a long passage with a high, open ceiling, the glass roof shattered.

To each side were several floors of crumbling balconies above. Nezka slowed to a near walking speed as he passed another twisted statue at the middle, one covered nearly head to foot in some odd plant. At the end of the long passage, glass lifts hung, stuck on various floors. But by the bent metal and broken glass, they were no longer in working order. Someone had come through here at some point and tore the building apart. Nezka could even see the marks from explosive damage and bullet fire on the walls and floors. It might not be empty, but it looked it, and he saw no signs of others or any recent damage.

It would have to do for now.

He stopped the two-wheeler beside a lone stairway beside the lifts. He turned the vehicle off, and Elise released her grip on him. She stumbled as she got up to stand, and Nezka caught the blood on her leg, staining her white suit a dull red.

"You're hit." Nezka got off the two-wheeler to examine her.

She shook her head at him. "It's from a bite." When he gave her a concerned glare, she continued with, "From a fight with a particularly large drogin. They tried to patch me up so I wouldn't bleed out, but they clearly did a shit job."

She looked pale. Her eyes were dark, lip cut, and face slightly swollen on one side. She looked like she was about to pass out as she hunched over, her eyes blinking slowly. "When's the last time you ate or drank?" Nezka asked, taking the bag off her shoulders to look inside. She didn't protest, though she looked ready to.

"A half a day or so, I think," she said hesitantly. As in she wasn't sure.

Nezka rifled through the bag. Only one food pack remained. The clothes were gone. Somehow, miraculously, her canteen had been spared, but it was empty.

"What happened to you?" she asked. Her eyes flitted over his face with what he thought might actually be a smidge of concern. He couldn't help smiling.

"That's a question with many answers."

She touched at her face, and he frowned. There was blood on her hand too.

"Let's start climbing. I want higher ground before we assess the damage," he said, throwing her bag over his shoulder.

She nodded her head at him and holstered her gun as they started for the stairs. Nezka halted only a few feet up to turn back to her, watching as she limped her way up to follow him. He hadn't noticed before how badly beaten she really was, but at the time, his focus had only been on getting them away. Now he could see she was in great need of help. He knew, however, what her answer would be if he even asked. But watching her struggle up the flights of stairs would be tortuous. Deciding quickly, he descended the fews steps back to her and bent forward, grabbing hold of her hips and swinging her up over his other shoulder.

"What the hell are you doing?" she cried, her legs flailing, trying to kick him.

"I'm carrying you, obviously," he answered as he took the steps two at a time.

"I don't need you to carry me. I can do it myself." Her fist hit his back in frustration.

Nezka blew out a small breath of air in a half sigh, half laugh. "Yes and take the rest of the day to do it, while tearing the wound further as you went, wasting the energy needed to recover." He was already to the second floor, but still, she continued to protest. He let her argue, let her squirm, but by the time it was worth anything, they were to the final floor, where he placed her down firmly on the landing. She hit his chest with the side of her fist then turned from him, huffing as she limped on. He followed her quietly down a wide hall filled with open doorways, watching for signs of others. None could be found as he searched the rooms, so he deemed it safe enough. The rooms were all empty save for a few broken pieces of statues, frames, or skeletons of some animal he could not identify.

There were inner glass panels and displays in some rooms, but they too were empty. A room at the end offered a wide-open space with a dome of glass at the center of its roof, a pinkish hue from lights above falling through the few broken panels. The room also had windows and a set of glass doors leading to a balcony where a small portion of the city could be seen below. There, past a low wall, were a few rows of tight alleyways and roads. Smatterings of people moved through them amongst colorfully lit shops and tents.

"Wow. Didn't think regular folk lived down here," Elise said beside him. "Figured it was all crime lords and their followers."

"All dark places carry some innocence," Nezka said. From the corner of his eye, he could see her studying him with a strange expression. He dropped her bag and looked back around the room. In one corner, a cushioned longseat was shoved against the wall along with a twin set of cushioned chairs. One table lay next to them, its leg broken in half. Nezka brought the two chairs over to the windows and forced Elise to sit in one as he took the other.

"I can do it myself," she said half-heartedly. But she didn't stop his hand, only grew a little tense as he examined the wound on her leg. "Are you going to tell me what happened to you?" she asked after a pause.

"Maybe." He withdrew his hand and stood. "I'm going out."

"What? Why—"

"We need supplies. I can't fix you up with nothing. I won't be gone long." He grabbed her bag, clipping it to his belt beside his mask, and started for the door.

"I could come with—"

"No." He stopped and laughed quietly before looking back to see her annoyed expression. "And if you try to follow, just know by the time you make it to the bottom, I'll likely be back to carry you up here again. So, stay. I won't be long."

She sighed. "Take my gun then, at least." She began to unclip it, but he held up his hand for her to stop.

"I won't be seen." At that, he left her, quickly making his way back down. He found a back exit out to some road, then he hopped the wall they had seen from above and started searching.

In no time at all, he had a bagful of items ranging from strips of cloth to healing salve similar to the kind found back home, being sold by a lygin; packs of food and water, fire starters, and even painkillers (also sold by the lygin), all stolen from the various shops as he had no way to pay. Coming back, he took a moment to explore the other floors for anything and found a thick curtain draped around another empty display, which he tore off, and a few scattered bits of canvas and scraps of paper which he also took. As he continued his way upward, he concluded the building might once have been a museum or showhall but had long since been raided of its goods. He stopped one last time to drag up a thick piece of metal broken off a statue that could serve as a fire holder then returned to the room where he found Elise still seated in the chair.

As he set the bag and piece of metal down carefully, he came around to the chair and saw her eyes closed, head tilted away. Only by the movement of her chest and slight whistle of breath did he know she was only resting. Gently, he placed a hand on her arm and she started, head snapping up, eyes wide. As she saw that it was him, she began to relax, though her eyes remained wary. He went back for the bag and took out the salve, strips of cloth, and canteen which he had filled in some back kitchen. He handed her the canteen which she took gladly, then he sat back in the chair opposite her to watch and wait. When she drank her fill and handed the canteen back, he took some for himself then leaned forward, grabbed her hand, and spilled some of the icy water onto her wound. Elise let out a small yelp and tugged her hand back.

"I can do it myself," she said again. Nezka studied her for a long moment, deciding whether it was worth it to argue, then handed her back the canteen.

"Clean the wound out then smear this over it." He tossed the bottle of salve on her lap.

Not wanting her to think he saw her as incapable of taking care of herself and also considering her need for privacy, Nezka turned away to let her dress her own wounds, concentrating instead on making the room more comfortable for each of them. He took the curtain he had found and placed it across several windows along one end of the room in hopes it would keep them better hidden from prying eyes searching from below. Then he took the metal piece of sculpture enclosed like a misshapen bowl and tossed the pieces of canvas and paper inside it, setting them aflame with a flick of the firestarter. The smoke drifted up and out through the open pane of the domed glass roof above, not so large that he thought it would be discernible, especially in the dark. He brought the longseat closer to the makeshift fire pit and picked up the broken table, snapping it into smaller sizes for firewood later.

When he deemed the area reasonably comfortable enough, he turned his eye back over to where Elise sat and saw the slender frame of her bare shoulders and back before him. He stilled, watching as she cleaned out a rather nasty-looking wound between her shoulder and neck. Blood, once dried and caking, now trickled down her back, diluted with the water she used to clean with. Nezka's gaze drifted downward to where the skin wasn't marred and showed smooth, soft skin.

A heat prickled along his stomach and made his spines tingle along his lower back. He had a sudden strong urge to close the distance between them and graze his fingers down the arch of her spine, to feel the warmth there. He let his imagination drift momentarily and saw her tilting her head to the side as his hand traced up her back and along her neck, feeling her shudder not with fear but with pleasure at his touch. He'd wipe away the blood-colored droplets that now coated her back and bring them to his lips, tasting what he imagined to be a sweet and earthy flavor.

Her head turned to lock eyes with him. She froze, giving him a questionable stare, and he responded by turning away, leaving the room to find more scraps for the fire or anything else that might be of use. Any reason to go, just so that he could clear his head.

He was not in any way denying his emotions. He wanted her. He knew he wanted her the first time he saw her back in the drogin station. It had been strong too. Stronger than the first time he had ever laid eyes on a human woman. That part was what made him curious, if not only slightly concerned. He'd had many women before, all of different kinds, of shapes and sizes, all unique in their own way. He'd wanted to experience the humankind the first time he'd encountered them, and that urge for something new and different hadn't changed once discovering them again. That feeling had only grown more intense now in this short time with Elise.

He thought maybe it was just a strong drive to want to connect. That powerful animal need that was always so great in him and was intensified through her. But there was something more there, lurking in the deep dark of his psyche. Something he was unfamiliar with. Something that crawled to the surface every so often. Some nameless thing swimming around in the black sea of his thoughts and desires. It had appeared when they had first fought; it had appeared again when he took her from the collapsing tunnel and watched her sleep; then again when he'd seen her above that pit, and once more just now in that chair with her back exposed to him. It tugged at him as if to pull him under, and though he let it attempt to do so, he did not move an inch, merely watched it with ever growing curiosity and that slight inkling of concern.

Nezka stopped inside one of the rooms and closed his eyes, remembering the burst of colors that made up Elise's aura. Her "spirit." *It must be that*, he thought. Her fire was so bright, so alive. Very few he'd found in his time to have such a passionate flame. And the colors pleased him more than those few. Yes, while others might have been just as beautiful or alluring to his eye at first glance, he was never fully drawn to them. But Elise's spirit caught at him. That must be what it was. He found her exceedingly...pleasing.

He laughed and rubbed a hand over his eyes. Not to mention her pouty face or look of surprise whenever he shocked her. The way her slender neck arched and looked his way with an intense gaze. Yes, he wanted her...seemingly in more ways than one.

He dropped his hand and opened his eyes, staring at the wall of nothing.

But she could only ever be a piece in his mission. Whatever he felt, however strong, he had a job to fulfill. He couldn't afford to feel...whatever it was he was feeling. And thinking such things seemed inappropriate in the moment. She was wounded, they had just come from a rather rough chase, and there was more to come as soon as they left their haven. He needed to get his head in the game, needed to focus on getting her better so that they could move on, to stop thinking about such...such *trivial* matters.

Determined to put it all aside. Nezka slipped out of the room and into the dark halls, concentrating on searching the grounds and planning their next move.

When he returned, he found Elise still sitting at the chair, her suit, now covering her shoulders, still unclasped at the back. He made a sound, so she knew he was behind her, and she looked around, caught eyes with him, then looked away.

"I um...think I got most of them." She waved the bottled salve in her hand. "Only..."

He waited for her to continue, and when she glanced back around, he saw her skin deepen to a reddish hue.

"Are you sick?" he asked, assuming the redness of her skin meant perhaps a fever.

The hue of red deepened, and she looked away. "No, I'm not..." She sighed. "I think...there's one left." She shifted uncomfortably in her seat. "But I can't reach it." She lifted a hand around her side, and his eyes fell to where she tried to touch. He could see a mark across her middle to lower back, along the spine. "Think it happened in the fight when I was thrown against the wall and my suit caught."

Nezka dropped the extra scraps for the fire on the ground and slowly approached. He dragged the extra chair over and sat down behind her. Neither of them moved for a brief moment until Nezka put out his hand for the salve. "I'll be gentle, I promise."

Elise, though still looking tense, nodded. She placed the bottle of salve in his hand and straightened out. Nezka waited as she carefully dropped her suit once more from her shoulders till her back was bare and he could better see the wound.

It wasn't deep, thankfully. Just a bad scrape if anything. Nezka picked up the canteen off the ground and poured a small lap of water down her skin.

Elise jerked, inhaling sharply. "Cold," she muttered when he froze. He continued on till the dry blood was gone, leaving only small cuts of open skin. Setting the canteen down, he took the salve, a clear jelly-like substance, and rubbed some between his fingers before reaching down and touching the small of her back.

Elise jerked once more and hissed through her teeth. "Also cold," she said. Nezka hesitated then continued to rub the ointment against her skin. Beyond the rough scrape of her wound, she was as soft and smooth as he imagined. His mind started to drift again (odd, as it usually wasn't this hard to keep his thoughts clear and focused), and he decidedly forced his fantasies back, keeping the touch impersonal, professional. Elise shifted a little but began to relax, probably in convincing herself he wasn't going to slice her in half. He worked the ointment gently into her skin, making sure it was thoroughly covered.

"So, are you going to finally tell me what happened?" Elise asked after a turn of silence.

"What happened to what?" Nezka answered.

She turned her head slightly to look back at him and pointed to the side of her face. He took it to mean she was asking about his own.

"Ah, that." Nezka shrugged. "A bad step on my part."

"A bad step?"

"In dodging the tentacled beast, I found myself in direct line with one of the fire bombs. The fire got close enough to sear me as well as a part of my armor which forced me to discard it and take another.

Clothing from one of the fallen Red Blades was the closest I could find."

Elise looked at his face curiously. "It just seems...shouldn't that have killed you? A wound like that, besides probably hurting like hell, would be too exposed to infection. And losing all that skin..."

Nezka huffed as he continued to dip into the salve and touch at Elise's back. "My skin is not prone to infection, and the wound will likely heal itself completely in a week or so."

Elise twisted around, forcing him to stop tending to her wound. "Wait, seriously? You're saying it will grow back?"

"That is what I am saying."

"Your skin can just regenerate?" she asked, slightly dumbfounded.

Nezka smiled. "Yes. Though the new skin tends to take on a different shade."

Elise's eyes widened. Her skin, once red in coloring, went pale. "Are you saying..." she said as her eyes flitted down what parts of him that were bare, mainly his hands, neck and face. "Are you saying that those aren't tattoos or markings on your skin? That they are...?"

Nezka looked at his hands where parts of the knuckles and fingers were white as bones. Small slashes that ran up his wrists and, if he took off his clothes, could be seen all the way up his arms and across his shoulders. "Yes," he said. "I may regenerate, but the scarring leaves the new skin altered."

She said something in what he assumed was her own language, but its tone sounded like a curse. "That's..." She turned back and shook her head. "I don't even know what to say." She sat quiet for a moment then turned slightly once more to study him. "Impressive."

Nezka's smile widened. "I think so too."

She shuddered, looking away from him, and Nezka froze as little bumps formed along her skin. Too tempted by his curiosity, he brushed a finger over them, and she shivered once more.

"Is it good now?" she asked.

Nezka pulled away and capped the salve. "Yes."

Elise shrugged her suit over her shoulders and clasped the back till it covered her body. Nezka stood and she gazed up at him.

"Thank you." She seemed to be deciding her words carefully. "I won't bother asking how you found me but," she laughed softly, a surprisingly light tone that made his heart thump a little heavier, "I'm actually really glad you did. Imagine that." Her smile faded, and her eyes fell. "If you hadn't, I would be..."

Nezka remained still. "Would be what?"

She looked back at him with a frown. "Somebody's plaything I imagine. Or worse off than I am now." Cautiously, she stood, her expression pained as she straightened, feeling out her aches. "So, I guess I should say thank you again. For coming to get me." She looked everywhere but at him at first until their eyes finally met, and, as if finding her courage, she stretched her arm out to him, presenting her hand. "I guess I owe you a lot. You've saved my hide more than once now" She smiled at him, and his heart thumped again. "Even if I don't care to admit it," she concluded.

Nezka looked down at her outstretched hand. Uncertain of this human gesture and what she expected him to do with it, he brought his own hand up and placed it lightly against hers. She laughed again, dropping her outstretched hand and lifting her other to grip his hand firmly and shake it.

"What does that mean?" he asked.

"It's just a show of gratitude between two people," she said. "Or when making a deal, but that's different." She clasped his hand a little longer before letting it fall. Something passed over her eyes, a strange look he only barely caught. She cleared her throat as if uncomfortable and passed a hand along the top of her head, through her hair. "Anyway. Once we get some rest, we can make plans to leave, maybe get out of this dump before night tomorrow."

It was Nezka's turn to stare at her in bewilderment. He had no proper words at first until all he could do was laugh.

Elise glanced back at him in surprise. "What?"

"We aren't leaving here. Not for some time."

She stared back at him, confused. "I'm sorry?"

"We are staying here."

"I...what do you mean staying here?" she said in a more forceful tone.

Here we go.

"I mean exactly that. We aren't leaving this place until I deem it safe to do so," he said firmly. "Or if by some bad chance we are forced to."

She crossed her arms in a defensive stance. "We can't stay here. My people are waiting for me. We don't have time."

"We have no choice. You are in no way ready to continue on in your state. You can barely walk. If you try to so much as run, you'll aggravate your wounds even worse. We would need to stop every hour just to put on more salve to keep the wounds from being infected. And when the time comes when we have to fight or run from whatever enemy we face, I won't be able to carry you, and you won't be able to defend yourself properly. So." He dropped the salve back into the bag and picked up the painkillers along with the canteen, handing them to her. "You will take these. You will rest. The salve will do its work but will take at least a few days—"

"A few days!" she nearly choked.

"—and a couple more after that just to be sure," he concluded. "You also are malnourished, the wounds draining your energy even more. Until you are healed and able to run and fight on your own, we go no farther."

She opened her mouth then closed it again, unable to find a response but wanting to argue all the same. "You don't understand. My team doesn't have a few days. Who knows what the Red Blades are going to do to them? Who knows if they'll be alive in a few days?"

"That is a risk we will have to take," Nezka said. "But if they've kept the first group for as long as they have, chances are whatever they have planned is not yet ready to be set in motion. My guess is because they are still searching, hoping to find you. Or perhaps waiting on more humans to come. Who knows? What I do know is I didn't get you this far just to see you die at the next gate. Because that is what will happen, Starling, if you don't stay."

She remained quiet, looking up at him still with an eye of defiance until her expression changed to one of confusion then annoyance. "It's Stirling," she said and turned from him to plop herself down on the longseat. She sat there seething and thinking, and he watched, waiting, until she finally looked back at him. "Fine. But if I am able to recover quicker than you say and can prove it, do you promise we will go?"

He looked at her for a long moment then came over and put out his hand. She huffed, gazing out the window, hoping he wouldn't catch one corner of her lip curling ever so slightly before she took his hand and shook it.

CHAPTER TWELVE

Elise took the first day in stride, trying her best to be patient, to just let herself rest and heal, knowing if she exerted herself and fell back on her recovery, Nezka would see to it that they stay longer, and she couldn't let that happen. She knew fighting him was useless as she was too weak, and if she even tried to leave on her own, he would likely find her and carry her back.

In truth, she wasn't keen on attempting to leave anyway. For one, she knew her emotions were driving her too much. She could hear Adrien's voice in her head, telling her it would be foolish to go on in her state, that the smart move would be to hunker down and wait till she was at her best and ready to complete the mission without fail. It was the smart, logical thing to do, even if she hated sitting or lying around doing nothing. And boy, did she hate it.

So, the day wore on, and she slept some and took what food Nezka found and drank as much water as he could fill in the canteen, part of her grateful for his help while another part was irritated that she needed it at all. She grew uncomfortable at the thought of being so dependent on him when he could so easily disappear and never return. But though he disappeared often, usually to find more goods, he always returned and was there when she woke up, turning the fire or preparing some meal from a package or can that she couldn't identify but forced herself to eat. He was silent for most of the day, and Elise was fine to just watch him in a half-sleep state as the painkillers kicked in, putting her in a sort of light daze.

When night approached and it grew dark, Elise became more restless. She wanted to get up and walk, but Nezka deemed it unwise, and she heard Adrien's voice in her head again, so she let it go, if only for tonight. It helped to know that the salve worked faster when she was at rest, and when Nezka checked her wounds, he concluded that they were healing at a good rate, faster than he expected which meant they might very well be on their way sooner, and that gave her hope, so she did her best to be patient.

She sat in her chair, sick of sleep, the painkillers beginning to wear off, watching as Nezka rekindled the fire. When he was finished, he sat opposite her and sifted through her bag. He'd gone on his last run for the night, returning with several food packs and a refilled canteen. He'd also found several other items in his search—another canteen, a small green block of something she didn't recognize, and a single cord of metal rope, which he hung on his belt. She asked him where he acquired such things, and his answer was in no way shocking.

"Some loner on my way back from the alleyway," he said.

Elise shook her head. "I know we need to survive and may have been forced to take a few provisions, but now you're just blatantly stealing."

He tilted his head in a shrug. "I take what I need."

Elise watched as he took up his new canteen, unscrewed the cap, and drank. A spicy, strong scent struck her, stinging her nose. She eyed him and the canteen suspiciously.

"Is that what I think it is?"

Nezka took one more swig before setting the canteen on his lap. He didn't smile fully at her, but his eyes glowed bright enough for her to recognize his sly, amused expression. "What do you think it is?"

Elise stared into his eyes, and he stared back. "Care to share?" she asked at last.

Nezka hesitated, considering it. "It might be unwise..."

She rolled her eyes and reached out her hand. "I've eaten enough. And the painkillers are nearly finished."

He paused a second more then offered up the metal bottle. Elise took it and sniffed the top before taking a sip.

Yes, it was exactly what she thought. The spicy liquor burned as she swallowed, making her eyes sting. "Ah, who knew?" Elise choked. "The drogin are skilled in rum-making too." She took another drink despite the burn then offered the canteen back to Nezka. "I know it's super egotistical, but I never thought there would be so many things that were similar to Earth and here or anywhere else for that matter. Makes the universe seem...small." She watched him drink again then said, "Is it like that where you're from too?"

He set the canteen on one leg and looked up at the domed window above. "Yes, some." His eyes flitted back down to her. "Though things might be similar, they are still different—unique—in their way."

"Like what?" Elise asked.

He shook the canteen. "Our drink which is similar to this is called liquid bluym. It derives from a certain nectar in a plant. The actual bud can be smoked, and there are different breeds."

Elise smiled. "We have something of that kind too."

Nezka gestured to the window, to the bridges and towers above. "The city I live in is not so different from this one. There are more ships, and the cloud cover is thicker, foggier, but the lights are similar, though we have more tech, more bots. We also have more levels, and they are better sectioned off."

Elise could envision it well enough. She thought of home and knew it couldn't compare. "Earth's cities aren't nearly as impressive. We don't have an undercity like here, but we have bad parts that look just like it. Our buildings aren't so tall, and the cities aren't even close to as big." Elise shook her head. "I thought they were quite the achievement but after seeing this? Well, the higher city, anyway. Yeah, we still have a long way to go." Elise picked up her small gun by the chair and turned it in her hands. "Our weapons can't compare either. Kinda scary to think we are more behind than we thought. But it's good to at least know what we're up against. And some things you can only improve so much. I mean a gun is a gun no matter what it spits, and a blade is a blade no matter how it cuts, right?"

Nezka tilted his head, and she felt her face heat up. Maybe that drink was making her talk nonsense.

He set the canteen on the ground then took out, from one of the inner pockets of his armor suit, a set of blades. They shined with a dark purple that almost seemed to glow. She'd seen them briefly before when he had been practicing with them. He flipped one with ease in his hand, and Elise could see they were unbelievably thin and sharp, the handles cut with some complex symbols and designs out of a material that looked like black stone or metal. He threw one across the inner wall, and it was so fast Elise didn't even catch it, but it stuck true and deep into whatever material made up the wall. Then, with a flick of his wrist, the blade returned back to his hand. He threw it again, this time at the floor, and there, it struck deep also, only the floor was made of a far thicker material, maybe stone or marble. He flicked his wrist again, and there it appeared, in his hand.

"How?" Elise said after a moment of frustrated shock.

Nezka smiled. He flipped them one more time before they disappeared back into his inner pockets. "You remember the guns the Red Blades used," he said, "how we couldn't use them because they are locked to their signature?"

Elise nodded.

"My blades are the same in a way. They call to only me, to my pull. It may seem...fantastical."

"More like magical," Elise said.

"But it is an old tech. They are connected to me like another appendage only separated. The pull might be something magnetic or maybe of a more complex physics, but my cells lie within. Where I go, they go."

"So much for a blade just being a blade." Elise laughed softly. "Where did you get them?"

"I've had them since I was a childling. I don't remember a time I didn't have them."

Elise looked at him oddly. "So, as in, you were born with them?"

"I don't know. I don't remember that far back," Nezka said, his eyes glazing over for a brief instant. "I only remember them being in my hands as they took me from the ship, along with this." He brushed his fingers along the beaded necklace at his throat.

"And your parents were just cool with you having blades as a kid?"

"I didn't know my parents, so I couldn't be sure."

Elise opened her mouth in a silent 'oh.' "I'm sorry," she said and found she truly meant it. "What about others of your kind? Did they have blades too?"

"I don't know. I've never met others of my kind," Nezka answered.

Elise's eyes widened, and she grew still with shock. How could someone have never met another of their kind? She thought about what he said before, about not remembering how he acquired his blades, and it started to click. "When you say 'they took you from a ship,' are you saying you were taken? Like..." Using the word abducted seemed wrong. "Like someone kidnapped you?"

Nezka didn't say anything for a moment. He picked up his canteen again and took another drink.

"I'm sorry," Elise said, thinking maybe it wasn't her place to ask. "It's none of my business."

Nezka's gaze fell to the fire. His eyes flickered against the flames as if they were made from the same source. "Or I was saved. I can't be certain," he said in a low voice. "But it was then I was brought to the city and..." His gaze directed back to her. "I was trained."

Elise thought over his words carefully. "Trained to be a bounty hunter?"

He lifted his hand, tapping at his ear.

"Does that mean yes?"

"Yes," he said.

"That explains...a lot, actually." She could still vividly remember the fight back at the pit.

"Does it?" He tilted his head.

"It certainly explains why you are such a good fighter and tracker and know the things you do," Elise said and blew out a short breath. "Guess I should have gone into bounty hunting instead. Maybe then I wouldn't have gotten my ass handed to me in that pit."

"You got a taste of what the training is like at least," Nezka replied indifferently.

Elise frowned. "They throw you in a pit and make you fight?"

"It was to weed out the strongest among the weak," Nezka said. "If you came out alive, you could continue on with your training."

"That's barbaric."

Nezka shrugged. "It works."

Elise thought that over and realized he was probably right. When your life was at stake, you learned to give it your all or die trying.

A light went off in her head with a crazy idea.

"Could you teach me?" she asked. "I mean to fight like you?"

She expected him to laugh but was surprised instead when he didn't. He gave her an inquiring stare then seemed to seriously consider it.

"You are in no position to train in your current state," he said, looking her over.

"Right, I get that," Elise said. "But when I am better I mean. I was trained to fight too and always considered myself pretty good at it. But after what happened in that pit and seeing you pretty much wipe the floor...I could afford to relearn some things."

He was quiet for a long moment, and Elise let him be. As he looked away from her to stare out one of the windows, Elise took the chance to study him better. To really see him. It was odd to think that this alien she believed she hated was now someone she was considering to be her teacher.

And maybe she didn't really hate him so much anymore. Sure, he had been a real jerk at first, but knowing what she knew now and realizing how alone he truly was, she was beginning to see him as just...a survivor. A lone wolf who had to fight to stay alive. And sometimes that really roughened up a person, made them hard and not always nice. He was violent and harsh because it was what he knew. But she had seen another side of him now, a side that was loyal and sincere, and that darker part was not the whole person. In a way, she could say maybe he wasn't so bad.

He turned from the window to gaze back at her, and for a moment, Elise felt a slow heat rise up her neck and face as if he might have heard her thoughts. The way he looked at her made her feel exposed.

He lifted his hand slowly and tapped his ear.

"Yes?"

"Yes," he said. "When you are recovered enough and ready."

Elise smiled and sat up a little straighter, feeling the swell of excitement building in her already. If she could learn to move like him, to strategically strike and dodge in a way no human had, she might actually have a chance at defending against these tougher aliens, have a chance at fighting her way to her team without having to worry about another bad break like in that pit. She wasn't always for violence, only when it was necessary. And something told her any chance of negotiating would be slim to none. So, if she had to fight, she'd do it with all the ferocity she had witnessed in Nezka. "This partnership may not be so bad after all," she confessed.

Nezka smirked. "Was it always so bad before?"

Elise shrugged, taking the canteen from him and another quick swig, letting the liquor slide down her throat before saying, "It's had its moments. I didn't really care for the big squid."

His pupils sharpened to a pinpoint, and his smile grew. "Too bad. I quite enjoyed that part."

Elise arched a brow at him. "Even when your face got blown off?"

"It did hurt a bit."

"I'd hope so. If you didn't feel pain either, I'd think you were a god or something."

"A god of what?" he asked, curious.

Elise reclined in her chair, studying that broken part of his face. It was awful, to be sure. But the rest of him wasn't so bad. "God of death," she said, watching his expression closely.

Nezka didn't look offended. He considered it seriously then seemed to agree. "I'd say that is fitting enough. Even if I don't particularly enjoy death."

Her brows rose. "You don't?"

"Not entirely, no," he said, throwing another piece of broken canvas into the fire. "In fact, I'd say I enjoy life even more. Especially the ritual of creating it."

Elise had to sit there for several seconds to understand exactly what he meant. When she thought she knew, she felt the heat rise in her face again. A particularly explicit image shot through her mind, and she quickly swatted it away, her body growing warm.

He might be an alien to her, but he was still a man, she realized, who still had wants and desires. She remembered all the slightly vulgar—if not flirty—remarks he'd made when they first met. She figured they were only meant to rile her up. They definitely had but she never wondered if they might hold any weight to them.

It probably meant nothing, she thought. *And it's not like I would ever consider...*

She cleared her throat and took another long drink. "Let's play a game," she said, thinking to change the subject.

"A game?" He looked intrigued.

"It's called 'never have I ever.'"

"Never have I ever...?" he repeated.

"It's a little juvenile, admittedly, but we get to use this," she lifted the canteen, "to play."

His eyes glanced to the bottle then back to her. "All right."

"It works like this," she began. "I say something I have never done before. If you have done that thing, then you take a drink."

"That's it?"

"For the most part. Oh, also I might be lying about never having done something, but I don't have to tell you unless you take a drink. If you do, then I have to drink as well. For example," Elise thought for a moment then said, "never have I ever taken a straight punch to the face." She handed him the canteen, and Nezka took it, gave her a 'seriously?' sort of look, and drank. She took it back and had a sip herself. "See?"

"Seems simple enough," he said.

"Okay, I'll go first." Elise thought for a moment. "Never have I ever...driven a ship."

Nezka took the can and drank. "You really never have?" he asked after.

Elise shook her head. "Jerico and Tom pilot at take-off, then the ships usually just sail on their own till we get to our destination. Sometimes they have to land too."

"So, no human has ever owned their own ship?"

"Some of the richer ones might, but most ships are military or company owned," Elise said. "Do you have your own?"

"Yes, many."

"Really? So, you can just go wherever you like?"

"Within reason," Nezka said.

"Must be nice."

"It has its advantages." Nezka swirled the canteen around in his hand. "I have never shot off any weapon by accident or hit someone I didn't intend to hit."

Elise made a face and snatched up the can, taking a drink. "I was ten, and it was my uncle's foot. But from what I know, there hasn't been another incident since. Dad made sure of it."

"Your father trained you?" Nezka asked.

"When I was a kid, yes. Me and my sister at first then..." She looked into the fire and frowned. "Then just me until my step-brothers came around."

"Step?" Nezka asked.

"Not related by blood," Elise said.

"Ah." Nezka seemed to hesitate, then he took the can from her and drank.

Elise smiled. "Ha! I knew it."

Nezka smirked. "I was young too. Don't know how many cycles. I was trying to impress a girl."

"Oh, god, tell me you didn't hit her," Elise said, leaning forward.

"No. But her animal companion had to have an ear removed."

Elise covered her mouth with her hand, trying not to laugh. "That's awful."

"Yes. We didn't talk much after that."

Elise laughed softly. "Never have I ever broken a bone."

"That's a lie," Nezka said.

"It's true...but I have sprained both my legs and an arm," Elise confessed. "Thick bones, I guess. You?"

"Several."

"I had a feeling."

Nezka took a drink then looked around before glancing back at her, giving her a wicked smile. "I have never fainted."

Elise grimaced. "That's not fair." She took another sip and could feel her mind going fuzzy. She should probably stop while she was ahead before she made a fool of herself, but she was starting to get curious and figured she could take a few more shots. She eyed Nezka for a long moment then said, "Never have I ever been to prison."

Nezka's smile didn't fade, but some shadow passed over his eyes as he took a drink.

"How long?"

"Not very," he said. "And it was to find a...bounty."

"That sounds like an interesting story..." Elise murmured.

"For another time maybe," Nezka said. "I have never stolen something personal from someone."

"That's a total lie!"

Nezka's eyes narrowed. "Even so..."

Elise huffed. She looked around at everything but him then sighed and took a drink. "It was from my friend's brother. A toy lizard he loved, but they were moving away, and I wanted something to remember him by. I still regret it to this day. I was a kid and didn't know better."

Nezka tapped at his knee as if wondering whether to believe her, then he took his shot.

Elise studied him again for a short time then blurted, "Never have I ever drank someone's blood."

Nezka stared at her. She waited for him to drink, but he didn't.

"Just making sure you don't have any weird dietary needs," Elise stated.

"Not of that variety," Nezka replied. His hand clenched and unclenched on his lap. "Never have I ever been with another kind other than my own."

Elise stared back at him. He waited, and when she didn't drink, he took another sip, his eyes never leaving hers. Well, it wasn't like she hadn't figured that after what he said about especially liking sex. And since he mentioned he'd never seen another of his kind, it only made sense.

"Pity," he said. "Do your kind not care to explore others, or is it a moral dilemma?"

Elise shifted in her seat. The liquor was starting to have a dizzying effect, making her insides warm. "I don't know," she said, determined to not let him make her feel uncomfortable. "We only have one other race in our system, the gyda, and I've only heard rumors..." Elise could feel her skin turning hot, but she wasn't sure if it was the drink or their talk. "There was also this scientist who, as the story goes, ran away with an—a non-human partner. She hasn't been seen since, but those who saw them leave swore they were...intimate." Elise shrugged, hoping her play of indifference convinced him. "I'm guessing out there in the bigger systems it's not so shocking."

"Not at all," said Nezka, just as indifferent. "In fact, I feel sorry that your kind hasn't had the chance nor the pleasure to gain more experience. Although some would find that enticing enough, seeing how new you are."

She had it in her to believe he was deliberately trying to embarrass her, and whether she saw it as a challenge or it was just the liquor affecting her brain, she was inclined to outshock him.

She leaned forward and gave him a sultry stare. "Well, maybe if the right type comes along, I'll let them have a taste." She said it in the most sensual voice she could muster.

A dark shadow passed over Nezka's eyes, and his mouth curled ever so slightly. "Yes," he said in a low voice. "When the right *type* comes, you might just be surprised at what you're missing." He leaned back in his chair, observing her with sharp eyes. "I'm willing to bet your men don't know as much as they like to think. But there are those who could...enlighten."

"Like yourself," Elise said, trying to ignore the heat that was beginning to simmer low in her stomach, hoping her face hadn't given anything away.

Nezka grinned, showing off his twin fangs, and Elise felt herself shiver.

"I'd like to think I'm knowledgeable enough," he said slowly. "And can teach in more than just fighting..."

Elise licked her lips, not daring to let her eyes fall from his. Her heart did a sort of jolt in her chest. Dark images fluttered in her mind again, and she brushed them aside. She forced a smile to try to hide her thoughts. His gaze said enough, but she didn't know what to make of him; she was still uncertain whether he was serious or just badly messing with her.

Elise finally broke from his gaze. Weary of this game already, she shifted in her seat. "Never have I ever swam in the ocean."

His smile lessened, and the fiery glint in his eyes faded. He tilted his head, studying her briefly. He did not drink, and Elise took the canteen from him and pressed the top to her lips, taking her final sip.

"You really have never swam in the ocean?" she asked.

His gaze was quizzical, as if he were confused. He blinked and made a gesture at his throat. "No. I have never been."

"Seriously? Even with all the worlds you've likely been to?"

"I never had the chance," he said.

"I used to go all the time," Elise said. "Back before my active service. It's one of the most beautiful things, especially when the sun is setting, all the oranges and reds." She met his eyes and noticed how they shined like liquid fire.

Nezka's expression softened. "You look tired."

"It's the drink." Elise passed a hand over her face and laughed. "I'm going to regret this in the morning."

"Likely so." Nezka rose and took the can from her, placing it back in the bag. Elise got up to move from the chair to the longseat. She stumbled as her head spun, falling against the seat. She laughed softly, embarrassed, wishing she hadn't drunk so much. She laid out on her side with her knees bent. Either the liquor was stronger than she thought, or it had been a long while since she drank.

"If I get sick, I'm sorry in advance," Elise said and groaned. She looked up to find Nezka setting the canteen beside her. "No more."

"It's water," he said and turned away. "I will be close by. Sleep."

Elise watched him through half-lidded eyes. She wasn't really that tired in truth, but the alcohol made her sluggish enough to think she was. Better to lie there and sleep it off than make a fool of herself.

She watched him rekindle the fire one last time and set the bag aside to search around. The flame's light made him nothing more than a shadow in the darkness.

Elise closed her lids fully. She thought of her sister then of her team, hoping they would be alive, and she would make it in time to save them. She thought of home, of the ocean. She thought of Nezka swimming in it beside her.

Or maybe that was just a dream.

CHAPTER THIRTEEN

Two days passed before Elise was able to walk properly without limping. Her wounds were already scabbing over, some even peeling, the effects of the salve working quicker than they both anticipated. Elise was proud to say she also managed to rest for the majority of it, only walking around briefly to stretch her legs or relieve herself. By the third day, however, her patience had all but faded. Feeling infinitely better, she waved off Nezka's remarks about overexerting herself and went to walk the grounds. In truth, she had a feeling he was relieved to have her up and about. The last couple days had been nothing but sitting around and talking; more than she'd probably talked to anyone in a long time. He had asked about her homeworld, and she asked about his. She learned more about his homeworld and the other planets in its system; about the city he lived in and his travels. He didn't get into much detail about certain things, maybe because they were too personal, but she found she didn't mind telling him more than he likely needed to know. It was strange how comfortable she felt talking with him. Maybe because he was never overly critical. Elise guessed that, being a part of such a huge galactic empire inhabited by so many other people and cultures, one needed to have a very open mind.

The things he spoke of from his world, the advancements in tech and social structure, fascinated her. She never admitted it out loud, but she found herself wishing she could see it for herself. She hoped that once her people were returned safely home, they could start to communicate with those of his territory. He hadn't seemed especially enthusiastic about this idea, but he didn't reject it either.

So, as the third day was spent just walking the grounds, gauging her ability to climb stairs and run across rooms, Elise was confident by the fourth day she could start her training.

Of course, Nezka had other ideas.

"Before I teach you anything, you have to show me you can truly exert all your energy without any issue," he said as they stood by the edge of the stairs. "Take laps around each level."

Elise gave him an exasperated look but decided not to argue. She did as ordered, and when she returned, she was in a full sweat, knowing she probably stunk something awful, but Nezka didn't seem to care.

"That was a warm-up," he said. "Follow me."

They went down to the very bottom, and from there, he had her trying different sets of exercises to gauge her strength, stamina, and dexterity. When he was finally satisfied, he took her to a long inner courtyard situated to one side of the building. Most of the ground was cleared away, leaving only soft black sandy dirt. What the area had been used for, she couldn't guess, but it worked for their benefit.

The rest of the day was spent reforming her fighting stance, learning to move in a manner that was quick and effortless, maximizing her energy for swift blows. Nezka tapped at her hips, arms, and legs to correct her, explaining each technique.

"Don't think, react," he said. "When I move, you should always move in some other way. Don't stand and wait for me to come at you or to attack and have me dodge you. Read my body—every little movement can be used to determine where I will step, how I will strike, notice the tension in my legs and arms. If you concentrate, you can predict what I plan to do. It is the same for others."

Elise watched him closely, circling around him with her fists raised. It was difficult, but after some time, she could see the slightest tension building in his muscles before he struck, giving her a good read on how to block and dodge. She kept herself ready for every move he made, reacting accordingly.

Despite her efforts, she ended up on the ground more than once. She didn't let it faze her and was always up and ready to go once more. His strikes were so powerful, so quick, even when he slowed for her benefit, but Elise was determined to learn and stay humble. After all, he wasn't human. He fought like a fierce predator.

"When you strike, release your energy right before the blow. A quick but powerful strike in the right place or even right angle can damage an enemy significantly." He showed her the most vulnerable spots, some she didn't even know or think of. And the ones she did know, he showed her how to strike in a different way for a more effective hit. "Use the sharp angle of your knuckles or the connectors in your bent fingers." He showed her, taking her hand and molding her fist so that her fingers were bent outward, almost like a paw. "Jab them in the neck." He took her hand and placed it to his throat. "Or between their cheekbone." He lifted her hand to his face. "Or eyes." He aimed her hand accordingly then let it drop. "Uppercuts are especially effective also. Aim up into the center of their jaw."

The remainder of the day was spent in the courtyard until the natural light was lost to them and only the artificial remained. Elise went to bed that night sore and aching but deeply satisfied.

"We will make tomorrow our last training day here," Nezka said. "I think it's time we planned to move on."

Elise couldn't agree more. Even if she was happy to be back to her healthier self, she was anxious to leave.

* * *

Early the next day, they started practicing once again in the courtyard. Elise practiced her sets, and Nezka watched and corrected when needed. They lightly sparred, and Elise was pleased to find she could better determine his moves, even if they were slowed down. She blocked and spun, always making sure her feet were moving, her back and knees bent slightly. Nezka moved with her, circling. After watching him, Elise thought she could read him well enough. As he swung an arm toward her, she dodged then kicked out her leg toward his chest. He slid back, and Elise took the chance, lunging at him. He blocked her blows, but she didn't let up. When he went to strike at her again, Elise ducked then swung her leg out once more, this time catching him in the lower stomach. Nezka backed away, pupils widening, mouth stretching into an odd smile. Elise dropped her guard and grinned.

"Looks like I'm catching up," she said, breathless.

Nezka dropped his stance and turned from her. "You're learning, and that's good. Let's take a rest."

"Oh, I'm not that tired yet. Let's just go one more," Elise said, walking toward him. She frowned when she saw him bend forward then drop casually to one knee. "Are you all right?" she asked.

He laughed quietly as he wrapped an arm around himself. He side-eyed her, and she thought for a moment he actually looked pained. His face seemed to darken as if flushed. "It seems I've let my guard down a little too much."

She glanced downward and saw him clutching his stomach just above his...

"Oh." Apparently, she'd hit a little lower than she thought. "Sorry!" She stepped closer as if to help him, and he put out a hand to halt her.

"I'll be fine, assuming nothing has shriveled up inside me." He let out a low hiss, and Elise covered her mouth, trying to stifle her laugh.

"Sorry." She choked down a giggle then forced herself to look serious. "Sorry, that wasn't funny."

"No. It was. And you did the right thing. You went for a vulnerable place." He shook it off, righting himself.

Elise backed up a step then placed her hands on her hips. "So, what's this about letting your guard down too much? How easy are you making this for me?"

Nezka tilted his head in a shrug.

Elise threw up her hands. "How can I learn to get better if you go easy on me?"

"I'm trying not to put you back into the same state you were in when we first came here."

"But somebody else might," Elise countered. "If I can be faster than them, then there's a lesser chance of that happening."

"Maybe." Nezka started back across the courtyard.

Elise went after him, catching his arm. "One fight," she said, walking beside him. "At your best. I just want to see."

Nezka snorted. "No, you don't."

"I do!"

She watched him roll his eyes then stop and look down at her. "You really don't know what you're asking. I could seriously injure you. Remember how you said you'd never had a broken bone?"

"I trust you won't mess me up that much."

Nezka laughed. "I don't trust me."

He went to move, and Elise caught his arm again. "Please."

He glared down at her, and Elise shot him with her best dolly-eyed look. He turned toward her and sighed. "One. One fight. But as soon as I make a clear hit, we are done."

Elise grinned. She moved back into the courtyard and took position, raising her fists and taking up the stance he taught her.

Nezka placed himself opposite her and didn't so much as lift his arms. "Ready?"

Elise nodded. "Yes."

"Go."

Nezka shot over and was on her so quick Elise almost missed her block. He swung so fast and hard that all she could do was dodge and shield herself from his blows. Even with her armor, she could feel the hits to her arms all the way to her bones. She circled, jumping back, never hesitating for a second, trying to keep up with him. To her dismay, she found herself retreating farther from the middle of the courtyard until she was at the door. She never turned her back to run, but his attacks never stopped. Heart racing, she led him down a passage and back into the main foyer where she was also forced to step around fallen pieces of glass and metal while escaping his blows. At one instance that she ducked his punch, his fist landed on the side of a stone obelisk in the middle of the room, and a piece of it shattered and crumbled to the ground.

Elise cursed. Thinking quick, she rolled to the side then jumped up. As he turned, she saw an opening and went for it. She swung out her leg, hoping to strike his midsection, but Nezka was too quick. He swerved away from her kick and instantly stepped to the side, snapping out his arm.

His fist collided with her chest, and she went flying back, the air sucked out of her lungs as she landed on her ass and slid across the floor. She lay back, stunned, the glass roof above going in and out of focus. She thought she heard a growl from somewhere and tried to lift her head when Nezka was beside her, lifting her into a sitting position. Elise blinked and gazed up at him.

He looked pissed.

"Are you hurt?" he asked in an angry growl.

Elise opened her mouth but for a moment couldn't seem to speak. She touched at her chest and looked down and found the armor plate cracked on one side. Oops.

She took a deep breath but was relieved to feel no real pain. She glanced back at him and smiled. Then quickly dropped the grin when his expression didn't change.

"I'm all right, honestly," she said. "That was incredible."

His eyes narrowed as he studied her. His hand lay flat against the middle of her chest, as if his touch could gauge whether she told the truth. His face came close to hers, and he closed his eyes. Elise went still, noticing his other arm was around her back. She watched his face, noting the skin was beginning to heal where it was burned, his teeth were nearly covered with a new layer, and she could no longer see his cheekbone. Now there was only pale new skin forming over it. Where he was still purple in shade, she was close enough to notice a set of small scales knitted tightly together, kind of like a snake, making what she assumed was a smooth surface. She had a sudden crazy urge to touch and see if it really was smooth. Her hand started to lift up when his eyes opened to look back at her and all she saw was bright orange.

"You're fine," he concluded. He released her and stood, pulling her up with him. Elise wiped dust from her suit.

"Well, at least I held my own for a small time. Next fight will be different when I've practiced more."

Nezka glared at her then let out a hiss of breath and turned for the stair. "If there is another fight. And don't expect me to go hard like that again."

"Oh, come on! It wasn't that bad," Elise called, following him to the steps.

"Not this time maybe..." she heard him mutter. "But I won't risk it again." She thought to argue when he turned back to her. "It's all we will do for now. It's time we started making plans."

Elise paused, gazing up at him, thinking about arguing still but deciding to nod her head instead. "Yes. I agree."

* * *

They returned to their room on the top level, Elise feeling a slight soreness building in her chest but nothing more. Nezka went over to the bag and took out the strange green block. He broke it in half and gave one piece to her.

"What is this?" Elise sniffed it. It had a minty, citrus sort of scent.

"Soap," Nezka answered. "Use the rest of the water in your canteen, and I'll fill it up when you're done." He picked up the other canteen that had once been filled with liquor but was now replaced with water and headed out of the room. "I'll return shortly."

Elise watched him go, curious about his reaction to their fight. She let it go for the time being and went to her chair. As she began to take off her armor and unclasp the suit, she grimaced as she smelled the inside and the stink of sweat. She peeled away the top half and shivered as the chill air bit at her. She washed quickly, scrubbing her skin with the block till she was red then washing the dirt away with cold water. When she was finished with her upper half, she risked doing her lower, assuming Nezka would warn her before he entered again. She washed and rinsed to the best of her ability, using up all the soap he had given her. When she deemed herself clean enough, she placed a little more salve on a few areas still healing. Then, with the remainder of her water, she rinsed out her suit, letting it dry some before forcing it back on. With her canteen now empty, she left the room to inform Nezka she was finished.

She walked down the hall and was about to call out to him when her eyes glanced over to a nearby room, and she saw him sitting by a faded glass window. She peered in closer, and her heart did a little flip. She slid back quietly, hiding herself by the open door. She remained still for a moment longer then slowly looked back in.

He was naked from the top, his back turned to her as he took his canteen and poured water across his shoulders. His back was filled with the same white scars as his face and arms, stretching across tight skin and sharp shoulder blades. His body was hard muscle along a slender but well-built frame that seemed larger, longer than any human's. It was an odd yet curious melding of a man's body and a primitive, animalistic power; like he had inherited the muscular complexity of a tiger or wolf. The scars even reminded her of a big cat, though his skin seemed more reptilian in nature. The sight left her breathless when she first noticed him because, for a split second, she thought he'd begun transforming into some hybrid werebeast.

No. No, that's just...him.

Nezka didn't turn to look at her, and she wondered if he really didn't notice she was there. Feeling embarrassed for staring, Elise started to open her mouth to make herself known when he bent his back and—

Elise's eyes widened, and she had to cover her mouth to stifle her gasp. She slid back from the door again and just stood there.

He had spines.

Not just a regular human spine but sharp protruding spikes that curved along his back like quills. They looked sharp and deadly as they rose up when he had bent forward.

Elise, though shocked, was just curious enough to dare another peek. She carefully looked around the door and saw that he was now standing up, the sight of his hard stomach and broad chest exposed in the dim light. He began to take off the rest of his gear, and Elise caught a brief look at the sharp line of his lower abdomen before she quickly turned away and headed back to the room, ignoring the sudden heat that ran across her body.

Whether from the embarrassment of watching or from something else she didn't care to name, Elise distracted herself by keeping busy, readjusting her armor to her suit then organizing their food rations. When she heard him return, she didn't look up, pretending to be focused on a snag along her suit .

He didn't seem to notice her unusual quiet as he took up the empty canteens and went to refill them. When he returned again, he sat down in the chair beside her and began to repack the bag. Elise eyed him cautiously and saw him wearing the Red Blade suit once more.

"I've looked over the map a few times while you were resting," he began. He touched at his band, bringing up the map before them. He focused on where they were now and what was ahead. The next gate wasn't far, but they were off their original course and would have to find another way through. "We have a few options on getting past but none will be easy," he stated. "We can head back farther north and find the trail we used through the tram tunnels..."

"I'd rather not go down there again," Elise confessed.

"I would agree. By now, they will be swarming with Red Blades," Nezka said. "So, that leaves another gate back south that may not be as heavily guarded but will put us at least a day or two behind and would force us back into the pack of car thieves' territory. Or there is the bridge."

"The bridge?"

Nezka focused on a part of the gate that was only a little ways east from them. There, they saw an opening unlike the others. Instead of a regular tunnel entrance, there was a bridge situated between the walls with what looked to be a building at its center. A deep river base flowed parallel to the gate at first then crossed below it, exactly where the bridge stood. "It seems that this is an old gate-house made before the other gates were built. It could not be torn down, likely due to the river-chasm below, so for whatever reason, the drogin left it and built the new gate across the old," Nezka explained, pointing to a crossway at the top that went over the gate-house and bridge. "The bridge is several spans long on both sides of the gate and doesn't end until the river turns off either to the north or south. It is the closest pass by far, and if we come out the other side, there is a road that can take us back to a path toward the energy deposit."

Elise observed the map carefully where the bridge and gate crossed each other. It wasn't far at all. The only thing standing between where they were now and the bridge was an expulsion plant —whatever the hell that was. After that, they could get a good look at the bridge and see what they were up against. If they could sneak past, they could gain some serious ground despite being a little off their course. Even the road he mentioned had to veer away a little before putting them back on their original path. Elise fixed her gaze on a portion of the map just past the bridge that the road went around. It was completely blank. "What's going on here?" She pointed to it.

"Uncertain," Nezka admitted. "Maybe an unmarked blockade. Or a hole."

"Hm. Too bad," Elise said. "If we could cross that particular section, it could make for a decent shortcut."

"Perhaps. But for now, I think our focus should lie on the bridge," Nezka suggested.

"Good point. I think it's a great idea. We should go for it."

"There's one issue." Nezka focused on the bridge. "What I've heard from others while out on my runs is that the bridge is owned by someone called Krow. The gatehouse now serves as both his own personal stronghold and as a sort of gambling entertainment clubhouse. They let people cross but for a price."

"Great." Elise sat back.

"I don't know what that price is exactly, but I assume he has his own pack and is armed to the teeth."

"Why else would he still have hold of the bridge and not the Red Blades, right?" Elise said.

"Exactly," Nezka said.

Elise shook her head. "They might not let me pass if they see me and know the Red Blades are looking."

"Not if they see you with me," Nezka countered.

She glanced up at him and could tell he had an idea in mind. "What are you thinking?"

Nezka smirked. "You might not like it."

"Probably not."

"I pass as one of the Red Blades bringing you back as a prisoner," Nezka said.

"You're right. I hate it."

"But it could work."

Elise exhaled through her teeth and crossed her arms. "Assuming they even believe it."

Nezka tilted his head. "Why wouldn't they?"

"I don't know," Elise admitted. She sighed and looked back at him seriously. "What would it entail, then?"

"You'd have to do as I say. You'd be bound, maybe gagged."

"Kinky."

Nezka gave her an odd but intrigued sort of look, and Elise felt her face grow warm. "A joke! But in all seriousness..." Elise looked back at the map to the bridge, shaking her head. "There's really no other way? Maybe we could sneak in?"

Nezka made a cutting motion at his throat. "No."

She really didn't like the thought of having to act the part of hostage. But his idea was sound even if risky. There were few other choices with less of a risk that she could think of. "All right." It pained her to say it." I guess...if you think it will work."

"I do," he said confidently. "Assuming they don't catch on, our biggest concern will be trying to convince this Krow to let us pass." Nezka tapped her arm assuredly. "It may take some time to convince him. A day or two."

"I was afraid you'd say that."

"But if we can get through after, the energy deposit is all that remains." Nezka closed out the map and rose. "We stay one more night, then tomorrow, we go."

CHAPTER FOURTEEN

They left at first light, taking the two-wheeler out to the nearest road and making east for the bridge-gate. Nezka had Elise keep hold of her gun, assigning her as lookout in case they met with anyone who posed a threat. Thankfully, those they did see were nothing to worry about. The drogin and otherkin of this particular part of the city were scavengers and poor folk looking to live peacefully and nothing more. They hid themselves when he drove passed, likely seeing his red and black armor and identifying him as a Red Blade. The real threat.

They passed the market and living district and drove on through to the factory zones where tall metal bots stood like dead corpses in mid-action, long since shut off and rusting. From there, they came to a wasteland of garbage and steel until they hit the expulsion plant. Large clouds of steam bellowed out from giant vents in the ground, making the way foggy and warm. It was here Nezka was forced to slow and where he warned Elise to keep her eye out and her gun ready. Shadows ran along the road and across the buildings, dashing in and out of sight. Nezka knew someone or something was watching them, following them.

Whoever they were, they weren't carrying guns for they never stopped nor did they fire at him. And that concerned him. He neared another set of buildings where several large fans turned slowly in front of two giant, empty vents angled toward the road. As he drove under a wide bridge toward them, a loud buzzer went off, and the fans started to turn faster. A wind picked up, and steam, along with other debris, began to spew out of the vents. Nezka stopped the vehicle as Elise called out to him over the wind. He hopped off the two-wheeler and dragged her with him into the shelter of the bridge.

"Someone is trying to force us back," Nezka shouted, pulling her with him against a thick blockade under the bridge. They huddled down as pieces of metal and chunks of concrete whipped by from the force of wind and steam. The air grew thick, and Nezka could see Elise had her mouth covered as if it was hard to breath. He too found it difficult and so ripped off the Red Blade's mask connected to his belt and tugged at the straps to loosen the bindings and widen the mouthpiece. Angling the mask, he pressed his face against hers, covering their mouths with the ventilator. Their breath mingled and, as intimate as it was, in that moment, Nezka could only think of the danger surrounding them, of the glass and dust and steam that could choke their lungs and the metal that flew by, powerful enough to shred them to pieces. His eyes shot around, preparing himself to shield Elise from anything that might fall on them when he felt the warmth of her hand cover his. He turned his gaze over to her, and their eyes locked. Her eyes spoke of her fear but also her fury and her will to endure, and in that moment, as time seemed to stretch, he felt again that pull—that need to bring her closer.

The wind died down and the steam lessened. Through the thick clouds, Nezka could see the shadows dropping from the bridge above and moving closer. Eyes narrowed, Nezka pulled away, forcing Elise to hold on to the mask as he pushed himself up and lurched forward, taking out his blades. The shadows began to band together until the steam drifted partially out of his view, and he saw a group with faces covered by scarves, bodies draped in scraps of black and gray. They each held a weapon in their hands, some with long swords, others with staffs. They crouched low, ready to attack.

Nezka didn't hesitate. Though his sight was obscured somewhat by the steam, he closed the distance between them, side-swiping one sword to block another then bending low and slicing across thighs and knees. A pair went down, and he leapt over them to the next, cutting their staff in half. The rest fell away into the steam, but he could see them circling, waiting. When he took out another attacker, there was yet another coming for him. He didn't slow, crushing each shadow that dared approach him. He heard someone bark in pain nearby, and when he snapped his head around, he saw Elise fighting them also, using the techniques he'd taught her.

Nezka smiled. *That's my girl,* he thought as he saw her strike one across the throat, sending them reeling and stumbling away. Nezka turned back to those about to lunge at him and moved swiftly. Though there were many, he took them out with ease, breaking their weapons and their bones, until the wind picked up, dissolving the clouds of steam, and he found none left standing near him. He twisted around in time to see the last one fall to the ground from a powerful kick to the face by Elise. The body fell with a thud, and Elise dropped her stance and turned to smile at him.

A strong feeling of pride overtook him, and Nezka moved toward her, grinning back. "You're a quick learner. I like that."

Elise shrugged. "They weren't so bad, honestly."

Nezka couldn't seem to stop himself as he drew close to her and lifted his hand, brushing a stray lock of hair from her face, checking for any signs of damage and finding none. She gave him a curious, almost timid sort of look, skin flushing slightly, her smile changing. She cleared her throat and stepped back.

"We should probably get going before..."

Nezka looked around and understood her meaning. Most of the attackers weren't dead, just injured. They would get up, and others might come. The vents down the road had shut off, and the fans were back to their slow turn. They should leave before they started again.

Nezka tapped his ear. "Let's go."

He lifted up the two-wheeler where it had fallen on its side. Some parts were tarnished and banged up somewhat, but it started fine. Elise got on behind him and, with her gun drawn once more, wrapped her arms tightly around him. Her warmth against him was comforting. He bent forward and kicked the two-wheeler into gear, speeding up fast as they turned off down one road, away from the vents.

* * *

As they neared the bridge, Nezka stopped briefly by a lone section of road beside the river-chasm to get rid of their bag (as it would look too suspicious to have) then to assess the gatehouse from afar. The bridge was long and wide enough for vehicles to pass. Besides broken off pieces of wall and a few burnt out streetlights, the road was clear up to the gatehouse where he could see the first gated doorway into what looked like a mote fortress. The windows were covered by shades made of thin sheets of metal. Some closed off completely, others open enough to see the glow of colorful lights from within. The stone and metal encased walls of the stronghold were blackened in several areas where pipes helped drain out putrid wastewater. From the front, Nezka could see several guards standing above the wide doorway that was meant to allow vehicles to pass underneath the building and on to the other side of the bridge. The guards had guns and long ranged weapons if anyone should be so stupid as to try to pass through without paying their toll. Neither he nor Elise had city credits on them, but Nezka knew they wouldn't ask for money. Perhaps a trade instead. Though they had little to bargain with, Nezka felt confident they could think of something to appease the bridgekeeper, Krow.

Before they went in, regardless, they needed to set up their lie. Nezka had Elise hop off the two-wheeler so that he could take her gun then bind her hands. She still wasn't pleased at having to give her weapon and wrists to him, but she allowed it to happen without complaint. He used the metal coil to tie her and suggested again a gag for added effect, but Elise had different ideas.

"I still look roughed up from the fights despite the healing," she said, touching at the bruised side of her face, now pale green instead of dark blue. "Just imply that the marks were from you to keep me quiet."

Nezka frowned, eyes narrowed on her face. "You'd need something fresher if they are to believe it."

Elise thought it over then looked at him. "Use one of your blades to cut me."

Nezka's frown deepened. Without shifting his eyes away from hers, he took out one of his blades and lifted it to her face. He knew they needed to be convincing, yet he still hesitated. Elise took his hand in both of hers and guided down to her cheek. Unthinking, Nezka cupped the back of her head, trying hard not to pull his bladed hand away from her face while keeping his grip tight to only let the blade nick her ever so slightly and nothing more. She winced, and he almost forced his hand back, but she let the blade make a small slice along her cheek, where tiny rows of blood beaded against her open skin. When he deemed it enough, he pulled the blade away and quickly pocketed it. His hand, cupping her head, brushed at the side of her face gently before falling. He suppressed the urge to wipe away the blood now trickling lightly down her face and took hold of both her shoulders, pinning her with a serious glare.

"For this to work, I will have to play your worst enemy. As soon as we enter inside, I will not be able to lift this facade. I will be cruel if I have to be. I will do what I please, and you will have to let me. Do you understand? If you fight me, I will have no choice but to..." He glanced down at the cut on her cheek then back to her gaze. The color of her eyes brightened to an almost golden hue he found to be frustratingly beautiful. "Do you understand?" he said in a low, quiet voice.

Elise nodded her head slowly, her hand coming up to grip at one of his arms, squeezing it gently. "I understand. Do what you have to, just get us past. Whatever it takes."

Nezka flinched at her words. Grimacing, he backed away, releasing her. He couldn't bring himself to look at her in fear she would see his sudden slip of emotion. He returned to the two-wheeler and ordered her to get on. When he felt her hands, now bound, clutching to his backside, he closed his eyes for a moment, taking deep breaths.

"Nezka?" she said from behind him.

Nezka opened his eyes and started the two-wheeler. He drove on until he reached the start of the bridge. From there, he slowed to make sure Elise didn't fall off as she clung to him tightly. As they drove straight on and approached the gatehouse, several men lifted weapons in their direction while another beside the doorway waved at them to halt.

A thin, scruffy looking drogin with markings across his arms came up and whistled softly. "My, oh my, is this a Red Blade I see? A real mean-looking one at that." He laughed, exposing crooked fangs. "Don't see your lot passing by here often." His watery eyes glanced behind Nezka to stare at Elise. "Brought a peace bearin' gift for the ol' Krow man, did yeh?"

"No," Nezka said bluntly. "I'm just here to pass."

The man grunted in surprise. "That so? What do you need to pass through here for? You lot own all the other gateways." He laughed. "Your brothers not letting you in for some reason?"

Nezka smiled. "There have been...problems with defectors and spies. I am ordered to return unnoticed."

The man gestured toward Elise. "Something to do with your cargo, huh?"

"Yes."

The man eyed Elise curiously. "I heard something about one of those...what do you call 'em? Humans? Heard the thornbacks had one. Then it got snatched up. You the Red Blade I heard about who beat up all of Roni's best fighters and took this woman?"

Nezka shrugged, and the drogin's eyes went wide, then he hissed out another cackle of laughter.

"No shit! So, you want to come on by so no one sees you with your little prize, huh? A gift to your boss, I'll bet. Well, you'll still have to talk to Krow. No one passes without his say. He'll be real excited to see you, though. The Red Blade who could actually fight without a gun at their side." He turned and howled, and those on top of the doorway lowered their guns. The gate blockading the doorway slid back to reveal a short tunnel leading to the other side. If it were in him to risk it, he would have taken that moment to speed on through. But with Elise, he didn't dare. As there were men before them on this part of the bridge, there were surely more on the other side. What's more, there were also several vehicles taking up space inside the tunnel and underbelly of the gatehouse, with groups of people lurking between them. Nezka drove the two-wheeler on through, ignoring the eyes that followed them as he parked against the tunnel wall. He felt Elise's hand tap against his back as if to reassure him before he shut the vehicle down and got off. He took hold of her bindings and didn't so much as look at her as he pulled her not so gently to him, tugging her over to a set of stairs on the side of the tunnelway. They followed the crooked-smiled drogin up the two flights where they were met with another pair of guards. The door before them opened, and they entered the gatehouse.

The first section led into a large red and blue lit room with a bar on one side and a stage on the other. Some sort of club. People lingered in groups, heads turning to watch them pass. At the next door was a small passage that brought them into a smaller red room, with a bar and tables along each side and lounge at the back. The center was a hexagonal ring with a set of stairs leading down to it, fenced in partially by sets of rails. Inside the space, two drogin were tearing each other apart in a brutal one on one fight, blood spraying along the floor. A small group at the back watched as they reclined in leather chairs. Nezka was brought around and stopped before a well-dressed drogin in an officer's uniform with slick gray and black hair.

The drogin's yellow eyes shifted over and sized him up. "Who's the corpse?" he said, eyeing his face.

"This is one of them Red Blades, Mr. Krow," said the gateman.

"You let a Red Blade in here, Jona?" Krow's eyes narrowed at him.

Jona's upper lip twitched back as he bowed his head. "Not intentionally, sir. The Red Blade is looking to pass."

Krow's eyes regarded Nezka now with curiosity. "That so, Red Blade?"

Nezka stared him down. "Yes."

Krow tipped his head sideways. "Odd way to come for one such as you."

"I wish to pass in secret."

"Hm. Your boss put you on a special mission, huh?" Krow's gaze fell behind him to Elise, and his eyes widened. "Ah. So, it's you. The thornbacks told me about you and your little human. Their leader wants your head real bad. Was looking to pay a nice sum if you should come this way. I didn't think I'd actually see you. Thought you'd be smart enough to pass through a different gateway." He leaned forward, crossing his hands. "But it's because your mistress orders it, not because you're stupid, I'll bet. Having trouble trusting her puppets, is she?" He grinned, showing off perfectly sharpened teeth. "I've seen a few trade in their guns for credits. They give away her secrets or turn to the other side then go running, scared of her wrath. Lady Moth is desperate to keep things under a tight hold, but even she can't control them all." He reclined back, regarding him sharply. "So, she sent you off to grab her lost human and bring them back without others knowing, am I right?"

"You're correct."

"And you think I will be willing to let you pass without issue?"

"No. I expect we will need to negotiate," Nezka said.

"Hm. Not like a Red Blade to do so. Usually it is all threats. But you are different, aren't you? Well, at least you respect my way of business, and for that, I'll do you the favor of not killing you and taking your human for the thornback's benefit. I hate that slobbering bastard anyway." He laughed. "But, yes, you will have to pay if you wish to pass."

Nezka waited as Krow waved one of the bar staff over and poured him a drink. Behind them, there was a sharp growl and a loud crack followed by a whimpering cry and the dull thud of a body dropping to the ground. Krow gave a short whoop and lifted his glass to the winner of the fight. "Good run, Ero," he said to the large, blood-covered fighter as he slunk out of the fighting ring. "That's one of my best there," Krow said to Nezka. "Trained to fight like the beasts they are." He chuckled.

Nezka said nothing. He felt Elise turn to look around, and he promptly tugged her sharply back. Krow's gaze fell on her again with curiosity.

"They are interesting, these humans. I've never seen one this close. Their faces are strange if not ugly, but she's not bad on the eyes. Bring her closer."

Nezka didn't hesitate, forcing Elise to the front. She stood tense as the drogin regarded her.

"You do that to her face?" Krow pointed to Elise's cut, still trickling fresh blood.

"Yes," Nezka said.

Krow nodded as if satisfied. "Keeping this one quiet, I imagine, put a toll on your patience." He smiled. "She's got a little fight in her still, though. I can tell by the brightness in her eyes." His hand lifted up and brushed at her cheek, and Elise flinched away. "There are those who'd pay a good chunk of change to have a go with one of these, you know. They get off to otherkin. Have you tried her yet?"

"No, I haven't," Nezka said, forcing himself to sound indifferent.

"Surely your mistress wouldn't care as long as she came back unharmed?" Krow tapped on his glass. "Let my men have a turn with her. Let us watch even, and I'll let you be on your way."

Elise whimpered, and Nezka tugged her back as if to silence her. "No."

Krow's eyes narrowed as he grinned. "Ah, so you prefer to have her for yourself?"

"She is not part of the negotiation."

Krow watched them both, his smile fading, then shrugged. "Your call. I was merely thinking of my boys, but in all honesty, it isn't the true entertainment I seek. It is you who I am more interested in, my wicked friend. I heard what you did to Roni's best fighters. I am impressed. And admittedly greatly intrigued. So, I tell you what." He drank down his glass and set it aside. "I'll make it easy for you—or at least what I assume should be quite easy. I want to see you fight my best just like you did those thornbacks. You give us a good show, and I'll let you pass. I want to see what you can do." Before Nezka could agree, Krow put up his hand. "But I warn you they are much more skilled than Roni's pathetic lot, so don't expect a clean sweep. You give me some good fights, and I'll give you my best accommodations. Honestly, you don't even have to win, though if you didn't, you'd probably not be in a state to continue on." He smiled, gesturing to the body still lying in the center of the ring. "Show me your savagery, and I'll show you the door to the other side."

Nezka paused only a moment, just to make Krow think he was considering it, then he bowed his head once. "Agreed."

Krow grinned and waved Jona back over. "Give them one of the good suites up top," he ordered. "We will settle on a match come evening."

Nezka turned and followed Jona back into the club and up a set of metal-grate stairs. They turned down a hallway and stopped at a thick steel door. The door slid open to reveal a bedroom and lounge area with another door leading to a second bedroom beyond.

"Make yourself at home," Jona said. "You get Krow's finest and I'll be your humble servant." He bowed low, grinning his crooked grin. "There is food and drink on the back bar and red haze for smoking— some call it bluym. I can bring up women or men if you're sick of the human's company, or perhaps—"

"I'm good," Nezka said, pretending to observe the room.

"You got it." Jona bowed again. "If you need anythin', ask a guard out in the hall. You can leave to wander any time, come downstairs and have a little fun. If not, I'll return for your fight. Be seein yeh'." As he left and the door slid closed, Nezka stood staring at it for a long moment until he felt Elise tug gently at her binds. He glanced back at her, noticing her look of concern.

"There might be another way," she said, uncertainly. "Maybe you don't have to do this."

"I do," Nezka said.

Elise shook her head. "You saw what happened to the loser of that fight. It was a slaughter. I know you did some serious damage in that thornback pit, but this is...this seems different. You could get really messed up here or..."

Nezka couldn't help smiling despite the seriousness of the conversation. "I'm glad to see you feel worried for me."

"I am," she blurted, and her skin turned slightly pink.

Nezka's smile dropped. He started to lift his hand as if to touch her, to comfort, then decided against it. "I'll be fine. It's not unlike the kind of fighting I've done before."

"Back when you trained?"

Nezka tapped his ear.

Elise nodded, her eyes dropping from him. "It's not just what will happen to me if you lose that I'm worried about..." She looked back at him as if she wanted to say something more about it but decided against it. "I know you will win."

Nezka stared down at her. He wasn't concerned about him losing either. What truly worried him was what Elise might see. What she might think of him after. Would she distance herself from him? Would she hate him or be afraid of him more than when she first met him? It bothered him to think it just as much as it bothered him that he cared.

Elise went to reach for his hand, and he let her take it if only for a moment. He felt the dark waters of his psyche stir, and he gently pulled away, making for the other room. "Don't worry about me. Take advantage of what we are given but stick to the plan, no matter what happens, no matter how I must act. Remember, I'm not your friend here, Starling."

He thought he saw sudden hurt in her eyes, but it passed quickly. "Of course," she said.

He looked at her one last time, almost tempted to move back over and pull her to him, then he turned and entered the other bedroom, closing the door between them.

CHAPTER FIFTEEN

IF THERE WAS ONE THING SHE COULD AT LEAST APPRECIATE given the situation she was in, it was the chance to have a hot shower. And by god, did she need it. Even the wash she'd given herself a day ago hadn't been enough to completely dissolve the smell of sweat and grime. She took her time in the water, bitter that such a luxury given the circumstance had to come from such a foul being.

She knew Krow was crooked, and she didn't trust him one bit. She couldn't put aside her worry for the deal he and Nezka had made. Unlike the thornbacks, that unsavory pack of thugs that had been as close to barbaric as one could get in the city, Krow and his kin worked on a deeper, more secure level. They were smarter, more cunning. A criminal organization disguised as a business for entertainment and indulgence. She'd seen it many times before. Sad to think nothing changed in the outer worlds. A city always held its demons.

But despite what she thought of Krow and the others, she wanted to be optimistic about her and Nezka's escape. She didn't think Krow would pull something like the leader of the thornbacks—that he would be true to his word and let them pass without a chase. But she couldn't pretend to think it would be that easy. He was just as deceitful as the rest of them. He'd get his entertainment, his fights. And he'd milk every last drop of his and Nezka's deal, maybe until Nezka broke.

After scrubbing herself raw until she was without a speck of dirt, Elise shut off the water and stepped out of the black box that was her temporary shower. She went over to the black mirrored wall and dried herself off, staring at the shadowy reflection of herself with a tight frown.

Krow never said how many fights.

She shouldn't be worried for Nezka. He'd shown her more than enough times that he was undoubtedly capable of holding his own. But still, she couldn't brush away her anxiety. All it took was one bad fight. And what then? And even if he did win them all, she'd seen how brutal, how violent they'd been. Could she stand to watch him lose his humanity? Because even she knew fighting could go too far. And despite what she might have thought of him before, she'd learned now that he wasn't a complete monster.

And Krow just might tempt him in every way he could to make Nezka forget why he was here. If the fights didn't do it, something else might. Some other temptation. She didn't touch the drugs laid out on the bar of her room, but she saw Nezka eyeing them. She thought of Jona's offer of sending someone to the room for his pleasure, and her stomach twisted, making her feel nauseous. She didn't know why it bothered her, but it did. He could do what he liked, but if he found himself too wanting of what Krow had to offer, he might just be enticed to stay longer than necessary and give in to such indulgence. Maybe it was a stupid paranoid way of thinking, but she couldn't seem to clear away such thoughts. He'd said himself he'd need to play the role, and Elise had no doubt he would. But she wondered if she could stand to play her part before she felt she might snap.

Elise turned to her suit laying out on the chair. It was filthy still, and there was no way she was going to put it back on after washing herself, so she started the water in the large basin meant to be a tub and threw it inside. As she watched the tub fill, she felt herself tense. She didn't like it here one bit and suddenly wished they'd tried a different route. She didn't want to go downstairs and act the part of a quiet, submissive captive. She didn't want to see Nezka tearing someone a part in that ring just because some psycho found it entertaining, and she didn't want to see the eyes of those men glaring at her hungrily nor the women eyeing Nezka, wondering if he'd take them to his room and screw their brains out after he'd split someone's head open. Already, she missed the broken down museum and their time in it together. She missed the stillness and the sounds of just their voices. But it was too late to go back, the bridge had been crossed. They had to keep going.

She just hoped it was worth it.

* * *

Nezka came back to her side of the room as night fell, ready to return down to the fighting lounge and give Krow a good show. She let him bind her again with the metal coil and pull her out to the hallway where two guards were stationed. They led them down to the club which was now packed, filled with all manner of people dancing to loud thumping music. They passed through the crowd, Elise having to shrug off a few hands, and stepped into the red lounge where a fight was just finishing up in the hexagonal ring. The winner ripped into the loser's throat with his teeth and tore a hole. The body fell, and the crowd watching cheered. Krow stood from his black leathered throne and, seeing Nezka, smiled, gesturing for him to approach.

"You see, now, that's a fight I can appreciate," Krow said as they came to stand before him. "But I anticipate you'll surprise me." He offered Nezka some 'liquid courage' which he declined then pointed to Elise. "You didn't have to bring her down. Could have kept her tucked safely in your suite."

"Where I go, she goes," Nezka replied.

Krow smirked and ordered one of his men to bring over a chair. "Then she can have the best view from here."

Nezka plopped Elise down in the seat next to Krow's and left without looking at her. Elise watched him step over to the ring, ready to enter.

"Hold on now there, tough guy." Krow laughed. "No shields, suits, or weapons. You can keep your pants if you want, but the pads go. This is a skin only sport."

Nezka hesitated for only a moment then began to shrug off the Red Blade chest shield with the arms pads followed by the inner long piece shirt. When he peeled it off and revealed his naked torso, Elise felt herself shiver, thinking back to when she saw him washing in the room. She turned her gaze away and saw the others watching closely, including a few women who whispered to each other, eyes lingering on his body. Nezka's spines rose across his back and the crowd "oohed" and "aahed" at the sight. Krow waved his hand to someone in the throng, and a very large, badly scarred lizardman—a grex Nezka called them—entered the ring.

Elise considered closing her eyes and just not allowing herself to watch, but she knew it would be a futile attempt. She sat up straight as the pair circled each other, waiting for Krow to give the word. When he raised up his arm and made a cutting motion downward, the crowd leaned in and so did Elise.

The grex hissed as he circled once more, venom dripping from his mouth. He struck fast, going for the jugular. Nezka was quicker. He swerved to the side and hammered his fist into the side of the grex's face. The grex turned to bite him, missing by an inch. Nezka landed blows on the lizard, but he didn't falter. Not like the others. His skin was tough to break and his bones too thick to crack. The lizard came at him like a savage beast, trying to rip and tear and bite. Nezka was backed into the wall. Even as his strikes hit, the grex kept coming. The lizard opened his jaws wide, ready to clamp down, and Nezka took hold of the skin and muscle around his snout and jaw, keeping his mouth from snapping shut. The grex tried to back up, but Nezka already had a firm hold on him. With strength Elise had yet to witness, he opened the grex's mouth wider, forcing him on his knees, and pulled his jaws apart. Elise heard the crack of his jaw breaking as the grex fell to its side on the ground. The crowd laughed and howled, and Krow clapped beside her.

"Not a bad first run," Krow said. "A little short for my taste, but I imagine many of them will be with you." He grinned. "No matter. I'll have to challenge you better."

Nezka's spines flexed before they lowered along his back. He didn't acknowledge the grex on the ground as he stepped closer to the rail by Krow.

"I'm ready for the next," Nezka said. Elise almost shook her head but stopped herself.

Krow looked him over for a long moment then bobbed his head. "All right." He smiled. He waved his hand again, and another fighter entered the ring.

Elise watched Nezka take out two more opponents before Krow decided it was enough for the night. The ring was colored red, pieces of fur and hair and teeth scattered along the edges. Nezka had taken a few bad blows, but they had barely slowed him. Krow whooped and hollered so much, leaping from his seat, shouting at Nezka to hit harder with each match, that he looked more tired than the fighters, sweat trickling on his brow.

"You are a treat. A real treat to watch," he said, slicking back his hair. "Best I've seen in a long time. And I'm bettin' many here made some good credits off of you. Yes, you are something."

"Good," Nezka said, barely out of breath. "I will take my leave tomorrow then."

"Oh, now, why the rush, huh?" Krow waved over a bar girl with a few glasses. "Your mistress can wait. You can tell her I kept you for my own benefit, I don't mind. Let us celebrate. Come on, have a drink and sit. The others are dying to meet you."

Both she and Nezka knew he'd not let them go so soon, but Elise was grateful that Nezka had at least tried. As he exited the ring, a slender, dainty drogin female came up and said something to him Elise couldn't hear. The woman whispered in his ear, and he tilted his head and said something back. The woman used a towel to wipe the blood off his torso, letting her hand move across his chest and stomach in a slow, seductive manner. Nezka didn't pull back, watching her with curiosity. They spoke a few words and Elise, realizing her hands were clenched tight in her lap, opened them.

Much of the crowd dissolved back into the club with smaller groups lingering at the various tables and bars. Krow had a table situated back by one side for him and those most loyal to him, including Jona. Elise dared not move from her seat, knowing if she got up, Nezka would be forced to put her back in her place, likely with a short cuff to the face for good measure, just to be convincing. She watched as Krow made room for Nezka, pouring him a drink and, as Nezka sat, the drogin woman made herself comfortable on his lap.

Elise turned her eyes away but kept a sharp ear to their conversations, most of which were Krow stroking his and Nezka's ego. Nezka said very little save to answer a question. From the corner of her eye, she could see him drinking heavily, his arm wrapped tight around the woman on his lap.

The night dragged, but Elise refused to let her patience thin out so quickly. When it was near dawn and the men and women had drank themselves stupid, Krow finally ordered them out. Nezka took Elise back up to their suite without so much as a glance her way. The drogin woman, who called herself Sona, had offered to come back to his room, but he had declined, saying he was too tired. Elise felt some relief in that, knowing she wouldn't have to listen to them pounding at the walls, but the relief was short-lived when the woman pressed herself against him and said, "Another night," and he smiled back with one of his wicked grins, tracing a finger across her neck like it was a promise. Then he took Elise back into their suite and didn't say a word as he unbound her and went to his bedroom, closing the door.

Elise sat up till morning, annoyed and wired. The fights had been as brutal as she feared. Worse than the ones he had fought in the pit which she hadn't thought possible. She didn't know if she could take another night of it, but she told herself she had to endure.

Eventually, she slept, and when she woke up, she was alone in a chair, her mouth dry and her stomach growling. She forced herself to eat what food Krow's men had left on the bar and drink water from the bath tap as they'd left nothing but booze. The day went by as she waited, pacing her room, trying not to knock on Nezka's door. When night finally arrived, his door opened. She started to say something but seeing his dark expression silenced her. Knowing there was nothing she could really say to better the situation, she gave him her wrists, and he took her back out.

The night went nearly the same as the last. Elise watched Nezka violently destroy his enemies in all manner of ways while Krow shouted beside her, rousing Nezka to be faster, deadlier. Elise felt sick after but kept her composure. After the matches, Nezka made another comment that he should be going, but once again, Krow shot him down, too intrigued by this lethal fighter to give him up so soon. Once more, they sat around and drank, Krow even offering Nezka some of the red haze which Nezka took without complaint; even, dare she say, gladly. Sona returned to take her place on his lap, giggling and whispering in his ear, and Nezka, in turn, trailed his fingers over her slender waist and back, making Elise glance away as a strange ache settled in her chest. Other girls fought for his attention, but Sona kept them away with a snapping growl, reminding Elise of one of those toy poodles her aunt had when she was a kid. Elise didn't so much as move from her spot though she was ignored well enough that she wondered if anyone would even notice if she left. Surely Nezka would.

Besides an occasional glance in his direction, she kept her gaze straight ahead. By the conversations she eavesdropped on, she could tell Nezka was warming up to them, especially to Krow. He talked more and—when she chanced to look—noticed that he smiled more, made himself more at home as he lounged back in his seat as if he were suddenly on a vacation. He was so relaxed, unlike her, but she supposed that was part of the act. Though she hated how easy he made it seem.

Once more, they stayed up till near dawn until Krow ordered them back to the suite. Thankfully, Sona did not ask to return with them, feeling too sick from drinking, so they entered the suite alone together. He unbound her hands like usual, but before he could leave her without a word, Elise grabbed his arm.

She opened her mouth to say something but was again frozen by his expression. His cold stare made her shudder, and she let him go. She stood staring at his closed door, her fists clenching and unclenching. She wanted him to talk to her, to tell her what he was thinking. She wanted to ask him how much longer, but she could guess the answer.

"As long as it takes."

* * *

Another day and night passed in Krow's domain. Elise remained in a corner as Nezka sat drinking with Krow and his group, grinning and talking as if they were close friends. He brought Sona close to him as she nuzzled his neck then bit his ear, her hand slipping down his bare chest. He'd elected to leave his gear off after the fights, and Elise found it increasingly hard not to stare. She wished she could say she was numb to watching him get touched all over, but she wasn't. If anything, she felt a sort of red-hot pressure growing in her head. She told herself over and over it was an act and that she felt nothing as she continued to untighten her fists and unclench her jaw.

She was just concerned for him, that was all. Though it was stupid to think he needed her concern. He was having a swell ass time by the looks of it.

Meanwhile, Elise had been dodging a pair of eyes on her all night from a drogin with a jet-black stare. She hoped he'd not be tempted to come near her if she didn't look his way, but when she did let her eyes pass over in his direction, he remained watching her intently. Thinking it couldn't be helped, she looked his way and locked eyes, hoping her glare told him enough that she wanted to be left alone.

No such luck.

He smiled at her and came over, seating himself beside her.

"You look so lonely over here by yourself, pet," the black-eyed male said sweetly. He had a sly sort of appearance about him, like a fox. He moved close to her, his hand lifting to graze knuckles against her shoulder. "I figured you could use some company."

Elise said nothing, uncertain whether she should. The man clicked his tongue as he brushed a finger along the side of her face, across her cut, making Elise flinch.

"That must've hurt." He dropped his hand. "That scary ass guy do that to you? What an asshole."

Elise was ready to tell him to fuck off when her eyes flickered upward and locked with Nezka's. As the others around him laughed and drank, he wasn't smiling as he stared over at her. Elise shifted in her seat, uncomfortable with this stranger so close, and Nezka looking like he might leap off the table and kill him for touching her.

Elise turned her head, pretending to ignore Nezka's dagger stare. "I'm not supposed to talk to anyone," she said. "He might hurt both of us if we talk. You should just go."

"I'm not afraid of that guy," the fox-like male said, rather stupidly. She could smell that he'd been drinking and was probably too far gone to realize the danger of his words. Even more idiotic, he put an arm around her and nuzzled into her neck, and Elise grimaced, pulling away.

She went to shove him off her when Jona appeared before them.

"Hands off, Nolin, ya prick," Jona said, pulling Elise up. "You wanna get your face turned inside out?" He laughed then turned to Elise. "Come on, sweet-eyes. I'll take care of ya." He took her back over to Krow's table, returning to his seat. "Why don't ya sit?" He patted his thigh. "I'm sure Nez here won't care." He grinned his crooked grin.

Elise looked over at Nezka who watched her as he drank from his cup, his little "lap dog" Sona glaring at her icily as she curled her fingers in Nezka's hair.

"Your little human was bound to have one of my boys come crawling over," Krow said. "They couldn't resist with her just sitting there all alone."

"I'm one of those," Jona admitted, pulling her to him. "Come on, join the fun."

Not expecting Nezka to stop him without coming off possessive, Elise forced herself onto Jona's lap, hating every second he touched her. Hands clenched tight, she tried to relax, but her body only seemed to tense more, as if ready to throw a few punches.

"Boy, she looks really uncomfortable, Jona," one of the men said, laughing. "She looks like she wants to bite your head off."

"He was never good at touching the ladies. They get all grossed out," another said.

Jona growled. "Fuck you, Lon. She's just nervous."

Elise squirmed as his hand grabbed her thigh. Her reflexes were giving in, unable to stop herself from fighting, ready and wanting to hit him. When her elbow clashed with his chest, he let out a sharp bark, throwing her off him.

"You little—" he growled, lifting his hand to hit her, and Elise put up her arm in defense.

"She only answers to me," Nezka said.

Jona dropped his hand. "That so?"

"Yes."

Jona huffed. He looked at Elise, frustrated, then turned back to Nezka. "Not that I don't like a little fight in em'." He shoved Elise over to the other side of the table. "Go on and take her then. Show me how you handle 'em. "

Elise stood by the table, trying to calm her breath. Nezka didn't move.

"What? Afraid she'll prove you wrong?" Jona bared his teeth. "Or you just trying to save her skin from my hand? Yours the only one good enough to hit her?"

"No one harms her," Nezka answered in a low voice.

"I don't see why one of mine can't have a little fun with her, Nezka," Krow commented. "Unless you're holding out. She's being wasted, doing nothing but sulking in the dark."

"No one gets her but me," Nezka said in a near growl.

That turned a few heads including Elise's.

"Oh, I see, so you *are* using her," Krow said, leaning back.

"I'm just implying that she isn't for use."

Krow seemed skeptical as he took a drink. "Well, that's a pity. Why so defensive of her innocence? Does your mistress demand she remain untouched?"

"No."

"Then why should it matter?"

Nezka tapped his glass as he glared at him, then his dark expression lifted, and he smiled. "You got me, Krow." He set Sona off him and gestured for Elise. Elise hesitated, knowing they were watching. She slowly came over and sat herself down on Nezka's lap.

The first thing she noticed was how ungodly warm he was, like she had just sat herself next to a radiator. He placed an arm around her waist while his other hand went over her thigh. Elise stiffened slightly at their sudden closeness but didn't squirm. She wasn't as uncomfortable as she imagined she'd be. In fact, she felt a sudden wave of relief, even if she was still a little nervous. Sona growled next to them, but Krow shooed her off, and she obediently went away.

Jona watched Elise closely with narrowed eyes. "So, you really got her tamed, huh?" he said. "Like your little pet, that it? And you don't want your mistress knowing you are giving her a squeeze at night."

Nezka only smiled more, though his eyes darkened. "It's a bad indulgence on my part that the boss wouldn't be too pleased to see." His hand rubbed against Elise's inner thigh. Elise tensed, feeling a sudden dull achy heat pull at her near where his hand touched. Her hand flinched as if to pull his own off out of sheer embarrassment, but she dared not break his little game.

Jona seemed uncertain as he watched them. "Think we could make a trade?"

"Likely not," Nezka said. His hand lifted to rub at her belly then higher still to brush against the underside of her breasts. Elise almost squirmed as her breath quickened. Beads of sweat began to dampen the back of her neck. His arm wrapped around her waist, tugging her closer, and she felt him squeeze her hip for reassurance.

"Too bad," Jona said.

"She's just a little comfort until I'm back to our stronghold," Nezka explained. "It means nothing. I just like to play with others. Once I get her back to my mistress, I'll have a new toy."

The men seemed satisfied with that and let Elise be. Though Jona still watched her idly, they finished off another round of drinks and played a few sets of some tabletop gambling. Elise let herself relax after a time, leaning back against Nezka, allowing the moment to happen, knowing she was better off where she was now than if she were alone without him.

Only, the heat festering in her body didn't go away which alarmed her a little. And was only made worse when he squeezed her thighs or nuzzled her shoulder while brushing his fingers across her breasts. Her heart fluttered in her chest, and those few times he touched her, she was sorely tempted to move her hips and rub against him, wondering how he might react. Would he get hard like a human man? Or would he not see the contact as arousing? She felt crazy thinking it, but she couldn't stop herself regardless. Feeling like she might be losing her nerve, she went for Nezka's cup on the table and took a long drink.

Nezka snatched the cup from her and pulled her back by her hair. "I didn't say you could take that," he said with a hiss.

Elise's heart did a flip. The others snickered around her, watching with bright eyes.

"Sorry," she mumbled. Her body warmed even more, whether

from the drink or from Nezka's sudden forcefulness, she wasn't quite sure. He let her go, and Krow laughed.

"The girl wants to have some fun too, see?" He poured her a drink and slid the glass across the table.

Elise didn't take the cup right away. She looked to Nezka first whose eyes flickered over her briefly before he tapped his ear. Elise took the cup and drank it down. She placed the glass back on the table, and when Krow offered her more, she shook her head. The liquor was strong, and she didn't want to get so trashed she couldn't think straight.

Nezka pulled her back against him, stroking her thighs. The fiery liquid settled quickly in her stomach, and in no time at all, she slipped into a daze. Despite the circumstances, she felt relaxed, even euphoric. She listened and watched the men play their games without thought or care, even almost laughing at one of their jokes. She leaned her head back against Nezka's shoulder, liking the warmth of his hands massaging her, and closed her eyes.

"Get the fuck out, you lot," came a loud voice, waking Elise instantly. Krow stumbled to his feet, hand slashing the air, nearly knocking glasses of the table. "I'm tired and want to have a squeeze before I pass out cold." He called them vulgar names as his men carried him out from the lounge, laughing and stumbling. Elise blinked several times to clear her head. Dawn must be coming again.

She looked around at Nezka who glared back at her then gently set her off him. Jona still remained at the table, swallowing the last of his drink, watching them.

"I'll follow you upstairs," he said and gestured for one of the women at the bar to come. One slunk over, and he took her hand. Nezka rose and grabbed Elise, pulling her back into the club.

Others still mingled inside, a few couples pressed together against the dark walls, moving to their own slow rhythm. Elise side-eyed them, and an image of her and Nezka in their place popped into her thoughts. This time, she didn't readily swat it away. Her gaze fell to his backside, to the flat spines and tight lower muscles and she shivered, her body suddenly feeling heavy. She glanced back behind and caught Jona watching her. He smiled as they made their way to the stair.

As they came to the door to their suite, Nezka pulled Elise inside. But before the door could slide shut, Jona blocked the doorway, setting his hand against the frame. He pushed the woman he had brought with him into the hall and told her to get to his room as he stared back at Elise then at Nezka.

By his lazy expression, Elise could tell he was nearly gone from the drink. He swayed a little on his feet and gave them a crooked smile.

"I get you're not gonna let me have her even for a moment," he slurred, gesturing to Elise. "But I can enjoy the sight of her at least. If you're gonna have her, at least let me watch."

Elise stared back at him, at first in shock then with disgust. She looked to Nezka, expecting he'd tell Jona to get his ass out, and found the hunter smirking, not in an expression of amusement but that of annoyance, giving the drogin a deathly glare.

"Come on, Nez. I won't even move from this spot. Won't make a sound," Jona said.

Nezka stared at him for a moment longer then looked away and laughed. "As if I'd let you. Please."

Jona's face twisted as he bared his teeth. "Why not, huh?" He took a step, his hand on the door frame turning into a fist. "You know, Krow's been more than nice with you, giving you all this shit just for a few fights. Lettin' you sit at his table amongst other fighters. Bet you didn't know I'm one of his best. Yes, that's right. I might not look it, but I'm a mean asshole and damn good at a brawl. If I asked him, he might reconsider allowing your little pet to be shared. He only spares her because he wants to see you fight, and he's being nice, that's all. You think others haven't come along asking the same for their mates and got the same treatment?" He fixed them with a nasty grin. "No. And it's not like you could fight us all, huh? We could take her if we really want, and there's nothing you could do. So, come on, throw me this bone. It's the least you can do."

Elise stood there, too flustered to speak. She stared at Jona then turned back to Nezka whose expression, to her surprise, hadn't changed.

"You're just drunk. You won't even remember what you saw in morning, let alone anything that happened in the last hour," Nezka said, brushing his threat off. He went to turn toward his bedroom when Jona growled violently.

"No. You'll do it, Red Blade, or I tell Krow you're too arrogant and disrespectful for your own good and wouldn't indulge me. He takes my word seriously. He'll see you pay for it. And her."

With his back turned, Elise couldn't see Nezka's face, but she saw him tense and heard him hiss. When he looked back over, there was murder in his gaze.

"You want to see?" he whispered.

When Jona bowed his head, Elise found herself being swung roughly around and shoved over to the bed. Yelping, she tensed at first, unprepared. He pinned her down hard and tugged open the clasps to her suit, nearly ripping it in half. Breathing heavily, Elise kept up her submissive act, knowing if Jona saw that she wasn't so "tame" after all, he'd suspect Nezka of lying. It happened so quickly regardless that Elise felt she had little time to react before her suit was pulled down to her wrists, exposing her chest. Nezka ripped off her binds and pulled the suit the rest of the way down until it lay around her ankles with her armor pieces scattered across the floor. Her body tensed as she felt him press hard against her back side, deliberately shifting her around in a way that his body blocked most of hers from Jona's sight. She felt him pulling at the clasps of his pants to free himself and she breathed sharply through her teeth. Heat bloomed unexpectedly between her legs, goosebumps spreading across her skin. Heart thumping hard in her chest, she waited for the feel of him inside her. His hand rested firmly on her back as he re-positioned, placing himself against her center. But he didn't slide true. Instead, he slipped himself firmly through the space between her legs, resting himself alongside her core.

"That good enough for you?" Nezka said in a low, seething voice that Elise barely recognized.

Jona grunted. "That's it?"

Nezka slowly rose his hips and pressed himself back down. The heat in her center burned hotter as he rubbed up against her. He was hard as steel but curiously lubricated. She shivered as she felt the odd shape of him slide over her. An ache began to settle over the heat between her thighs, and she was nearly tempted again to move her hips. Nezka rose again, ready to press back down, when a shout came from down the hall. Nezka froze, and Jona turned away to look down the passage.

"What?" he called to someone unseen.

"Need you at the gate," was all Elise could hear.

Jona grumbled. He looked back and shrugged. "I guess you'll have to finish without me. See you tonight, Nez." He smiled and turned away.

Nezka didn't move an inch. The door slid shut, the sound of their breathing all that remained. Elise turned her head and swallowed hard, wondering what Nezka would do. If he continued, she wondered if she would try to stop him or let him carry on.

"Nezka...?" she whispered, unable to see his face.

In an instant, quicker than she'd ever seen him move, he was off her. She twisted around and only for a brief second caught the sight of his male organ before he turned and reclasped his pants. He looked to her with deep concern. "Are you all right?"

Elise blinked. "I...yes."

Nezka bent his head, studying her intensely.

"I'm okay," Elise said honestly. Though her body still burned.

Nezka gazed at her for a second more before standing back. He went for his bedroom door, and Elise sat up.

"Nezka," she called.

He stopped but didn't look at her. His hands turned into tight fists. "I need to go and be calm before I kill someone..."

"Don't," Elise said. "Just wait."

He turned his head away, and his body shook. "I can't," he said so softly she barely heard him. Then he said a little louder, "I should go, or I might compromise everything..." He looked back at her. "If you are hurt..."

" You didn't hurt me." She let out a short, nervous laugh, the heat and liquor making her feel lightheaded. "Although I was afraid for a minute that you—"

"Afraid?" His burning eyes flickered over her body. His expression turned pained. Elise, forgetting her nakedness, flushed, covering her breasts. She was about to say "afraid he would rip her suit in half," but his face stopped her from saying more.

"I have to go," he said again in a tone of anger that she knew wasn't meant for her. Before she could call him back, Nezka flung himself into the other room and shut the door.

CHAPTER SIXTEEN

Elise sat on her bed, staring around the room, most of the time eyeing Nezka's door. She hadn't slept much at all since their incident, and when she did sleep, her dreams were filled with surreal and erotic scenes, mostly between them. Her body had been so lit up by his touch, by the way he moved against her, that once he left, she was beside herself, the ache eating at her. When she dared to finally venture down between her thighs with her hand, she found herself drenched. She'd had many men in her life, a few exes spread over the years of her training. She wasn't a prude by any means. She even considered herself knowledgeable in more than a few dirty acts. She knew her body well enough, knew how it reacted to certain moves or touches. She thought she knew what she liked, what really set her off. And she certainly didn't think it was other-worldly men.

That is until Nezka...

She laughed softly to herself. That was it. Until Nezka.

Elise closed her eyes and took a few deep breaths. Come night, she didn't know what to expect. But she didn't know if she could take another repeat of the last few. She didn't think Jona would ask to watch again, but they would need to keep an eye on him and be careful. He was as manipulative as his master.

Elise took another slow breath then fell back on the bed. She knew she should just be focusing on them getting out of this mad clubhouse, but all she could think of at that moment was the hunter in the other room. The memory of her dreams in the little time she'd slept passed through her mind once more, and she let them take over.

The most vivid one of all had also been quite scary. She'd been in a very dark place, some castle made out of black stone. She sat at a long table filled with all kinds of food. A feast for a whole town, but it was only for her and for the demon on the other side of the table. He looked like Nezka save that he was larger, and his eyes burned true fire, like twin suns. His fangs were longer, and the row of spines across his back went up his head. His face was horrifying, with burned flesh exposing his sharp teeth, his eyes set in sunken pits. They sat together at that table with no one else around. Through a set of open windows, the ocean raged, waves crashing, colored red.

He'd called to her, and Elise turned to him.

"Convince me," he purred.

As if she understood in some dreamsense what he meant, she rose from her seat and went to him. She sat on his lap and let her hands and mouth possess every part of him, and something in the back of her mind told her if she didn't please him, he wouldn't keep her. He'd give her to someone else. She'd be back in the jungle which now grew alongside a dark city.

It had been the last dream, and it had woken her with a cry. She'd taken a cold shower after, but her body still felt hot.

Now, night approached again. She could tell by the fading light coming from the slated metal shades which didn't so much as budge at her pulling grip.

She heard voices out somewhere nearby, two people laughing and talking though she couldn't make their words. A woman and a man. Their steps went down the hall then seemed to stop close to her door. They passed by close until she thought she could hear them on the other side of Nezka's door. Frowning, Elise went over and listened and heard a man's low voice and a woman's soft one. She heard giggling then moaning and the wall thumping. Heat burned up her face as Elise backed away.

He wouldn't.

But why not? He wasn't hers. He could do what he pleased. He'd left her looking just as in need of release as herself, so why wouldn't he find someone to fulfill his needs? Why did she think it should be her?

Elise paced the room as the voices grew louder. She covered her ears, her breath quickening. She knew she needed to be logical, but her emotions drowned any logic out, and the next thing she knew, she was going for Nezka's door and flinging it open.

The room was dark. And empty.

Relieved, then confused, Elise noticed there was a door on his end leading to the hallway. She went over and opened it and found a male drogin pressing a female lygin against the wall, her legs around his waist.

"What...?" Elise began to say and the drogin saw her and nearly dropped the lygin. He barked in surprise, covering himself.

"You mind?" he said.

"Sorry." Elise started back into the room, but the drogin called back to her.

"He's downstairs already. I'll take you in a moment."

Elise frowned and nodded her head. Looking at him, she realized he was one of the hallway guards.

She let the door slide shut and stood in the dark. Then she laughed softly, rubbing her forehead. By the way the noise carried, she thought it had been coming from the room. Now that she was no longer worried about finding Nezka in bed with another woman, she was concerned with the fact that he had decided to leave her in the suite without him.

Elise went back to her side and waited until the drogin had finished. When he eventually came to her room to take her down, he bound her wrists, and she let him, only to keep up appearances. He didn't pull her away like Nezka but allowed her to follow.

When they entered the lounge, Elise froze in place as she witnessed Nezka already in the middle of a match within the ring, blood dripping down his back from several large gashes. The lygin he faced looked like an unhinged panther with blood dripping from his snout and talons.

Elise took a deep breath, ready for another awful night of watching these sickening fights, made even worse by the fact that, this time, Nezka was badly injured already, and she would have to endure seeing him in such a state, unable to say a word in fear of giving them away. She allowed the guard to bring her over to her usual seat next to Krow who was too fueled up by the match to notice her. The room was well packed already with early betters, anticipating Nezka's next win. Elise watched their jeering, shouting faces with anger and disgust. Her gaze drew back to Nezka, and her stomach turned, a deep ache settling in her chest.

Despite his wounds, Nezka got the better of his opponent in one powerful strike to the face and eyes, sending the lygin to the ground. In little time, they removed the body and sent in his next opponent, a large bull-like drogin. Elise eyed Nezka's wounds and wished she could make him stop, wishing she could make the others disappear. Instead, she could only sit and watch yet again.

The fight didn't last long as Nezka's sudden rage seemed to energize him. He seemed driven to fight till he blacked out from exhaustion. His seething expression could not be overlooked, even if the others chose not to regard it. But Elise could see he was pissed.

"You're one lethal son of a bitch, Nez," Krow said beside her, smiling. "Really incredible. Let's get this man a drink," he ordered a bar girl. "Come on out and celebrate."

Nezka didn't move from the ring. "Another," he growled, huffing. The wounds on his back still bled badly.

"Now, don't get greedy." Krow laughed. "You'll have plenty more—"

"Another," Nezka hissed. He began to pace the ring like a caged beast.

Krow's smile faded as he too eyed Nezka's wounds. "All right, but let's have someone wipe you off at least, eh? Have your little pet do it. Here." He grabbed Elise's arm and pulled her up, shoving her. Elise silently cursed him while grabbing a towel offered by one of the men and moved over to the stair. She caught eyes with Nezka who hesitated before approaching. She had half a mind to shout at him for being so stupid. She lifted the towel with her bound hands. Nezka said nothing as he turned around, letting her wipe the blood from the wound.

"You're an idiot," she whispered. "Are you trying to get yourself killed?"

"Maybe." Nezka laughed bitterly.

"This isn't funny," Elise hissed. She wiped harder at his back, avoiding the spines that rose an inch. "Why are you doing this?"

Nezka said nothing, and Elise looked around to see who was watching. Krow was occupied with one of his men, and the crowd's attention was on each other.

"You're mad, I get that, but don't injure yourself over it," Elise warned. "I need you to get us out of here."

"Then you need to let this happen," Nezka said in a low voice.

"I hate this," Elise blurted.

"Really?"

Angry heat burst from her body. "You honestly think I enjoy seeing you like this? Or seeing you drunk every night with some girl on your lap?"

Nezka looked around at her with a fiery expression she'd never seen him give her before. It wasn't anger but something else in his gaze that made Elise almost flinch back though she refused to look away. For a moment, she thought he was going to turn around and do something drastic like kiss her or shout at her, giving them away, but instead, he whispered, "If you can't handle it, then go."

They stared at each other for what felt like a long time but was only a few seconds before he turned from her and stepped back into the center of the ring. Elise stood there with the bloody towel in her hands before one of Krow's men grabbed her shoulder to pull her back. She turned on him, giving him a death glare.

"He's ordered that I be taken back to our room," she said, trying to sound as calm as possible.

Krow's man looked around at Nezka then back to her. He took hold of her binds and led her away, and Elise refused to look back.

* * *

Elise threw another glass cup at the door, watching it shatter to pieces. Red-faced and panting, she paced the room. She hated being alone and without Nezka in this place, but she also hated the idea of watching him perform again for Krow's benefit.

She hated Krow and his men for everything. She hated the people too. She also, undoubtedly, hated herself for not being stronger. For not keeping her emotions in check. She was tired of it all. Tired of pretending. She just wanted to get out of this place. She wanted to find her team, she wanted Nezka to stop fighting, she wanted him to...

Elise stopped and stared at the hallway door and the glass on the ground. Then she turned her head to look over at the door to Nezka's bedroom. She thought again about her dreams and about what happened the night before. She thought about how he looked at her just now down in the ring. She thought about how she had felt pressed against him with his arm protectively around her. And lastly, she thought about how scared she had been when she thought he'd come back to his room with someone else.

She closed her eyes and rubbed at her temples then paced the room a little more before stopping at Nezka's door.

Fuck it.

Elise went for the door and flung it open. The room was dark still save for a soft red light around the minibar. Elise closed the door behind her and stepped toward the bed. Unlike hers, it was a large canopied bed with four posters made of slick, shiny steel. She placed her hand on the end then sat down. She stayed there for a few seconds then got back up, realizing she'd probably be waiting a long time before Nezka returned.

Damn it.

Annoyed, she paced his room then went over to the bar and poured herself a small drink. Guess this gave her time to figure out exactly how she wanted to approach him. She figured if he came and found her sitting in his room, he would be more inclined to let her stay and...talk. But as she looked down at herself in her ratty suit, she didn't feel so confident. Heart fluttering, she turned her thoughts around as she sipped from her glass. She looked over to the bathroom door beside the bed. Setting her cup down, she stepped over to look inside.

His was much larger than hers and had a bigger tub. Figured. Elise went over to the jacuzzi-sized tub and crossed her arms, thinking. Before she lost her nerve, she reached over and started the water.

When the tub was filled with hot, steamy, water, Elise took off her armor plates and shrugged off her suit then carefully stepped inside. The warmth relaxed her, easing her tension. She let herself lay in the water for a long time, just thinking over what she was going to say when Nezka returned. When the water began to cool, Elise rose and stepped out, wrapping a towel around herself.

She returned to the room and sat back on the bed. Thinking there was no way he would return until late, Elise prepared herself to wait for a while. She scooted herself up on the bed and started to lay back when she heard loud footsteps coming down the hall and the door slid open. Bolting up, Elise tensed, ready to fight off the intruder when she saw Nezka step inside, closing the door behind him. He didn't see her at first as his eyes were fixed on the bar. When he realized someone was on his bed, he jerked around and growled. He choked it back and froze when he saw it was her.

"What are you..." He froze as he looked down at her bare legs and the towel that barely wrapped over her.

Elise was shocked at first as well. He had come back so soon. And judging by the little blood on him, someone had wiped him down again. He looked tired and still pretty pissed along with the shock of seeing her.

Elise scooted up to the edge of the bed, heat burning up her neck and face. "I...um...I wanted to talk."

He stared down at her, his head tilting slightly. "Talk...?" His sharp gaze flickered down again to the towel and back up.

Elise rose from the bed. "About everything. And the other night."

Nezka seemed to tense, his mouth widening in annoyance. He turned from her and went to the bar. Elise took a step closer as he took her glass and filled it. "You shouldn't be here," he said.

"Why not?"

Nezka didn't respond. He lifted the glass to his mouth and drank slowly.

"Nezka, I know you're upset about what happened," she said softly. "You know I don't blame you."

Nezka placed the cup down on the bar and laughed low. "Upset? No, I'm not upset." He turned toward her, and Elise took a step back. "I'm enraged. Do you want to know why?" he said in a hushed tone. "Because I had to almost force myself on you because of that insufferable crooked-fanged piece of shit. And despite what you might think of me, Elise, I'm not fine with that. I know I've come off like some kind of brute, but I don't like my women to be disgusted or afraid. In fact, I hate it." He got real close, backing her against the bed. "I don't want it." He placed his hand on the metal poster behind her. His body shook. "I cannot bear to be with someone who is afraid of me. Who loathes my touch. I want them to be hot and dripping for me, just me. I want them to want it so bad I make them scream," he whispered, leaning close. "I want to see their pleasure and know it is for me. And I want to feel it too."

Elise barely moved or breathed.

"Tell me you don't want me, Starling," he continued. "Just say it, and I won't come near you ever. Not even if someone tries to force me. I will kill them before I lay a hand on you like that again. Just say it."

Elise didn't speak. Nezka went to move back and turn from her, and she stopped him, the tips of her fingers lightly grazing his chest. Nezka stilled, watching her fingers fall along to his stomach. Quietly, Elise loosened her towel and let it fall to the ground. Nezka's pupils widened, eyes glowing hot. Elise grabbed his wrist and placed it on her waist then down to her hip.

"Show me," she said softly. "Teach me."

Nezka didn't move. Elise released his wrist, but his hand didn't drop. He seemed to hesitate for a mere second, as if to just be sure, watching her expression, her eyes, carefully. When she didn't look away from his gaze and even dared to fix him with a little smirk, he moved, closing the distance between them, gripping her hips with both hands.

She was on the bed in an instant with Nezka on top of her. He unclasped his pants and pulled them off, exposing himself fully to her. Elise looked down and found the lower half of him was just as breathtaking as the upper. Though the part between his legs was alien in itself (the rimmed shaft situated above a hardened, slated shell), it still held a human-like appearance that made it recognizable for what it was. Nezka took hold of her thighs and spread them apart.

As if by some well-thought-out assumption he might have had, he lowered his head between her legs and slid his long tongue along her center, twisting in and around her most sensitive place then dipping deep inside. Elise gasped and felt heat burst in her lower belly and between her thighs. She moaned loudly as Nezka slipped his tongue out and lifted back his head. He pinned down her thighs, keeping her spread in place and positioned himself over her. His cock, already hardened and oiled on its own, rubbed against her core before he moved his hips back and placed the tip at her center.

Elise inhaled sharply as he penetrated then slipped deep inside.

The shape of him settled nicely against her, and she was surprised to feel almost every part of him. Goosebumps ripped across her body, and she shivered as a sudden lick of heat seared along her center. His body tensed, thigh muscles tightening. Nezka let out a low groan.

"You feel as amazing as I'd hoped," he whispered. Still keeping her legs in place, he began to move, slow at first, in a sensual beat that made her flush. Elise didn't think she had ever felt such intense heat in all her life. She moaned loudly again, uncaring who might hear on the other side.

Nezka's pace quickened with each bow, his groan turning into a growl as he bared his fangs, his face twisting, turning beastly amongst the shadows. Elise thought in any other circumstance, she might find it terrifying but was even more aroused at the sight. The aching heat coiled in her, tightening, making her breathless. She placed a hand on Nezka's chest, letting her fingers claw at him. He pressed himself deeper, hitting somewhere that sent her burning higher.

Her body tightened, and she let out a cry. Nezka hissed and seemed for a moment surprised. He glanced down between them, his expression shocked and annoyed as Elise felt a throbbing, liquid heat fill her. He drew back, cursing, and she felt something wet hit her inner thighs.

Elise lay back for a moment, her hand sliding down his stomach, enjoying the hardness and warmth of him. There was an odd scent in the air that reminded her of baked almonds with a hint of spice. She carefully sat up on her elbows and straightened out her legs as he released her.

"Are you all right?" she asked.

Nezka reached an arm out, brushing back the hair in her eyes then caressing her face gently. "More than all right. I just..." He dropped his hand and laughed softly. "Ah, it's been a long time since..."

Elise tilted her head. "Long time since what?"

He sat beside her on the edge of the bed and drew a hand across her inner thigh, brushing away some of the remains of his passion and rubbing it between his fingers. "Since I was unable to hold myself back. Not since my first time, I think. But I fear I couldn't stop, especially when you tightened like that."

"Oh." Elise smiled sheepishly. "That's a good thing, I guess?"

"Good and slightly embarrassing." He leaned down to her and nipped at her neck with his sharp teeth, flicking his tongue after. "I was just unprepared for the feel of you, my Starling."

The way he said Starling sounded less like her name and more like an endearment. *Star-ling.* Elise didn't mind. She smiled again, lifting her hand to draw lazy circles along his shoulder. "How did it feel?"

Nezka seemed to think for a moment. "Like...*Etharium*"

Elise fixed him with a confused expression. "What is that?"

"A place of pure bliss."

Elise gave him a doubtful look. "Are you trying to say I feel like heaven? Because that is simultaneously the most romantic and cheesiest thing I've ever heard."

Nezka shrugged and laughed. "Perhaps. But it is the closest I've ever been."

Elise laid back with a groan. "You're too much. Is this just what you say to all the girls after?" She laughed.

"No."

Elise looked back at him and saw he wasn't smiling. Feeling bold enough now, Elise lifted her hand and touched his face. He nuzzled against it, eyeing her. Elise lifted her body and pressed her lips against his. Nezka drew back a little in surprise then allowed her to kiss him again. She flicked her tongue out flirtatiously, and his gaze grew hot once more.

"I have an idea," he said in a husky voice. He picked her off the bed, setting her on her feet, then turned her around, placing her against one of the bed posts. Elise bent and gripped the sleek metal, tensing as Nezka entered her from behind. She moaned as he pressed hard against her, placing one hand on the post above hers and one on the back of her neck, gripping her firmly. "We put this room to better use. Then move to yours." He moved his hips out and back in, and Elise huffed but didn't complain. "Then we will take a bath."

"I just took one in yours," she said between breaths.

"You'll need another after what I'm going to do to you." Elise didn't need to turn around to guess the wicked grin he was sporting.

"And after that?" Elise said, biting her lip as he moved harder against her.

Nezka growled softly, and she could feel the vibration along her back. "We're getting the fuck out of here."

CHAPTER SEVENTEEN

NEZKA REMAINED, SO FAR, TRUE TO HIS WORD. AFTER THEY HAD
put the rooms to better use and cleaned thoroughly afterwards, he
bound Elise one last time and pulled her down to the lounge.

Though the night was nearly gone, and dawn soon approached,
there were still several groups that remained. Krow, Jona, and several
other men sat at a table at the back, smoking red haze and talking softly.
When they saw him, they stopped, Krow greeting him with a tight grin.

"Come down to finally join us?" Smoke blew out from his mouth.
"A bit late now, but we can make room—"

"I'm giving you one last fight, and then we are leaving," Nezka
said.

The table went silent, the men glancing at Krow. He took another
hit from his pipe as he glared at Nezka. "That so?"

"Yes," Nezka said, keeping his grip tight on Elise's binds to have
her stay close.

Krow blew out another cloud of smoke then placed his pipe
down. "But I have so many other fighters wanting a piece of you. You
are quite the spectacle but have yet to face even my best."

"Which is why I plan on doing so now." Nezka looked over to Jona. "I take him on right now. I win and we leave. No one comes after us."

Krow tapped his fingers along the table. "What makes you think he's my best?"

"He's your second in command," Nezka answered. "He wouldn't have gotten there just by giving you respect and loyalty alone. He would've had to prove his worth in the only way you see fit. Tell me I'm wrong."

Krow said nothing, and a second later, Jona rose from his seat. "I accept your challenge."

"I didn't say you could fight him, Jona. Sit your ass down," Krow ordered.

"I can take 'im." Jona turned to his leader. "I've seen his moves. I can take him."

"You are too impatient," Krow said. Nezka saw the look Krow gave his man, and it was as Nezka had both predicted and hoped for. Krow knew Jona might lose. Badly. And he didn't want to lose his closest servant and partner.

It was just the kind of revenge Nezka wanted. For them both to suffer, Jona the most.

He knew getting Elise out of here was to be his top priority. Beating Jona until there was nothing left was just an extra treat on the side.

"Let me beat this freak and show you I'm still the best," Jona implored.

Krow glanced between them, considering it. "I'll let you fight," he said after a pause. "But you're gonna be doing guard lookout for a full cycle if this is what you want," he warned Jona.

"Fine. Deal." Jona grinned.

"And you." Krow directed his hand toward Nezka. "If you lose, you not only don't get to leave but your little pet gets to stay in Jona's room. That clear?"

"Yes," Nezka said without hesitating. He thought he heard Elise whimper behind him, but he didn't turn his head.

Krow waved his men off. "Get to the ring then. Let's see this play out."

Nezka placed Elise back in her usual spot by the ring, forcing himself to ignore her gaze, knowing if he locked eyes with her, he might slip even just a little, and Krow would see he wasn't the only one with something to lose. He threw off his gear per usual and stepped into the ring with Jona jumping in with him. Groups huddled in, reawakened by the excitement, their voices turning into static. Nothingness. Nezka focused in, seeing nothing but Jona with his crooked smile.

"I'm going to enjoy this," Jona said, circling.

"I was just going to say the same." Nezka smiled back. He would make this quick.

One signal from Krow and Nezka was forced back by Jona's sudden swift attack. The drogin was small, but he was extremely agile. Jona shot away before Nezka could get a hit on him, attempting to get around to Nezka's back. When Nezka turned to strike again, Jona ran for the rails of the ring then jumped away again, staying out of Nezka's reach.

Nezka knew what he was playing at; putting himself in retreat, waiting for the right moment to make a move. He was also hoping to outpace him, making Nezka drain his energy. Nezka watched him carefully, moving in unison, realizing he'd have to let Jona get his attack in before he could make his own.

Nezka lunged forward and deliberately missed, letting his fist go long to see what the drogin would do. Jona slipped behind him and jumped on his back in one quick move, wrapping an arm tight around his neck.

His grip was impressive, Nezka had to give him that. He was probably really good at knocking his opponents out this way. And quickly too.

Too bad it wouldn't work.

Nezka tried to elbow him first in the gut, but the blows slipped past as Jona swung himself back. Nezka went for his groin next, but once again, the drogin kept his body back while tightening his grip. As his vision began to blur, Nezka bent low, moving his body to the side then behind, swinging Jona around to his front then quickly grabbing one of the drogin's legs and throwing him up, forcing him to lose his balance and his grip. With the drogin now in his grasp, Nezka threw him off, slamming him down on the ground.

Jona scrambled to his feet, but Nezka was faster. He took hold of his ankle, dragging him back. Jona tried to kick himself free, but it was too late. Nezka threw himself on top of him and started throwing heavy, violent blows.

For a brief instant, everything went red. He couldn't recall the last time he'd allowed that to happen, but he wanted Jona to pay. In blood.

When he finally came out of his sickening rage, Nezka had to remember for a moment what he was even doing before he could make himself stop. He pulled himself back and rose, breathing heavily, trying to make himself calm. The crowd shouted, but he barely heard them. His head was buzzing; his spines, standing straight, trembled as his back tingled. He shut his eyes tight then opened them slowly. He glanced down and no longer recognized his opponent. Jona lay unmoving. There were claw and bite marks on Nezka's arms and torso where Jona must have tried to force him off, but it hadn't worked.

Nezka's eyes flicked upward and met Elise's, who stared wide-eyed, looking pale, almost grayish. Afraid. He wished he could comfort her but knew he couldn't. Not yet. He shifted his gaze to Krow, who hadn't moved, not even to applaud. He looked back at Nezka with a not-so-amused expression then called one of his men over and said something Nezka couldn't hear.

Nezka left the ring, took the towel from the girl offering to clean him and wiped himself off instead. He put his gear back on as Krow ordered his people to get out and for his men to carry Jona away.

Krow watched Nezka closely then fixed him with a tight smile as his eyes read murder.

"I'd congratulate you, Red Blade, but I'm afraid I wasn't all that impressed this time," he said, his smile tightening as his eyes narrowed. "But I am a man of my word, just the same. Even if you nearly killed my guy..."

Nezka came around and grabbed Elise. "And you won't come after us. That was the deal."

Krow's smile slipped a little then stretched back into a grin. He shrugged, took up a glass from nearby and drank. "Yes. I won't come after you. You may pass with your pet. We won't try to stop you." Krow dropped his glass on the ground, letting it shatter. "Now get the fuck out. I'm done with you."

"Sounds good."

Nezka pulled Elise away. Krow's men let them pass, following them out of the lounge and through the club.

The light of dawn was just beginning to break as they came down the stairs and walked under the gatehouse over to his parked two-wheeler. Elise stirred behind him, muttering something low, and when Nezka glanced around, he saw the men casually leaning against their vehicles, eyes fixed on them. Nezka unbound Elise and got on the two-wheeler, his hand itching to unclip her gun from his belt and start shooting. Instead, he waited for her to get on and situate herself behind him, then he backed up and moved slowly forward to the other end of the tunnel. When the men were out of earshot, he turned to her. "Hold on tight. Once we start on the bridge, it's going to get rough."

"You think they are going to chase us?" Elise said from behind him.

"I don't know." It was an honest answer. He knew trusting men like Krow to keep his word was foolish. Better to be prepared. "Get your gun ready if you can."

He felt her hand against him as she fumbled with the clasp on his belt and pulled the gun free. As she gripped the gun tight, he felt her arms wrap around him.

The exit was ahead, and Nezka picked up speed. As they shot out of the tunnel, he pushed the two-wheeler even faster. He heard no roaring of cars behind him, and when he looked in the rear sights, he saw no one following behind. What he did see was several guards on top of the gatehouse roof watching them go.

No. Not just watching.

Nezka's eyes narrowed on one in particular, crouching at the edge. As he focused in, he saw him holding a long range weapon.

The first shot went off with a sharp crack and a flash of white, like lightning. Nezka heard the woosh as the bullet passed, hitting the road. Nezka cursed and swerved the two-wheeler to one side. Another shot went off, the bullet hitting right below Nezka's foot. He swerved again and again, back and forth, hoping to make them miss each time. The jolting from side to side kept Elise holding tight. The end wasn't far, but the bullets kept coming and wouldn't stop until they were out of sight.

As Nezka straightened out, Elise twisted around and let off her gun. The blades of light didn't meet their targets but did make them halt and cover. Elise fired until the weapon's energy bank was empty. With the gun finished, Elise tossed it away with a shout of rage. Holding on once more, Nezka swerved, dodging another bullet.

The end was just ahead. Once they were off the bridge and into the city, they would be safe. Nezka focused on the road and buildings ahead.

They were going to make it.

A bullet hit the back of the two-wheeler, and smoke hissed out from the wound. Elise called out to him as another sharp crack sounded, and her shout turned into a sharp cry. They exited off the bridge and flew down the road, Nezka determined to get as far away as possible.

The bullets ceased as they raced on past crumbled and burned-out buildings. When they came to a large city square, a wall met them ahead, forcing Nezka to decide whether to go right or left.

Before he could choose, Elise's grip on him loosened, and she began to slip. Cursing, Nezka skid to a halt and grabbed her arm just before she fell over and hit her head on the road. He let the two-wheeler drop on its side as he quickly pulled her up.

"Elise?" he said as he grabbed her waist. Her head fell back, face pale, sweat beginning to break on her forehead. Cursing again, Nezka hooked his arm under her legs and carried her quickly over to a broken statue of some drogin general on top of a horned beast, carefully lowering himself below it. He sat her up and examined her back.

She had been hit. He tugged off the now cracked armor plate and tore the hole in the suit wider so that he could better see the broken skin. The wound wasn't deep at all, but that wasn't what concerned him. What concerned him was the shade of purple and black spreading around the wound and across her back.

The bullets held poison.

Elise moaned as Nezka shifted her to lay against him with his back to the statue. "Elise, stay awake," he said softly, wiping away damp hair from her face. "Stay awake." He searched frantically around, as if he might find something that could help, but the square held nothing but broken statues and uprooted trees. He wrapped his arm around her and brushed his hand along her head as her body began to shake. If he didn't find help soon...

Elise's chest fell as she shook, each breath a low, gurgling wheeze, her head falling back on his shoulder. Her lips moved, but no sound came out.

"Just breathe, Elise, breathe." Nezka held her close, knowing his only options were to either carry her until they found help—if they ever did and if she could make it in time—or to leave her momentarily so that he could find aid on his own. He hated the idea of leaving her, especially with Krow's men not far away, but he didn't think he'd have a choice. Closing his eyes tight and baring his teeth, he prepared himself to lay her out in order to start ahead and find an antidote—anything—that might save her.

As he opened his eyes and began to lift her up, Nezka looked across the square near to the wide, vacant wall and saw a hooded figure. They locked eyes, and the figure lifted their hand. Nezka tensed, ready to place Elise on the ground beside him and fight if need be. The figure was small in size but could be armed. They took a step toward him, and Nezka growled.

They both stilled in surprise.

"I mean you no harm," came a gruff, low voice from under the hood. "My name is Worik. I am merely a watcher of the wall, and I saw you drive in."

Nezka brushed his knuckles across Elise's cheek, studying the figure carefully. "Show me your face, and maybe I will believe you harmless."

The figure lifted their hood, and Nezka saw it was just another drogin only older, with long shaggy hair growing on their head and face. He looked innocent enough, though he might be hiding a weapon under his robes. But with Elise, Nezka had very little time to gauge whether the man was truly honest. They had nothing of value now, and if he had wanted to kill them, he would have already attempted it. Nezka decided the risk was worth it. "Can you help us?" Nezka asked before lifting Elise up again.

"I can," Worik said. "But the poison takes her fast. We must act quickly. Follow."

Nezka pressed Elise close as he lifted her up and carried her across the square to the wall. The drogin went over to one side of the wall where a control box stood and opened it, turning on several switches. He closed the box then walked up right next to the wall and looked back at Nezka. "Follow." He stepped through the wall and disappeared.

Nezka hesitated for only a second before he stepped over and cautiously crossed through. There was a flash of darkness before he found himself standing on the other side. He looked back at the wall.

A few feet away, the drogin closed up another control box then gestured for him to follow.

They had come into some sort of forest or park. A path stretched across an open field with sections of trees along both sides made of white bark and dark blue leaves. Several marks ahead was a large, ancient looking building. There were no bridges or railways that crossed overhead like in the rest of the undercity. Here, not even the massive towers blocked the sunlight. It was open and bright, and Nezka wondered how no one from the high city wouldn't have noticed it.

Time for answers later. Now, he only cared for Elise. They raced down the path and came to the doors of the ancient site which opened at their approach. Inside was dim and warm, with lanterns guiding their way. Other robed drogin walked past, hardly noticing them. Worik took him into an inner chamber where a large female drogin sat beside two basins of water.

"Modella." Worik bowed. He went up to the woman and whispered in her ear.

She looked over at Nezka and waved him to come closer. "Lay her out. Worik, get the others, and make sure they bring my mixing kit."

Worik bowed again and left as Nezka laid Elise out beside the woman, who gave him a tight glare.

"Did you do this to her?"

Nezka glared back. "No."

"But you are not so innocent as you claim, are you?" Modella shifted forward and placed a hand gently on Elise's brow. "You are one of those Red Blades."

Nezka was uncertain at first whether to be honest or not but, judging by how different they seemed to the others he had encountered, he chose to trust them. "I am not. I stole this gear so that I could get past the gate."

"That so?" She eyed him curiously. "Your voice reads truth enough. You will reveal yourself more to me in time." Her hand lowered to Elise's neck. "She is waning." Modella touched last at Elise's chest. "Where are my maids?" she shouted.

The door to the chamber opened, and several other women scurried inside. They circled around, and Nezka stood aside. As they crouched around Elise, placing several jars on the ground, they rolled her over and began to unclasp her suit. Elise's eyes were shut, but Nezka could still see her chest rising and falling. He closed his eyes and could see that the colors of her spirit had not entirely faded but they were dimming.

"Now get out," the older female snapped at Nezka.

Nezka opened his eyes. "I'm not leaving until she is well."

Modella waved her hand, and her maids stopped. "Then we do not fix her. You go and leave us to do our work, or you stay and watch her die."

Nezka would have given her credit for such stubbornness if not for the circumstances. He stepped back, letting his eyes fall on Elise, anger and guilt swelling in him. "Fix her. Whatever it takes." He turned and left the room.

CHAPTER EIGHTEEN

The waves crashed over and over, a deafening roar that filled her ears. Elise opened her eyes and saw the ocean, bright and blue and beautiful. She sat up and stared, unaware of anything, of where she was or time itself.

"You're doing it again," came a voice from beside her. Elise looked over and saw her sister sitting only a few feet away, her red hair billowing in the wind. She had her knees up to her chest, arms wrapped around her legs. She looked over to Elise and smiled.

"Doing what?" Elise said, as if seeing her sister there was no surprise.

"You're sulking." Her sister tilted her head.

Elise glanced away with a frown. "I don't know what you mean."

"You're waiting for that moment," her sister said.

"What moment?"

"The one that will let you move forward."

Elise pulled her knees up and wrapped her arms around her legs. "It was supposed to be you and me."

"I know."

Elise sat silent as they stared at the waves.

"Let death be your moment, Elise."

Elise gazed back at her sister, ready to scream at her that she never would. Not again.

But her sister wasn't looking at her. She, instead, peered over her shoulder at something behind them. Elise looked around and saw the ruins of a black castle. Beyond a row of broken pillars, a long table lay on its side, rotted food scattered on the ground. Nezka stood between them and the ruins, watching her.

The scene changed, Elise finding herself in a dark jungle, her sister gone. She was alone, wrists bound. A shadow with pits of fire for eyes grabbed her and dragged her up.

"He's waiting," the shadow said.

Elise didn't care to know who he was. She clawed and bit at the shadow, but it hardly budged as it pulled her through the dark. Elise heard the sobs and cries of those nearby, becoming louder.

No. Not again.

Darkness swallowed her, and she smelled a whiff of smoke before a dull light brought her back around. Elise blinked and shut her eyes tight then opened them again. She stared up at an ornate stone ceiling with a narrow skylight. Groggy and a little light-headed, she didn't stir until she could clearly make out her surroundings. She was lying naked on a soft, thick blanket in a dark-tanned room with lanterns sitting in shallow alcoves. The dim light falling from the skylight coupled with the flickering flames of the lanterns showed Elise a small chamber with strange carvings on the wall. She studied them for a moment with confusion, wondering where she was. When she turned over to her side, she found Nezka lying close to her. His eyes were closed, his breathing slow. He appeared to be sleeping.

Elise watched him for a long time, studying his face. He really was one scary-looking guy. But he was rather beautiful too. His dark, sharpened features made him look mysterious and wild. A terrifying and magnificent creature from some other realm, lost now in hers. Without thought, Elise reached over and touched the side of his face, the one now nearly healed over from his burns. His skin was warm and smooth, and she felt that she'd never want to stop touching him if she could.

Nezka stirred, and his eyes slowly opened to meet hers. They stared at each other without a word for a long while before he lifted his hand to take hers. "How are you feeling?" he asked softly.

"Like...what's the opposite of *Etharium*?" Elise said.

Nezka smiled, if not sadly. "*Sucarium*."

"What's that?"

"A state of agony."

"Ah." Elise shifted. "Maybe not that bad. More like just a bad hangover."

Nezka released her hand to brush a lock of her hair from her face, his smile slipping.

"What happened?" Elise asked after a pause.

"You were hit. It was my fault," he said.

"How was it your fault?"

"I should have protected you better. I should have..." He closed his eyes, and Elise sighed.

"Typical. Well, for what it's worth I don't blame you." Elise smiled. The scene started to come back to her. "I was in the line of fire. It couldn't be helped. I just wish I had a better gun." She could see Nezka wasn't much happier with her response so she added, "If you want to apologize, I will forgive you."

"I'm sorry."

"I forgive you."

They lay silent again for a long moment as Elise listened to the sounds of the roaring of trams or ships somewhere in the distance. So much quieter now than usual.

"Where are we?" Elise asked.

"Some sanctuary. That's all you need to know for now," Nezka replied. "The people here are kind."

Elise nodded her head. "That's nice for once." She looked back at him as he watched her, his gaze lingering over her face, neck, and shoulders. She might as well ask since she could see the look of concern in his expression. "How bad was I?"

Nezka's eyes flicked up to the ceiling then back to her. "Pretty bad. The bullet wound was shallow. Thanks to the armor, it didn't even pierce all the way through. But the poison..."

"Ah. That explains why I felt awful after," Elise said.

"Yes."

Elise nodded. "Well, I guess it's good you found help in time."

"More like help found me. But, yes, I agree," Nezka said, his hand squeezing hers gently.

Elise knitted her fingers with his and shifted a little closer. "It was worth it, though, you know. I would have rather died than been left at that gatehouse."

Nezka frowned. "I would have never abandoned you or let them keep you."

"I know. But I'm just saying...even if you hadn't got us out. If the worst had happened and you hadn't won that fight—"

Nezka huffed.

"—I would have fought to escape. I would have let them gun me down before becoming their plaything or their slave."

A shadow passed over Nezka's eyes, and Elise shivered. At the sudden realization of her almost-death, Elise wanted to tell him everything. To just open herself to him and let it all come falling out. It was hard, but she wanted him to know. She wanted to let the fear go.

"I had a sister a long time ago," Elise began. "Only a few years older than me. Her name was Grace. It's an older name on my world, but Dad was always old-fashioned. Anyway. He trained us both to be the best we could be. But Grace was always his shining star. I lived in her shadow for a long time, but she was always there to teach me. I wanted to be just like her. I wanted to be brave and tough and strong. Just like her." Elise closed her eyes and took a deep breath. "She died of sudden heart failure. Just one day—gone, just like that. We were just about to enter our junior training academy together. I had to go on alone.

"It was hard for a long time. My father remarried, and I got a couple of step-brothers. He looked to them to be the best, but I never stopped my training. I never stopped trying. For Grace." Elise cleared her throat, refusing to cry in front of him. "When I got promoted to a high rank soldier and started with my team, one of our first missions was on a newly-registered world. There wasn't even a full base there yet. The gyda, the first race of nonhumans we ever encountered, had a small reservation there on the base. Only a few months in, half the gyda from the reserve went missing. We were tasked to go and find them. The planet was an awful, jungle landscape, the most uncomfortable heat I've ever felt. There were rumors of a company looking to extract resources from the planet, working somewhere deep in the jungle. There were rumors the gyda might have been taken there. We went looking and found the company's base but no gyda. None that we could see, at least, from the outer walls." Elise paused for a moment, closing her eyes. Nezka lay quietly beside her. "We decided someone would have to go in. I volunteered first because I knew it was what Grace would have done. I disguised myself as a lone intern—a student—doing her research on the company. Little did we know the company was working with a terrorist group, bent on enslaving the gyda. They found me walking the jungle nearby and took me. They suspected me right away, but that didn't keep them from putting me to good use." Elise opened her eyes and saw Nezka watching her, listening carefully. "I found the gyda. They were stuck in some warehouse making machine parts. Some had been beaten bad, others even mutilated. I knew where they were before I saw them because I could hear their cries..." Elise squeezed his hand. "They made me work just like them. They hit me a few times but never beat me like they did the gyda. I kept my composure for most of it but as days passed, I began to slip. Being controlled was the worst thing I had to endure. I nearly knocked a guy's teeth out, but I knew if I attacked them, they would put me away somewhere, and I had to stay with the gyda. Weeks passed, and I heard nothing from my team, even after I had let out the signal confirming the gyda's whereabouts. I was starting to worry something had happened, that they weren't going to come. It was the first time I felt doubt for my team. It was also the first time I really felt terrified. Afraid I was stuck there with the gyda with no hope of escape. I was ashamed, as stupid as that is. But I couldn't help thinking of my sister. How she would have been stronger, braver." Elise sniffed, looking away from him. "Any-way...eventually, my team did come, and I was able to help the gyda escape. They called us heroes. It was a successful mission in the end, and everyone congratulated me on my bravery but..." Elise looked back at him. "Still to this day, those weeks come back, something random triggering the memory, and I just...I fear someday I'll slip in front of the others, and they'll know. They'll know I'm not like my sister at all."

Nezka's face darkened considerably even as he drew his other hand up to brush a comforting touch on her arm. "You are brave, Star-ling. More brave than you think." His voice held an edge to it, and he seemed to tense. His reaction was strange, but Elise chalked it up to him being uncomfortable. But then, maybe it was something else. Maybe he had endured something like it once himself. She felt better, anyway, after telling him. A little lighter, at least for the moment.

"My team and the others might be thinking the same now," she said after another pause. "They might be thinking there is no hope, that no one is coming. I have to keep going for them. Or die trying." She leaned in and kissed him. "Thank you for helping me." She smiled. He didn't smile back but he allowed her to touch her lips to his. He said nothing, but that didn't bother her.

His hand continued to caress her, and for a moment, his expres-sion actually looked pained, but she couldn't imagine why.

"I felt terrified too," he said suddenly.

Elise fixed him with a confused frown. "When?"

"Just a few hours ago. When I thought I was going to lose you. I don't think I felt that sort of fear in...in a long time."

"Really?"

"Yes."

Elise smiled again, feeling better. They would find her team and the others, and she and Nezka would be together to save them. She could envision them now, side by side as they brought her people back to the ships, seeing their happy, relieved faces. And then they'd be settled, and Elise would ask Nezka to join them and maybe...

Elise pressed herself close. She released her hand gently from his, letting her palm slip over his bare chest, down to his stomach. He stilled as he watched her touch him, his eyes alight with fire though his expression remained dark. When her hand reached the clasp of his pants, he grabbed at her wrist.

"You must be tired still. You should sleep," he whispered.

"I don't want to sleep." Elise rose and pushed him onto his back, placing herself on top of him. "I want more of what we did at the gatehouse." She kissed him again, biting his lip. He hissed softly, gripping her hips, allowing her to grind against him. He seemed to hesitate, as if uncertain, until she flicked her tongue between his lips and rubbed harder against him, and he finally snapped. He rolled her onto her back, and Elise could feel him harden as he pressed himself between her thighs. Elise gasped and threw her head back, and he, in turn, nipped and bit at her throat then down to her breasts as he unclasped his pants and freed himself. His tongue traced circles on her skin, and Elise felt the heat rise instantly. She moaned as he grazed his teeth and tongue along her stomach. Lifting her leg up and bending the other, he spread her out. His tongue swirled and slipped along her center, and Elise let out a shuddering cry.

Nezka lifted himself up, letting his body settle on top of hers. He bent himself down to her and kissed her roughly, needfully, his tongue slipping between her lips, grazing against her own. He rose back up and slid himself deep. As he moved slow against her, Elise noticed his expression still remained dark—troubled. She lay a hand on the side of his face, and their eyes met. Nezka's rhythm increased, his upper lip curling up to expose his fangs. His slow beat turned frantic as he caught hold of her wrists and pinned her. But there was something different in the way he moved, something less primal but just as intense. Something in his gaze flashed hot, and without warning, he let out a low growl. He slipped out of her then forced her onto her knees and moved hard on her again.

Elise, uncertain how their hosts might react to the noise, pressed her face into the blankets and moaned loudly, letting the cries fade into the soft bed as the pressure and heat overtook her. Her body tightened, harder now than before, and she let herself go, moaning sharply into the blankets, her limbs shaking. Nezka pressed his hand to her back and let out a low hiss as he slowed, and Elise felt the warmth of his heat inside her. He groaned and crumbled on top of her, nearly crushing her. Elise could feel his heart beating hard against her back in time with the throbbing between her legs. He shuddered against her, drawing his arms around her.

He mumbled something as he nuzzled her neck. She thought she heard him right, but she wasn't entirely sure.

"I can't let you go," she thought she heard him say. "I can't."

CHAPTER NINETEEN

The room had darkened as night returned. Nezka lay on the mat, not stirring an inch as he watched Elise's chest rise and fall, her mouth parted ever so slightly as she slept soundly beside him. When he closed his eyes and placed his hand on her arm, he could see her spirit was bright again as ever.

He let out a slow, deep breath.

Her body had recovered from the poison, but he couldn't stop checking to make sure there were no lasting effects. To his relief, her fire hadn't dimmed. Yet still, his worry remained. His hand fell from her arm, and he lay quietly, letting his eyes wander over her, memorizing every part of her.

Emotions of every kind ate at him. He wondered if he had ever felt so...*much* in such a short amount of time. When he had been a child, it had been harder to quell his thoughts and feelings, but they had always been the same back then, always anger and fear, until eventually, they just slipped away into nothing. He'd taught himself to overcome, to control.

Now, in the most unexpected way, things had changed. And perhaps for the first time, he felt uncertain of everything.

Nezka closed his eyes and covered his face with his hand.

This was supposed to have been a simple mission.

But now it was far from it. And he would have to make a decision.

Vesra had been like a father to him. It was he who had taken Nezka in after he had been taken from the ship. Those who discovered him had wanted to put him out or lock him away, but Vesra had convinced them otherwise. He'd saved him. He'd put him through the training, and it had been brutal, but he told him it was so that he would never have to be afraid again, that he would always be prepared for any enemy, for any fight.

But there was one fight, one enemy, Vesra couldn't prepare him for. The darkness of his psyche had boiled over, and the thing lurking in the deep smiled at him. He finally realized (or maybe admitted to himself) what it was, and when it reached for him and grabbed him once again, this time, Nezka allowed it to pull him under without a fight; he wouldn't be able to pull himself back, and he wasn't sure he wanted to. Because the grip of the mating bond was a powerful beast he had no hope of defeating.

In a way, he'd known she was for him even when they first met, first locked eyes. He'd known, but he'd been too wrapped up in the mission, in everything, to believe it.

Nezka dropped his hand and opened his eyes, staring once more at Elise.

'I hope someday you know how it feels to love someone,' said a female voice in his head. *'...and you feel the pain.'*

The soft, seething voice of the human woman on Nihl cut through him like one of his sharpened blades. Her warning was now a prophecy.

He couldn't let Elise go. But he was bound to this mission. To Vesra. When Elise had told him her story about the jungle, he felt his heart turn cold as ice. He almost revealed himself, almost told her everything right there. But his fear of her knowing the truth, knowing she and the other humans were to be taken back to Xolis, then seeing her hate him once more, had silenced him. Worse, he knew if he told her now, she would try to make for the deposit on her own and jeopardize her life along with her own mission to save her team.

Thinking of his mission now made him feel venomous. A deadly, possessive rage took him at the thought of those nillium men touching her. No. He would lose himself entirely if she was given to them, so he knew for one thing she wouldn't be taken from him. No one could have her, not even Vesra. He would hide her. Or intimidate Vesra into paying off one of his debts to him. Some way, somehow, she would be saved.

But of the others...he could not be certain. And still, she would hate him if he took them.

Deeply troubled, Nezka touched at his Starling's soft brow then silently rose. Whatever he might feel, he couldn't stop now. Not when they were so close.

* * *

"You've come around at last, as I knew you would, shadowstalker," Modella said as she ground some kind of strong-smelling plant in a bowl. She did not look up at him, and he wondered how she knew he was there. "But you are pained. Is your woman not faring well? I was told she had recovered, and I know my medicines to be strong."

Nezka took a moment to turn over her words before saying, "She is well, thank you."

Modella grunted as she continued to turn her bowl. "Then tell me what troubles you. What is it you fear?"

Though curious about her powerful insight, Nezka did not ask how she knew his emotions. He remained silent, uncertain whether he cared to tell her.

"You are not one of those Red Blades, it's true. Worik knew too, which is why he let you in here," Modella said when he didn't respond.

"And where is here exactly?" Nezka asked. "Because judging by the map, there is nothing here. The wall is an illusion, and something tells me those above see something completely different from below."

"It is true," Modella answered. "This is a sanctuary. It used to be a gathering for many. When the gangs and their leaders began to overtake the undercity, destroying everything in their wake, we made the choice to hide. To protect this sacred place. A place once made for those to find peace and hope. Those who are still in need may enter, and those who seek to harm may not."

Nezka could have guessed well enough by the ancient look of the place and the robed men and women who inhabited it, reminding him of the oracles from Xolis.

"So, enough trying to escape the question," Modella said as she set her bowl aside and picked up another.

"What question?"

Modella glanced up at him and gave him a fed-up sort of look. "What do you fear?"

Nezka fixed his gaze with hers. "Nothing."

"Don't try that lie with me. It won't work." Modella waved her mixing tool at him. "You have that human with you, and I see the way you look at her. But you fear to lose her. You fear that she will see you for who you really are." Modella went back to her bowl. "You are not a Red Blade. But you are like them. Tell me I am wrong."

"No," Nezka said in a low voice. "You're not wrong."

"So, you come from far away, a lone beast hunting by its master's orders. You caught your prey, but you find yourself unwilling to give it up. Am I wrong?"

"No."

Modella glanced back up and smiled. "You don't have to be the monster your master has carved you into. But you will have to decide in the end what you want to be. The hero or the villain." She set her bowl aside and wiped her hands on her robe. "She will find out, you know. She will see what you truly are. And you will have to decide."

Nezka kept still, not breaking from the shadows where he stood. "Tell me," he said at last.

"You will lose her as you fear. She will either turn from you when she learns the truth, or she will be taken. You must decide how you wish to part."

Nezka did not breathe. His lips curled back, and his hands slowly turned to fists. "Is that all then?" he whispered.

Modella's eyes fixed him with a sharp, all-knowing stare. "No. Did you not hear me? You must decide how you wish to part. You can be what you have always been and let her be enslaved within that jungle of steel and marble with your master. Or you can save her and lose yourself. The moment will come, shadowstalker. And you will have to decide."

Nezka felt his heart turn once more to ice. "Then I will lose myself. Tell me how."

"I cannot readily say." Modella sprinkled her crushed plant into a pot of hot water and stirred carefully. "But the moment will come, and you will know. And perhaps, if you play it right, what was once lost can be reclaimed. If not through life, then through death."

Nezka did not care to ask what she meant by that, though he could guess enough. "We leave at dawn," he said after a pause.

"Then go." Modella waved him away. "And be ready for what is to come."

* * *

Nezka couldn't go back to the room. Not yet. Instead, he found his way to the top, onto the temple terrace, and sat out for some time, watching the night pass by. Not far ahead was the energy deposit. He could just make out its domed shape past the wall. He'd been so wrapped up in getting him and Elise to this point, he hadn't even thought about how they would actually get inside. He knew he should be more concerned about it, but he could think of nothing else save for Modella's words. Black thoughts raced through his head, and he began to lose track of time. He was deep in some other place when a sudden small pinging noise cut him from his thoughts, and his techband lit up. He blinked down at it, nearly forgetting he had it, then saw that someone was calling him.

Silfres.

Nezka took the call. "You made it out. I thought maybe you hadn't lived up to your name."

"For a second, I thought I was a goner too," the lygin admitted. "Would have certainly been upset about my reputation."

Nezka let out a short, bitter laugh. "And the others?"

"Jazlin went on ahead. I only caught up to her today. We've hidden ourselves close to the deposit, taking turns to keep watch. Vijnn was with me for a time until he took to the sewers. Ruumas and Wruk are gone."

Nezka might have felt something for the loss but, either from years of training or from the other emotions still grating at him, he couldn't feel much of anything. "Too bad, they were good men. I assume they got caught in the bridge attack?"

"Wruk did. But Ruumas was a different story. Something real nasty got to him."

"What do you mean?" Nezka asked.

"I don't know. Right after we found a way out of the gate, I saw him fighting...something. Whatever it was, it was on the Red Blades' side for sure, though it didn't wear their signature gear and mask. It could fight like nothing I ever saw. Once me and Jazlin caught sight of it and saw Ruumas practically gutted, we went into hiding and started making our way slowly to our mark. Shit wasn't easy. We had to go way out of our way to slip through one of the less heavily guarded gates that had a few cracks in its wall, which was lucky in itself. I had got your message and agreed it was better not to contact you until it was safe...I was going to wait until I heard from you again, assuming you were getting close to the deposit. You are close?"

"Yes. Only a little ways off from where you are now," Nezka confirmed.

"Right. I was going to wait. We had been trying to find a way in for some time. The place is crawling with men, no surprise, but it seems a lot less than we might have thought. And even less now. I think they've been ordered to spread out, searching for us and guarding the gates. Either way, it was going to be hard, but I figured once you got here, we'd make a plan."

"That's a sound idea."

"Until today," Silfres continued. "I got a message back from Vijnn. Thought he might have slipped away somehow but it turns out he had taken the sewers all the way up to our mark. And not only that, he found a back tunnel leading inside."

Nezka stilled. "You can confirm this?"

"He sent coordinates and images and everything. He didn't say much else, mind you, as he was trying to be discrete, but it was all the evidence we needed."

This was good. They could use this back entrance to slip inside. "Send me the information."

"You got it."

"Is Vijnn with you now?" Nezka asked.

"No, I think he plans to wait out in the tunnel. I'm sure he'll contact us soon enough."

The coordinates and images popped up on his screen, and Nezka looked over them carefully. Yes, it was perfect. Already, he could feel a plan forming in his head. He could lead Elise in through the sewer up to the tunnel entrance and meet with Vijnn from there. They'd go on through together while Silfres and Jazlin attacked from the outside. "I want you and Jazlin to wait on my signal," Nezka said. "You will distract from the outside while me and Vijnn make our way inside." He hesitated a moment then continued with, "One of the humans is with me too. One of the women from the team back at the station. She is helping as well."

"Really? You got one of them out?"

"Yes," Nezka said flatly. "Why? Did you see what happened to the others?"

"No. I assumed the Red Blades got to them or they got crushed.

We were fighting our way through one of the tunnel passageways when all the chaos happened."

He'd hoped to get some good news to tell Elise but all would have to wait till tomorrow when they saw for sure. As nice as it was to know they now had a plan of attack and wouldn't have to wait by the deposit to look for a way in, Nezka's mood was still a raging storm he couldn't quell.

"Be ready for tomorrow. We move at sun up," Nezka said. He ended the call and stared out at the half-moon shaped dome in the distance.

No matter what happened after, whether for the sake of his mission or for Elise, he would find the humans and get them out. He would make certain of it.

CHAPTER TWENTY

Nezka stood alongside Elise by the temple's back doors as light began to filter down from above, accompanied by a heavy mist that clung low to the ground. Those of the temple, including Modella and Worik, came to see them off and give them a small pack of provisions. Though their journey wasn't far, Nezka took them gladly.

They also gifted Nezka a set of new armor plates to replace the mediocre ones of the Red Blade's and a new gun to Elise, equipped with a heatscope. Her face lit up as she handled the gun and clipped it to her side, thanking them.

"What need does peaceful folk such as yourselves have for weapons and armor?" Nezka asked with a half-amused expression.

Modella huffed. "We don't. They were just precautionary items found while scavenging by the walls."

"We can't thank you enough," Elise said as she adjusted her now gray and worn-looking armor.

Modella trotted over and clasped Elise's hand. "Be safe. Find your people. Trust in yourself." She released her and stepped away. "If you ever have a need to return to the undercity, you are always welcome here. But I hope that you won't." Modella's eyes met his. "I hope you will find peace."

Nezka felt an icy knot tighten inside him as he nodded back to her. "Farewell."

Worik led them down the temple steps and onto a path toward the eastern wall. They walked in silence, Nezka's mind turning over what was to come, when he felt a warm hand in his. He tensed and looked over to see Elise smiling up at him.

"Whatever happens, I'm glad it's you and me. Together." She squeezed his hand, and Nezka could barely return her smile as the icy knot grew, touching his heart and rising into his throat, making it hard to speak.

He squeezed her hand in turn then released it, his eyes shifting away from hers. "We're almost there."

Worik brought them to the edge of the wall and slipped over to the control box. A wave of energy shimmered along the wall that Nezka had not noticed before.

This is where I leave you," Worik said at his return. "Good luck to you both."

"Thank you," Nezka replied, bowing his head. "For everything." He took hold of Elise's waist and drew her close against him.

As they walked through the wall, Elise stretched out her hand as the darkness took them momentarily then in an instant was gone, leaving them on the other side of the wall.

Nezka did not let go of Elise right away. Instead, he pressed her closer and buried his face in her hair, filling his lungs with her scent. Before she could say a word or wrap her arms around his waist, he let her go, pretending not to see her look of confusion.

"We make for the sewers," he said, shifting his gaze away to focus on the section of buildings and road ahead. "There is a path leading into the energy deposit from there."

"You saw on your map?" Elise asked with growing excitement.

"Not I. One of the other hunters." Nezka lifted his techband to message Silfres as they made their way into the shadow of a large building.

"They finally contacted you?"

"Yes. Three have found their way here. Two will be waiting on my signal to attack from the outside. One will be meeting us in the sewers." Though he had not yet heard from Vijnn, Nezka assumed he was waiting on his command just like the others. Nezka's assumption was confirmed when Silfres quickly replied back, stating that the corax had messaged him last night. He was ready to go and would be waiting. Nezka messaged both Silfres and Vijnn to let them know he and Elise were on their way.

Keeping close, they ran on down the road, Elise taking up her gun, having it ready for anything unexpected. But the streets were dead and the buildings empty. No one met them as they found an entrance into the sewers along a dried up waterway. They slid carefully down into the slime-filled sewage canal and stopped at the half-grated tunnel entrance.

"Why didn't we think of this before?" Elise asked as they stared into the mouth of the tunnel.

"I had back when we first started out but quickly learned that pumps deep within drain the water and sewage out every thirty minutes. We would have either been washed away farther from our destination or drowned. So, I considered it unsafe."

Elise nodded. "You definitely made the right call then. But what of your teammate? How did he make it through?"

"Corax are impressive swimmers and are equipped with gills as well as lungs," Nezka stated. "Vijnn likely had no problem."

"Makes sense." Elise did not move. "How much time do you think we have?"

"Not much. But the path isn't far. Let's get moving."

Together they slipped into the tunnelway. As soon as the light faded and the darkness took hold, Elise clicked the light on the top of her gun and Nezka turned on those attached to his wrist plates. Nezka took the lead as they made quick work through the murky tunnels. Several unsavory scents hit his nose and oily filth splashed against his boots, but he cared little. He listened for the sounds of metal grinding or of the rush of water and found only the sounds of his and Elise's footsteps. Small creatures scurried around their feet as they passed but nothing larger met them. He stopped every so often to check the map then they would continue on as before. They were getting close.

When they were just before the deposit, they heard a dull thumping noise that grew louder as they approached. Judging by the map and the sound, Nezka theorized it must be a large reactor settled beneath the building. As they turned a corner and headed down the last tunnelway, Nezka could feel a low vibration.

The deposit was in working order, generating what must have been a good chunk of the undercity's power.

They exited the tunnel and came to a small end chamber with a welded ladder leading to the top. Nezka cast his light at every corner and frowned.

"What is it?" Elise asked.

"Vijnn. He should be here." Nezka brought up his techband and began to message the corax after telling Silfres to stand by.

"Do you think he went to the top?" Elise said, pointing her light up at the door.

Nezka couldn't be sure, but an unsettled feeling began to brush at him. He cast his light once more around then made for the ladder. "Wait here."

Elise stood close by as he climbed swiftly to the top then started to push at the door. With some effort, he was able to shift the heavy metal back until it left an opening wide enough for him to poke his head through. Cautiously, he looked over and found a darkened room. Large steel barrels made up most of the space. Quietly, Nezka slipped out and looked over the room. He was about to message Vijnn when he heard a sharp clanging close by and saw a shadow move. In an instant, he had his blade in hand, ready to strike. He moved toward the noise and cast his light up just in time to see Vijnn directing his gun at him.

They stared each other down for a mere second, neither dropping their weapon, when Vijnn relaxed first, lowering his aim.

"I was wondering when you'd show," he said, black eyes regarding him warily.

Nezka slowly relaxed as well, letting his blade-hand fall. "You were supposed to meet us below."

Vijnn looked over at the hole behind Nezka with a frown. "Yeah, well...no one comes in here. And I was getting sick of waiting in that muck. Sorry."

Nezka's eyes narrowed on him, studying him carefully. The corax looked paler, his natural blue-gray skin now a dull ashen color. He seemed on edge, a spark of fear in his eyes. Nezka also spotted dark markings under his jaw and throat.

"Have a tough time getting here?" Nezka asked casually.

Vijnn shifted his eyes away, his fingers rubbing along the side of his gun. "We should get going."

Nezka watched him a second longer than turned back to the sewer door. He aimed his light down and saw Elise looking up at him with concern. Water was beginning to splash along her legs, rising slowly. Nezka could hear the grinding of the pumps. They couldn't turn back now.

"Come. It's safe." Nezka reached his hand down. Elise quickly climbed the ladder and allowed him to lift her out. She righted herself then looked over to Vijnn and nodded. The corax looked at her, confused, but nodded back all the same.

"There is a door over on this end." Vijnn gestured over to the far wall. He started for it, and Nezka stopped him.

"Hold. Silfres and Jazlin are outside. I'm going to have them attempt to make their way in." Nezka lifted his techband. He looked to Elise. "Ready?"

Elise regripped her gun. "Ready," she said through her breath.

Nezka gave the signal to the others then took up his blades and made for the door. "Let's go."

As they slipped out of the room, they found themselves in a tight hallway passage. Nezka allowed Vijnn to take the front while keeping Elise at his back. Other rooms they passed were empty save for a few barrels. When they came to the end of the hall, they paused at the next door. Vijnn's hand shook slightly as the entrance slid open and brought them out into a very large open space serving as a warehouse. All around, Nezka spotted rows of equipment, weapons, gear, even vehicles and, yes, a few ships. Above, in the center of the roof, Nezka could see a sky entrance that allowed the ships to come and go as necessary.

Carefully, they made their way to the other side, over to a large, thick metal door. They stopped, and Nezka noticed it was locked. Vijnn went over to the keypad in an attempt to unlock it while Elise stood with gun ready, watching from the door. Nezka too looked around, and the same unsettled feeling brushed at him again.

"We should have met with someone by now. Guards if anything," Nezka said aloud.

"Maybe they are all at the gates?" Elise said. "Or outside."

Nezka began to pace around, his eyes searching the dark corners of the warehouse when his techband went off. He lifted it up and saw it was Silfres.

They saw us coming, the message read.

The unsettled feeling quickly turned to alarm.

"Get back!" Nezka threw his arm out toward Elise as Vijnn unlocked the door and it slid open. Out from the opening came a loud hiss followed by a wave of smoking gas that engulfed them. Nezka threw up his arm to cover his mouth while using the other to shield Elise and back her away as she coughed and choked. The gas worked into his system almost immediately, making him feel sluggish. He continued to back away from the door with Elise beside him. Stumbling, she buckled down and he stopped. The smoke dissolved away, and in its place, more than two dozen Red Blades with faces covered and weapons drawn surrounded them.

Nezka stepped in front of Elise, gripping his blades tight as he looked them each over. If not for the smoke, he would have already been cutting them down. But now he moved too slow, blinking continuously as his vision went in and out of focus.

The Red Blades tightened their circle around him and Elise. Vijnn remained outside the circle, still standing by the door, uncovering his mouth. They locked eyes, and Nezka saw the look of fear and shame in the corax's gaze.

Three more Red Blades appeared from the doorway. Two men with a woman between them. The woman's armor, unlike the rest, was the color of blood, her face covered by a sleek, red mask with an X over the mouth.

"You've come to us at last," she said, voice grated by the vent of her mask. "Though I had hoped it would have been sooner."

Nezka kept Elise behind him. She gripped his arm as she weaved on her feet. With a shaky hand, she aimed her gun at the woman, who merely laughed.

"She's a brave one. No whimpering or crying like the others. Nice to know they aren't all like that." The woman lifted her arms and took off her mask.

Cold black eyes regarded him, and for a mere instant, Nezka was convinced he was looking at his master, Vesra, only now in the form of a woman.

But no. It was not him. Only someone who looked uncannily like him.

The woman smiled with pale, wide lips. "It's been a long time, Nezka."

CHAPTER TWENTY-ONE

THAT COLD KNOT TIGHTENED FURTHER AROUND NEZKA'S HEART and throat, making it hard to speak. "I don't know you," he whispered.

The woman's eyes widened. "Oh? I think you do. Though you were but a child last we saw each other." She gave her mask over to the Red Blade beside her and stepped closer. "Right before my brother exiled me from his city."

Nezka grew still as he stared at the woman, turning over each memory of his youth until he remembered a woman who had come to meet with Vesra on one of Nezka's first training days. A vain woman who cared not that she was disturbing Vesra's work or disrupting Nezka's training.

"Pyra." Nezka's voice cracked.

"Good, see?" she said sweetly. "You do remember." She came closer, ignoring Elise's gun on her, looking only at him. "When I learned that you were in the city, I admit I was...ecstatic." She smiled. "And when I learned that you were coming here, it felt personal. Like a friend coming to visit. How is Vesra, by the way? I keep up on his dealings in Xolis, but I don't ask my little spies about his health." She took a step back and tilted her head, regarding him. "You should know better than anyone, after all."

Nezka glared back at her. *No,* he thought, *not this way.*

"Hm?" Pyra tilted her head more. "You are still working for him, aren't you? Haven't gone rogue on him?" She giggled, her laughter piercing in his ears. "It's all right if you have." She approached him again, this time placing her hand on his chest. "Because I was hoping you could work for me now? Seeing that me and my brother have the same goal in mind."

"Like hell he would," Elise said from beside him. Pyra looked to Elise, and Nezka had to stifle a growl. Pyra dropped her hand from him to study her closer.

"My spies were right. You really are good, Nezka. You didn't even have to drag this one all the way here." She giggled again softly. "You've somehow convinced her that you're on her side."

Elise shifted behind him. "What is she talking about, Nezka?"

"Oh, let me save her from her confusion, Nezka, please," Pyra said. "And you don't know either, do you? About my little business here. Why I have been collecting the humans too." She grinned, showing pearly, silver teeth. "It's for the same reason my brother wants them. When I learned he was going to sell them off to the nillium, I desired to find them first. But I didn't have to look far. As fate would have it, they came to me. I wished to collect them and sell them myself, either to Vesra in hopes that he would consider a partnership and trade of resources or to the nillium themselves for a high price. I knew you were coming to take them to my brother but," she stepped back and gestured around her, "as you can see now, you needn't bother. We are on the same side, you and I. We can bring them to Xolis together."

"You're wrong," Elise snapped before Nezka could respond. "Nezka was hired to take you out and bring your head to the drogin officials. And now he's helping me save my team."

Pyra's hairless brow rose. She looked to Nezka with a curious, unblinking stare. Her hand slowly lifted, and her men aimed their gun's higher, toward Nezka and Elise's head. "Am I wrong, Nezka?" she said in a sweet yet venomous voice.

Nezka dared not unlatch his gaze from hers, keeping his expression cold and indifferent. If she believed him turned, she might very well kill him where he stood. She would take Elise regardless, but if he convinced her he was still Vesra's most loyal servant, she would allow him to live, giving him more time...

Such a plan, however, meant the inevitable betrayal he had so wanted to avoid.

"No," he said without wavering, his body turning cold, heart turning to ice. "You're not wrong."

He could feel Elise growing still beside him. "What?" she said in an exhale of breath. Pyra's grin widened, and she lowered her arm. Her men lowered their guns.

"I'm so very glad to hear it," Pyra said. "Like your corax friend, you've made a wise decision. Come, we have much to discuss."

"Nezka?" Elise said.

Nezka dared not look back at her, unable to meet her eyes. He sheathed his blades and stepped away from her, toward Pyra. Elise let out a cry of shock. "Nezka!"

He stopped and forced himself to look around, seeing past her. "You were a fool to trust me."

She lowered her gun in surprise. Then lifted it back up and aimed toward Pyra. She fired off but the bullets missed their mark as one of the Red Blades got in her way, taking the brunt of the shots then swiping an arm out and throwing her to the ground. Nezka forced himself not to move as they ripped the gun from her hands and locked her arms behind her back.

"No!" she screamed, struggling against them. "No!" She kicked and fought as they brought her with them, Nezka following Pyra past the warehouse doors and on through a large passage going deeper into the deposit. As he listened to Elise's cries and shouts behind him, he made himself absolutely calm as Pyra walked at his side.

"I know you are most loyal to my brother, but I think we can come to an arrangement. I've been waiting for more humans to come. But it might be some time before that happens. This could be the first batch, then others can follow. I have no doubts that you can persuade Vesra to my favor."

"Perhaps," Nezka said indifferently. Vijnn came to walk close to him with his head bowed low.

"Your corax friend took some convincing," Pyra said, eyeing him. "But he came around in the end, didn't you, Vijnn? He really didn't like the idea of bringing you to me, but he saw my way in the end. The other hunters are welcome to join too if Ryxok hasn't killed them already for attacking us." She laughed. "I probably should have mentioned to him to go easy. Ah. well. You are all I will need."

They came to the end of the passage, and Pyra went on through into the room beyond. They entered into what looked to be a large, central control room. She stopped beside a circular terminal displaying holographic maps of the city while her men dragged Elise past, taking her through another set of doors on the opposite side of the room. Nezka watched them go until the doors shut, cutting him off from Elise.

Shoving his need to tear the men apart and bring her back to him, he turned slowly to Pyra, who smiled. "I don't think you will regret your decision, Nezka. Vesra has a tendency to betray his closest allies. Look what he did to me, after all. But I can give you so much more than him. I don't expect you to fall completely to my will right away. Once we have a little chat with Vesra, you will see. I have so much planned for this city. Vesra has been losing his grip on his own. Especially since the death of the nillium prince. Things are chaotic in Xolis. But here, we can start anew." She looked to the rest of her men, who waited for her orders. "Back to your stations, the lot of you. I trust my shadowy friend well enough."

The men reluctantly relaxed their guns. Some slipped back through the passageways while others positioned themselves by the doorways. One door to the back opened, and Nezka tensed, baring his teeth in a half-snarl.

"Ah, Ryxok, you've returned," Pyra greeted the alien at the door.

The alien in question was not of a kind Nezka had encountered before, but if he had, he would have gladly challenged it in a fight just to see who was deadlier in practice and design. The alien looked lethal on its own, a solitary predator like Nezka himself. If things were different, perhaps he would have felt a sense of comradery or kinship with the intimidating creature, but instead, all he saw now was a threat.

Ryxok glared back at Nezka with blood red eyes, seeming to think the same thing. His tail, tipped with spikes, swished casually beside him. His head, piled with twisted horns, bowed.

"Did you find the others?" Pyra asked.

"Yes," Ryxok hissed. "In a building connected to ours. I injured one nicely, but I'm afraid the other took me by surprise. They ran. I expect they will be back."

"Maybe you should call on them, Nezka," Pyra suggested. "Tell them to come and we will not harm them. They could join us as well."

Nezka's eyes narrowed on the dark red alien before him. "In time. I want to hear your arrangements first. I will tell them to hold off until then."

"Suit yourself. But if they attack again, Ryxok will have to go after them. It might be wise that they come here unarmed."

"I will tell them not to attack."

Ryxok moved swiftly over, eyeing Nezka curiously. "I have not seen the likes of your kind before."

Nezka tilted his head. "Nor I yours."

"Have you not?" Pyra said. "I would think you would have encountered the vrisha at some point in your travels, Nezka."

Nezka made a swiping gestured at his throat. "No, I have not."

"They are a formidable race. Ryxok has never met defeat. It is too bad his kind have exiled him. A bad assassination attempt on one of the vrisha queens. But he has been my most faithful servant. Having you both here, I can't see anyone ever daring to challenge me." Pyra worked at the controls on her terminal, bringing up an image of several Xolis-made ships. "Now, with the last human female in our care, we can begin preparations for their departure. I will send a message out to Vesra. Once we speak, I will determine where the humans shall go. To Vesra or to the nillium's home world. I expect by now another ship of humans will be on its way to us, containing another team. Qorey has yet to confirm, but I know they will come again to save their own."

"You mean Councilman Qorey?" Nezka asked.

Pyra smiled as she glanced at him. "Yes, of course, he is one of my own."

The attack on the first gate now made sense. "Did you get them all then? The team of human soldiers?"

"Not all, I'm afraid. We left those who were too injured and were likely going to die anyway. Thankfully, they were only males."

"I see," Nezka said flatly. He fixed his gaze back on the image of the ships. "How do you plan to fly them out from the undercity with the threat of the ships powering down?"

"I will have to lift the shields momentarily. It will be a necessary risk. I don't expect any drogin fighter ships to be waiting. Qorey has seen that they remain too afraid to approach." Pyra brought up another map, this time of the inner workings of the energy deposit. He studied it carefully before she swiped the map away. "Enough talk of this for now. We wait on Vesra's call. Let us celebrate our inevitable partnership." Pyra turned away from the terminal to face him. She stepped closer and lifted her hand to the now healed side of his face, brushing it softly with her fingertips. "Then the final phase will begin."

CHAPTER TWENTY-TWO

Elise struggled all the way down the passage but couldn't wrench away from the grips of the Red Blades that held her. As they came to the door at the end, they forced her to stand upright as they stripped the armor plates from her suit. Now with no shields to protect her, they unlocked and opened the door then shoved Elise inside. With the gas still working on her brain, she fell to her knees on the hard concrete floor. Her vision swirled, and she thought she might throw up. The door shut behind her, covering her in darkness.

"Who's that?" someone whispered close by.

"I don't know, can't see," whispered another.

"Vince, turn on the light."

There was a moment of shuffling around then a clicking sound followed by the flicker of a flame. A silhouette of a man could be seen touching the flame against a strip of cloth, lighting it on fire then placing it into an empty bowl.

As the flame grew and the light burned brighter, Elise began to make out the edges of a room filled with mats and clothes and people.

"Elise?"

Elise blinked and looked around. She tried to make out the faces of those around her, but they all seemed to meld together.

"My god, it is her. Quick! Pull her up, and bring her over here."

Elise was pulled to her feet. She stumbled a few steps as a pair of hands brought her farther into the room. Supporting her still, Elise lifted her head as a large man came into view, setting a heavy palm on her shoulder. Elise blinked a few times before she could make out a face. "Bruce?"

"The one and only," Bruce said, fixing her with a smile that didn't quite meet his eyes. His other arm was wrapped from wrist to elbow, and his face had the faintest smattering of bruises that were nearly healed. He let his hand fall from her shoulder, and Elise looked to the pair that held her and saw Tom and Helen smiling back at her. Her throat tightened, and a low sob escaped her lips. Next thing she knew, she was being engulfed by bodies, arms wrapping around her, pressing her close. Elise let out a few more heavy breaths before she calmed herself and allowed the others to release her. She looked at each of their faces and saw that Amy and Reese were there as well. All of her team except for...

"Where are Adrien and Jerico?" she said softly.

She didn't have to guess, judging by their faces as their eyes fell as did their smiles.

"They were left behind," Tom answered. "We don't know...we aren't sure if they are..."

He didn't continue, and Elise didn't ask him to. She nodded her head as her heart sank to her stomach. "What happened at the gate?" Her voice cracked.

They each glanced at each other, and Helen patted her arm gently. "Sit down. Let me check you."

Elise did as commanded and sat down on a thin mat made of some foam-like material. Her gaze shifted around to the others, who all watched quietly by the walls. The Grayhart team of scientists. They whispered to one another as they glanced her way, their expressions curious as well as anxious.

Helen gripped at Elise's arms and legs then pressed against her sides and asked her to breathe normal as she checked her pulse. She had none of her medical tools, but she did her best to examine Elise as best she could. She unclasped Elise's suit partway to examine her neck and back and found the marks of her fight now nothing more than scars.

"How did you come by these?" Helen asked, brushing her fingers against the sensitive skin.

Elise clenched her jaw and stifled a shudder. "A fight."

"Damn, Stirling, you've been through some major shit too, huh?" Reese said close by.

She swallowed hard, her throat still tight. "Yes," she said, her voice shaking. Her hands turned to fists as her thoughts drifted to Nezka, and she shoved them away. Anger and despair rose quickly, and she closed her eyes, trying to stay calm. "Tell me what happened."

They didn't answer right away. Bruce leaned back against the wall nearby while Reese and Tom sat together with knees to their chests. Amy sat beside her as Helen continued her exam.

"The tunnel broke," Tom began. "I remember coming to and there were pieces of the tunnel falling onto the car, dust so thick you couldn't see anything outside the vehicle. Thankfully, the car was a tank and sheltered us from most of the debris. When everything went quiet, we got up, made sure everyone was okay." Tom shifted, his eyes dropping to his hands. The others stared out at nothing as they listened. "We were banged up a little but luckily nothing major. We could stand at least." He laughed. "We escaped the car and started looking around. We noticed you were gone and that the tunnel exit was nothing but a pile of rock. There was more rubble around us, but the tunnel hadn't collapsed fully. We could still see up the tunnel part way. But it looked pretty bad. We searched around for you, and that's when we saw Adrien and Jerico underneath the car. We scrambled to get them out, but by the time we dragged them to safety, we were overtaken by more of the Red Blades. They left them, thinking they were goners, and took the rest of us out through a tunnel passage. Bruce tried to break free and got his ass handed to him. Can't do much when you're bound up. Anyway, they brought us here instead of killing us. Not sure why."

"For the same reason why we are here," said a man on the other side of the wall. "They are collecting us for some outerworld purpose."

"Crazy..." Amy murmured.

Elise closed her eyes and shook her head. "No, he's right." She opened her eyes and saw them each looking at her.

"How do you know?" Reese asked.

"Because I was with one of the bounty hunters and..." She took a deep breath. "And I thought we were coming to get you all out, but he betrayed me...betrayed us. The head of the Red Blades is a woman named Pyra who is looking to sell us off, and the bounty hunters are in it to help her."

"Great," said Reese." And we thought the drogin were the only snakes in this trap."

Elise's brow furrowed. "What do you mean?"

"Someone, one of the drogin officials we think, is in on this little plot too," said one of the Grayhart members.

Elise thought back to their time at the station and their journey to the gate. "Why do you think that?" she asked.

"Because they were the only ones who suggested we make for the undercity. With nothing but a guide and a handful of soldiers," said a woman by the back wall. "They told us it was safe. We just wanted to see the beginning foundations of the city, to get an idea of how they built it from the ground up. Next thing we know, we are getting sacked."

"Do you remember which officials made the suggestion?" Elise asked.

"Official Dol, Official Rola, Official Joli," an older man listed off.

"They recommended it and enlisted our aid," said the woman. "They had to have gone to the head of command first to even meet with the suggestion."

"And that was?" Elise asked.

"Councilman Qorey."

Elise placed a hand over her eyes. She remembered the day they went into the tunnel and she had seen his face right before. She could have never guessed. "So, he planned to set the Red Blades on the gate in hopes to get to us right off the bat."

"Seems about right," said the woman.

Elise let her hand drop. It had been planned from the start.

She thought of Jerico and Adrien being left behind. Of the rest of them now trapped, waiting to be traded off. She thought of Nezka taking her, separating her from her team. She didn't want to believe he had betrayed her like this. She wanted to believe he was going to come for her—for them, still. But what hope she had was fading fast.

He let them take me away. He didn't so much as look at me.

Elise slammed her fist down on the ground. She bent forward and let the rage finally consume her. Body shaking, she opened her mouth, hoping he heard her scream.

* * *

The room lay quiet. Elise rested on her side, eyes open, peering through the dark. The others slept around her, some snoring softly or shifting in their sleep. They rested together though they had no way of knowing if it was night or day. Only going by when they began to feel tired.

After she'd come down from her episode, they offered her a meal bar, which she didn't take, and some water from a large jug which she only took a few sips from. Her team understood her anger, but they didn't know how deep it went and for what purpose. They were enraged by their capture. It only made sense for her to be as well.

But they had no clue what it had been like for her. What it had taken her to get to this point. All to save them. All for nothing.

She lay there thinking about how stupid she was for trusting Nezka. She supposed she hated him again, but there was still that small piece left that longed for him. She wanted to snuff that piece out with the heel of her boot.

She heard someone grumble softly in their sleep. She shifted her eyes around the room, unable to see anyone but knowing they were there. The Grayhart team had been shut away in darkness for so long she was surprised at how well they were holding up. One of the scientists, a man named Vincent, mentioned that guards came only once a day to throw meal bars at them and trade the empty jugs for filled ones. It was all they were living on, and by the last glows of the flame, she had seen how gaunt they had become. Soon her team would become the same. Too weak to fight.

They had talked of escape many times. But the door was sealed and there were no windows. The vents might be big enough but those leading to the room had small openings and were sealed tight. The only tools available to them were a lighter one man had hidden in his boot and the clothing they had come with. The Red Blades had taken all their gear and their weapons.

So, all they could do was wait and hope another team would come along and not make the same mistake they did.

"Meg might still find help," one of the Grayhart girls had whispered after the team told Elise their plans (or lack thereof) when she had asked.

"Meg is dead," replied another.

The girl, with wispy brown hair and round glasses, shook her head. "She's still alive. I'm sure of it."

"Who's Meg?" Elise asked.

"She was one of our engineers," replied Vincent. "There was a small scuffle when we were first brought here. The power had gone out for only a moment, and we tried to scatter. The Red Blades were ordered to bring us to this room and thought they got us all, but they didn't realize one was missing."

"Meg was always a wallflower, so it's no surprise," said one of the Grayhart men with a thick black beard. "Quiet too. They probably didn't even notice her from the start."

"But we haven't heard from her since," Vincent said. "Not that she could ever get past the guards."

"But they must have not found her either, or she would be back here by now," said the brown-haired girl.

"Or she did get out somehow and got killed trying to run. Either way, she can't help us," said the bearded man.

They had argued for a little while about whether or not Meg was still alive. Tom whispered to Elise that they argued quite a lot. But then there was nothing much else to do. When they eventually settled down to rest, Elise knew she would find no sleep no matter how much she tried.

It might have been a few hours now since she had laid down with the others, but her mind always remained in the same place.

No matter how much she tried to block him from her thoughts, she could not escape the hunter. Eventually, she gave up and let the thoughts pass. An awful swelling ache had settled in her stomach, growing larger by the minute until she was sure she would be torn apart. She thought about the hours before they had journeyed together to the deposit. About how aloof he had suddenly seemed. She had noticed his tension, his unusual quiet and intense focus but had chalked it up to his anticipation for the battle to come. But in reality, he was only preparing to push her aside.

And she had told him so much, opened herself to him, given herself to him. Hell, she had told him things she hadn't even told her teammates, her friends. She had felt so close. And he had only been playing with her.

Tears welled up at last, falling down her face. She brushed them angrily away. No. He wouldn't get her shame or her despair. If she saw him again, she would make sure he saw nothing but her dry eyes and her cold indifference. Just like he gave her.

A soft tapping started on the wall behind her. At first, she thought nothing of it, taking it for whatever the city's equivalent to rats was or maybe a leaking pipe. But the more she focused on the noise, the more she realized there was a pattern. She sat up and listened for a moment then turned her eyes to the wall. Some of the others stirred as the tapping continued, until Elise heard someone jolt up and cry out, "Quick, Vincent, the light!"

As Vincent flicked on his lighter, a woman with thick curly locks flung the jacket she used as a blanket off her and fumbled over to the wall, nearly tripping over one of her teammates. She pressed her ear against the wall and smiled. "It's them." She began to tap back in an obvious pattern as Elise's team sat up, their attention fully on the wall.

"What's going on?" Elise asked.

"It's the drogin," said Helen.

"What drogin?"

"Other prisoners like us. Drogin soldiers. The Red Blades didn't kill them all. Some they took to try to gain information. Or they are trying to force them into joining their gang," Helen said. "The Grayhart team has been communicating back and forth for some time now."

Elise shifted closer to the wall. "What have they been saying?"

"They usually just ask how we are holding up. Sometimes little pieces of information get passed. They know who we are. We know they are being interrogated."

An answering tap came after the woman paused, and she waved for them to be quiet.

"We've told them about one of the head officials being in league with the Red Blades," Helen whispered. "They think we are right. They've told us that the Red Blades are going to make a move soon. That their leader is readying supplies...and ships. If they can find a way out, they can free us, and we can make it to the supply room. Obviously getting out of this room is the issue, but they claim if there is a way to power off the reactor, it will cause an outage to all the systems, unlocking the doors."

"How do they plan to power off the reactor?" Elise whispered.

"They don't. They're stuck like us, but they think the last outage —the one that helped the engineer get away—wasn't an accident."

"They think there is an agent on the inside?"

Helen shrugged. "Maybe. But this person hasn't let themselves be known to the other drogin, so there's no way to tell. Either way, we're still stuck here with just theories, but it helps keep spirits up."

The woman tapped back one last time on the wall then stepped aside. "They say they've heard guards talking outside. Looks like we will be shipped off soon. They think in a matter of days now."

The others, now awake entirely, began to talk amongst each other, many of their faces tight with fear.

"I don't want to go. Oh god, where are they taking us?" one cried.

"What are they going to do to us?" asked another.

"Make us slaves, I'll bet," came a reply.

Slaves.

Elise saw the jungle again, now lit up in red.

"Tell me you saw Jerico or Adrien alive," Elise asked, gripping Helen's arm. "Tell me they were still alive before you were taken."

Helen shook her head. "We only had time to drag them out from under the vehicle. I couldn't get a proper read."

Elise released her and stood. She went over to the door, ready to pound on it, and instead placed her palms against the cool metal. She rested her forehead against the door, trying to keep her body from shaking.

She would rather die.

But that was just it, wasn't it? They wouldn't kill her. They would immobilize her, strike her down. But they wouldn't kill. Because they wanted her and the others alive.

The next time this door opens, I'm going to fight.

She repeated it to herself over and over. She would go kicking and screaming all the way. And eventually, someone had to let their guard down.

"Elise?"

Elise stepped away from the door and turned back to her team. She had no words for them. She was not her sister. But, like her, she was going to fight till the end.

A sick feeling swirled in her gut as she thought again of Nezka. If things were different, she imagined he'd be proud.

CHAPTER TWENTY-THREE

It felt like days had passed, but in reality, it might have only been hours. Elise sat against the wall, letting her mind wander. The others passed the time talking and playing games. One pair even started a round of 'never have I ever' but quit after only one turn, giving Elise a death glare because she wouldn't stop laughing. Helen watched Elise closely, and Elise knew her teammate was concerned for her, wanted to ask what had happened to her, but Elise never gave her a chance to mention it. She didn't want to tell Helen or anyone, afraid they would think she had lost her mind.

They had small talk instead. Reese and Bruce kept talking about all the food they missed. And the beer and the traveling and Bruce's dog, Po (who was going to take care of him?), and Tom wanted to see his kid, Amy wanted to see her sisters. Others walked the room to stretch their legs, a few cried, some whispered angrily in the corner.

They ate and slept a little more and waited. Elise glared at the door more than once, knowing any moment it had to open. When they heard footsteps coming down the passage, Elise jumped up and placed her back to one side of the door.

"Elise, what are you doing?" Tom asked.

"I'm taking them. Are you with me or not?"

The team looked at her like she was crazy.

"They have guns, Elise. And full body armor," Tom said after a pause.

"Bruce already tried. Did you not see his face and arm?" Amy pointed his way.

Before she could open her mouth to reply, the door opened. Thinking quick, Elise lunged forward and struck the masked man firmly in the neck. He went stumbling back, and she kicked hard to make him fall the rest of the way. She went to jump past him but was quickly blocked by two others. Remembering the moves Nezka taught her, Elise struck in the areas most vulnerable and where their armor was nonexistent. A few put up their guns but were shouted at by the group leader to not fire. Instead, he took out a long red glowing stick and hit Elise across the shoulders with it. The pain was intense and immediate, like a sharp, twisting cramp. Elise nearly buckled before he hit her again and she fell to her knees, gasping from the pain. Bruce and Reese, followed by her other teammates, were there at the door, ready to defend her, but were promptly pushed back with guns in their faces.

"Get back, the lot of you!" the group leader shouted. "Or I will order them to shoot your legs off. Pick her up," he ordered. "And bind her."

Elise tried to fight through the pain but was quickly overtaken by the group of guards. A couple, she was pleased to see, were on the ground clutching their necks and sides. The other men did as ordered and bound her wrists, forcing her to her feet. She kicked at them and one struck out, hitting her square in the face. Elise twisted away as her cheek burned and blood trickled from a cut on her lip. She spat the blood out at them as one man grabbed the back of her neck and shoved her forward.

"All men get to the wall," she heard the group leader snap through the open door. "Face it with your hands up."

The guard who held her backed her against the hallway wall and kept her there as the rest of his group blocked the doorway. There was shuffling from inside the room as the men of her team and of Grayhart's placed themselves along each side.

"Now each woman line up at the door," the group leader ordered next.

Reluctantly, the women did as told. From there, the guards bound them each and brought them out into the hallway. Seeing Elise, Amy fought against her holder, but with one hit of the red rod, she too went down. Helen tried to go to her but was held back.

With the women forced into a line, the Red Blades sealed the door back behind them then ordered them to walk. Elise, still struggling at the back, was dragged more than pushed.

The guards led them down the same passage that Elise had been carried through the first time. They entered into the main control room where they had the women stand in a row between a wall and the central terminal. Dragged to the end, the man holding her let Elise drop to her knees.

"What happened to that one?" she heard Pyra say.

"She got smart. Had to rough her up a bit," replied the group leader.

Elise made the mistake of glancing up and, in doing so, locked eyes with Nezka, who glared down at her from where he stood beside Pyra. Elise quickly glanced away and saw on Pyra's other side a demon who appeared just as menacing as Nezka. Elise shuddered at the sight of him. He looked familiar, as if she had seen his species somewhere before. She stared at him for a moment until it hit her.

Lazris.

She hadn't been there, but she had seen the footage and heard about it from others. The alien was the same kind as the one that had gotten out from that base after the incident. They had claimed the race was hostile while others said different. Judging by the one she saw before her, she'd say definitely hostile.

Pyra studied her from atop the control center and shrugged. "Some will have a bite to them. But can be tamed if need be. Now," she tapped at the terminal, and a holographic display appeared. A pale-gray man sat in a darkened room with cold, black eyes and a sharp nose. Elise could tell the resemblance between him and Pyra almost instantly.

"Hello again, brother," Pyra greeted the man.

"Sister..." The man looked over at Nezka. "So, your message wasn't some trick. You've got my man after all."

"He only wishes to aid me with the trade, Vesra," she said sweetly.

The man frowned. "So, you have the humans then?"

"See for yourself." Pyra tapped again at the terminal, and the image of the man faced them. He looked over each woman, his eyes flickering over to Elise last. His frown deepened.

"You are very clever, Pyra, I'll give you that," Vesra said in a grated voice. "But I don't take kindly to being schemed against."

"And I don't take kindly to being thrown out of my home, yet here we are," Pyra replied.

"You know why I threw you out. You were trying to overthrow my power."

Pyra huffed. "Only to equal it, dear brother. But I have grown quite a following where I hide now. I'm willing to forgive and forget. I'll give you the humans in exchange for aid to overtake this city. Nezka would make a most skilled servant, and I know there are other hunters in your command. Bring to me more of your men, along with a larger arsenal of ships and weapons, and I will send a ship of humans back to Xolis every third cycle."

Vesra seemed to think on it. He looked to Nezka again and gestured toward him. "I will consider giving you other men but not Nezka. He belongs to me. I will send out a larger ship with cargo in return for both these humans and him."

Pyra smiled. "Fine. I will not fight over one man, no matter how good he may be. Until the ship arrives, however, he works for me."

Nezka stepped forward. Elise felt her body tighten. "I would complete my mission despite the circumstances. Once the ship arrives, let me bring the humans back on my own. I can use more Ionx capsules to make less stops and return quickly."

Vesra and Pyra each looked to him with raised brows.

"I see nothing wrong with that," Vesra said.

"Nor I," said Pyra. "It is settled then." She clapped her hands together. "I await your ship's arrival. Until next time, brother." She tapped at the terminal one last time, and Vesra's image disappeared. Elise struggled to her feet as Pyra turned to Nezka, placing a hand on his chest. "I had hoped to keep you, but sadly, my brother is selfish. If he does ever betray you, know you are welcome at my side."

Nezka looked at no one but Pyra. "I will keep it in mind." He smiled, grasping her hand. "I would have a favor to ask you before Vesra's ship arrives."

"Oh?"

He gestured over to where Elise and the others stood. "I would ask to have one of the women sent to my room."

Pyra's eyes widened, then she laughed. "I have heard you take pleasure in all kinds. Did you not have that woman you came here with? I'd be shocked if you hadn't."

"I did, and I would have her again before I am to take her to Vesra. I fear he will be selfish with them too, and I want one more taste before she's kept from me."

Elise grew still with shock at what she was hearing. Then, like a living fire exploded in her chest, she grew hot with rage. "I wouldn't let you touch me!" she burst aloud. "I wouldn't let you touch me ever again!"

Nezka's eyes drew over to her, fixing her with an intense gaze filled with his own fire as his expression darkened into something she'd never seen before. Pyra started to laugh again when a map showing the deposit's outside doors appeared above the terminal and a light blinked near the outer edge of the screen.

"Someone is trying to gain access," said the devilish alien beside Pyra.

Pyra frowned and looked to Nezka. "I thought you told those other hunters to keep away."

Nezka's eyes bore into Elise for a second longer before turning to Pyra. "I did. They would not disobey my orders."

"Then who could it possibly be?" she snapped.

"I will go," replied the red alien. "If it is them, I will catch them this time." Without looking back, the alien left through another doorway, disappearing from sight.

"If they are under Vesra's command as well as your own, they would do well to come unarmed and aid in my cause," Pyra said in a low voice. Before Nezka could reply, she turned to the group of guards. "Take them back to the room. Except, I suppose, that one." She gestured to Elise. She glanced back at Nezka. "You can have her for now, but I would see you persuade your men to cease any attack and to fall on my command."

The guards moved to take the women back to the room. Trembling, Elise shook her head as she tugged her arm away from the men trying to take hold of her.

As the women struggled against their holders, the lights of the control room dimmed then brightened. Each head turned up in confusion.

"What..." Pyra started to say. Then the dull roar coming from the flow of energy in the room ceased, and the lights flickered out.

Elise, in a split-second decision, cut her elbow back and hit the man beside her square in the groin. He went down with a bark, and that seemed to trigger the others to fight. In the mass of chaos, Elise hit one wall and ran alongside it until a door opened. She shot through and started quickly down the passage. The shouts and screams of those behind her could be heard, followed by the firing of guns. Red beams of light brightened the passage. Elise didn't turn to go back for the others, knowing the men couldn't possibly be so stupid as to kill them in fear of their mistress' wrath. Likely, she told herself, they were only letting off shots to scare them and drive them back into submission. The only thing Elise feared was getting caught by a Red Blade, or worse, by Nezka himself.

As she turned down another passage, the lights flickered back on. A Red Blade, trying to find his way down the other end, saw her and put up his gun. He shot at her legs, but Elise jumped up in time and lunged at him. Wrists still bound, she swung her arms out and clocked him as hard as she could, square in the head. He hit the side of the passage wall and, as he stumbled, Elise kneed him in the head. He went down, and Elise didn't bother to hit him again. She ran down the hall as fast as she could until she found a stairwell at the end, leading down. Having nowhere else to turn, she descended the stairs. When she came to the end, she entered into another passage, one lit up in violent red. She heard the shouts of men nearby, but she didn't pause. There were doors on both sides, and she tried each as she passed but with no luck. She turned down another narrow passage connecting one corridor to another when she heard the voices of men at the other end. Halting, she started to turn back but heard footsteps growing louder from the way she came. Cursing, Elise stopped, knowing any moment, the Red Blades would turn the corner and find her. Readying herself for a fight, she put up her hands when, without warning, she was grabbed from behind.

Yelping in surprise, Elise found herself tripping back into darkness. For a moment she thought she had somehow passed through the walls themselves just like she had at that hidden place with the temple. But before her was an open doorway to the passage she had just been in. A silhouette reached out and closed the door, pitching her into nothingness.

Beyond her own breathing, Elise heard the shouts and footsteps of men pass by. Then slowly, over the span of seconds, they faded. When it was silent again, there was a soft tap as someone unseen clicked on a flashlight and aimed it at her face. Elise squinted, putting her hands up.

"You're new," came the low croak of a voice. "So, they did find others. Pity."

"Who are you?" Elise asked.

"Talk later. Follow me." The flashlight directed over to a large vent opening, and the shape of a woman crouched down and vanished inside. Elise hesitated uncertainly. She looked back at where the door must be and knew if she tried to leave, someone would find her. Not feeling threatened, she judged following the woman was her best option and so crouched at the vent entrance and slipped inside.

They crawled for some length, Elise shuffling on her elbows, her arms beginning to burn from the strain. Eventually, the woman stopped in front of a wide vent entrance and popped open a grate. She slipped out, and Elise followed. Beyond, a soft light from a cracked lantern bathed a small inner room in a warm yellow. Elise shifted through the vent and dropped out onto the ground. When she sat up, she saw the room was filled with equipment she didn't recognize. Seated by a monitor was the smallest drogin she'd ever seen. She thought for a moment it was a child but when it looked back at her, she could see it had the matured traits of an adult with large all-knowing eyes like Modella's.

"Come, girl, close up the vent," said the woman beside her. Elise twisted around and fixed the grate back into the wall. When she turned to the room, she saw the woman bending down to study her closer. She was older, with short gray hair and laugh lines around her mouth, though she didn't look like the type who laughed much. Her thin lips tightened as her eyes narrowed. "So, you supposed to be one of the rescue team? Ha." The woman straightened. "How far did you get before they caught you?"

Elise glanced around then stared at the drogin, who was back to watching the monitor, before saying, "They caught most of us at the first gate. I...got taken when I tried to sneak inside."

The woman grunted. "Well, at least there was an attempt. I didn't know if Grayhart would send anyone or not." She turned and set the flashlight down to sift through a duffel bag.

Elise shifted over, observing the room curiously then turned her gaze back to the woman. "Are you the one who got away? Are you Meg?"

"Yes. That's me. So the others told you." Meg looked around at her. "Are they all together then?"

Elise nodded. "They are keeping everyone in one room."

"How are they faring?"

"They are malnourished but surviving," Elise replied. Then, after a pause, she continued with, "You should know the Red Blades plan to ship them out soon. Along with my team."

"So, it's as we feared." Meg turned back to searching the bag. "We will have to work quickly then." She took out a pair of metal cutters. Gesturing for Elise to raise her arms, she cut into the binds on Elise's wrists, breaking them and letting them fall to the ground. "I was wondering if anyone else would get away. Though the power outages don't last long, I always hoped it would give someone enough time."

Elise stared at her, wide-eyed. "You did that?"

Meg laughed. "No, not I." She pointed to the drogin. "That's all Lo."

Elise watched the drogin working at the computer. There was a strange cylinder-shaped device plugged into the console that pulsed blue and several other machines that blinked on and off.

"How?" Elise said, shaking her head.

"Oh, Lo is one smart gal. Took her a while to acquire all the parts needed for an electromagnetic generator but once she got things going, she's been working on getting that damn reactor to turn down. Unfortunately, so far, she's only been able to cause short blackouts."

"She's the one the soldiers mentioned," Elise whispered. She quickly stood and crept over to kneel by Lo's side. "How long have you been here?" she asked.

Lo paused in her work to glance at her with a timid expression.

"Oh, she can't talk. Been mute since she was a kid." Meg crouched to Lo's other side as the drogin made gestures. "She says she's been here for several cycles. So, about five months give or take. The Red Blades brought her here some time ago to force her to help improve their shields and their tech. She worked in one of the high-end security sectors before that. Right, Lo?"

Lo tapped at her nose and returned to keying in short codes into the computer.

"She found a way to sneak out of her holdings, likely through one of the smaller vents since she's so tiny," Meg continued. "And she's been hiding since. She found me in one of the empty storage rooms and brought me here to help." Meg sighed and shifted over to set her back against the wall. "Too bad though. Was hoping that last surge would be enough to turn off the reactor and, in doing so, the shields, but no such luck. Looks like it's on to plan B."

Elise sat there for a moment in a daze. All the hopelessness she felt before started to dissolve away, replaced with hardened determination. Yes, this was it. This was the fight she needed.

They still had a chance.

"How can I help?" she asked.

Meg looked over at her and smiled. "You're a soldier, correct?"

"Yes."

"Now that the generator is too weak to work, we—or more so, Lo —had the idea of using an electromagnetic bomb. We got all the parts ready to be activated. The only issue is the bombs' radius isn't so large that it can be set off from here. It needs to be placed right near to the reactor, and it's safe to say there are Red Blades who watch and guard the chamber it lies in all day and night. Me and Lo would get our asses handed to us if caught, and honestly, I'm not that brave. But if we had someone to keep them out, maybe as a distraction..."

Elise nodded her head, and for the first time since being brought to the deposit, she smiled. "I can do that."

CHAPTER TWENTY-FOUR

Nezka didn't need to be told who was missing once the lights came back and the women were rounded up. As Pyra seethed beside him, Nezka felt the icy hold on his heart burn now with a deep vexation.

If it had been any other circumstance, he would have been thrilled to see that Elise had gotten away. He couldn't deny he was proud even to see that she still fought, that she hadn't given up despite everything.

But, be it as it was, he had greatly hoped to have had that moment with her alone in whatever quarters Pyra gifted him. Just so that he could talk to her, explain everything, tell her he was going to make things right. He had that sliver of hope when Pyra agreed to let him use his ship to bring the humans to Vesra. He knew he could have easily dropped the humans somewhere and taken Elise into hiding. Vesra had trusted him enough now through the years not to have his ship tracked. It would have been their best chance.

But he couldn't leave. Not without Elise. He couldn't leave her.

And not knowing where she was tore at him.

"Find her," Pyra spat to her men. "Break her if you must, but don't kill her. Bring her to me when she is found."

The men scattered. The women were taken back to their room, and the rest of Pyra's men began their search.

Nezka wasn't going to just stand there and wait. "A waste to have all these men look," he said, feigning arrogance. "Let me search. I can track better than all combined. If anyone can find her, it's me."

Pyra seemed to think it over. "All right. Go. But if I find you trying to leave the building, I'll make sure you go back to Vesra in pieces."

Nezka put a smile on his face for good measure. "Has your trust in me slipped away already?"

Pyra gave him a venomous glare before returning his smile. "Just a precaution, my friend."

Nezka stepped away and started for the door Elise had been closest to. As he slipped into the passage, he knew he would break bones before letting someone harm Elise again. He needed to find her first. She would fight him when he did, but he was prepared for that.

As he stalked the halls and found the other Red Blades searching, he ordered them away, fixing them with his meanest, most ass-kicking glare ever. They didn't argue. He was in the darkest mood he'd ever been in, and the urge to throttle each one of them was a hard temptation to fight.

As he went through every unlocked room, he knew once he found her, he needed to convince her to let him take her and the others aboard his ship. She wouldn't go easily, but he was beginning to feel fine with that. He had made his decision. He wasn't going to let her be taken. Not by anyone.

The humans were coming with him and not back to Xolis.

As he stepped into another darkened room and saw it was empty, he heard someone coming up behind him. When he turned around, he saw it was Vijnn.

The corax stared back at him, fear still showing in his eyes. "I'm sorry," he said.

"I know." And Nezka did. With the look on Vijnn's face and the marks on his throat, it wasn't hard for Nezka to put two and two together. They had tortured him.

"Tell me what to do," Vijnn said.

Nezka looked away, thinking. "I have a plan that I hope will work without the need for a confrontation. However, I can't assume nothing might happen." Nezka glanced back at him. "If we are to fight, I need to know you will be on my side, no matter what."

The corax bowed his head. "I will do whatever you ask of me."

"Good. If and when a fight happens, I want you to message Silfres and Jazlin and tell them to attack the outside just as planned. Then we will get the humans out. Lead them to the ships we saw in the warehouse."

"But if the shields are still up, we won't be able to fly one out of the undercity, possibly not even from the building itself," Vijnn said.

"Don't use it to fly. Not right away. Use whatever the ship has for its attack system. They are equipped with gun pods and launchers. I saw for myself when we passed them in the warehouse. They are battle-grade ships and should be able to take heavy fire if need be. Take out every Red Blade you see, and wait for me and the others."

"What will you do?" Vijnn asked.

"I'll make for the control room and see if I can somehow power down the shields."

"This is assuming we can even get past every one of these guys," Vijnn stated.

"True. Which is why I'm hoping it won't come to a fight. But if it does, this may be our only other chance." Nezka rubbed a hand over his eyes. "Just be ready. If nothing else, make it your sole purpose to get the humans out and as far away from here as you can. Will you do that even if I'm unable to go on for whatever reason?"

The corax gave him an odd sort of look. "Would it not be less of a risk to just wait for Vesra's ship? I mean, it sucks that he's forced to bargain with that bitch of a sister but it beats having to fight them."

Vijnn frowned. "Or are you trying to say you want us to...actually save these humans?"

Nezka dropped his hand and looked at him. "Would you betray my command again if I said yes?"

The corax's eyes widened. He looked over his shoulder then back at Nezka. "Vesra will have us hunted and killed."

"I know."

Vijnn stared him down, and Nezka didn't falter. "I thought I'd never see this day," he said in a shocked tone. "Nezka Voidstorm...is going rogue."

"I have a very serious reason for it," Nezka said, unwavering.

"That is?"

Nezka closed his eyes and opened them slowly. "To save my woman."

Vijnn took a step back in surprise. "That human?"

Nezka's eyes narrowed on him, making sure he understood how serious he was. "Do I have your word that you will do as I say or no?"

Vijnn rubbed at his neck then let out a soft hiss. "Fuck it. Yes. I'll do it. I have more respect for you, anyway, and I would see some payback for what Pyra did to me. Seeing as you aren't choosing to kill me for betraying you now, I'd say I owe you one."

"I'd say that is wise thinking. Let us hope it won't come down to a war. Once I find Elise and have her back with the rest of her team, I will prepare to take them far from here and from Xolis. You can join me, or you can stay and hide in the city, but until they are safely away, this will be the plan. Understood?"

Vijnn bowed his head. "Understood."

"Good." Nezka stepped around him and exited the room. "This mission is finished."

CHAPTER TWENTY-FIVE

It took Meg and Lo no time at all to assemble the parts for their bomb. Elise knew little about the kind they used—Bruce being her team's bomb expert—but it looked capable enough to do its job despite being as small as her forearm.

A blue light pulsed along its side as Lo carefully placed it inside her bag. They weren't going to wait for some better opportunity to arise. With Elise aiding them, the pair felt confident that no time was better than now to get to the reactor and set off the bomb. Elise couldn't agree more.

With the bomb packed, along with flashlights for each of them and a bag of tools at Meg's side, they were prepared to make their way down.

"One last thing," Meg said as she rummaged through a set of crates along the wall. She took out a long red rod that Elise recognized well enough as the same baton the Red Blade had used on her to force her down in her fight from the room. "Got real lucky, Lo did, in snagging this when one of the guards was sleeping. Bastards used this on my team a couple times. Hurts something awful. Might be hard to hit through their armor but I reckon you will make them feel it in some way."

Elise took it gladly. With her armor gone, she would need any and all help she could get. A gun would have been better, but even if she did acquire one somehow, she wouldn't be able to use it because of the Red Blades' trigger-lock security system. Lo claimed she could hack such a program if need be, but she would be too busy with the bomb to do so. They needed to get in and set it up quick before Pyra found out and sent down more of her men, namely those Elise knew she wouldn't have a chance at beating such as Nezka and the demonic alien Meg called the vrisha—a name Elise now remembered hearing before.

Elise tied the baton to a tool belt also given to her by Meg and, using a clip, secured her flashlight to her shoulder. The two women followed suit, strapping their bags tight to their waists and fixing their lights to their suit collars. Lo placed a small tablet-looking pad into an inner pocket along with a device that looked like a metal bug. When Elise asked what it was, Lo gestured that it was a B-connector and Meg explained it was like a wireless USB used to connect her coder with other devices and computers. Lo had several other gadgets on her person that Elise could only wonder what they did. The only thing she didn't seem to have, to Elise's disappointment, was a Ulink that could communicate with others from the outside.

"That's it then," Meg said, tugging at her belt. "Let's get this over and done with."

Together, they crouched by the vent. As Lo popped the grate, she took the lead, followed by Meg then Elise at the back.

Clicking on their lights, they crawled the maze of vents, Elise trusting that Lo knew where she was going. They climbed their way down one central airway as large as Elise was tall and went a short distance along another vent until Lo finally stopped at a small grate and gestured for them to keep quiet. Through the narrow openings of the grate, Lo kept watch while, behind her, Elise and Meg waited until the small drogin deemed the area clear. Popping off the grate as quietly as possible, Lo set it down then slowly slipped out. Elise waited a few seconds longer for Meg to slide out next before she pushed herself out into the room beyond.

The room was an impressively large, round chamber with a high, domed ceiling. At its center, just up a set of steps, was the reactor, a giant tank with dozens if not hundreds of cables and pipes, some as thick as her body, others as tiny as her fist all fixed to the seal at the top. A rush of red light pulsated from the base and along the floor, as if fires burned underneath the ground. A dull roaring vibrated under Elise's feet from the loud hum of the reactor.

Meg tapped on her arm and signaled for her to follow. They crept up to the reactor's side, over to a small terminal and control panel. Meg crouched down while Lo brought out the bomb from her bag.

"We just need to fix the piece on to the panel and set the charge," Meg explained. "Shouldn't take too long." Her eyes shifted behind Elise, and she quickly ducked, pulling Lo and Elise down with her. "A guard!"

Elise looked around and saw one of the Red Blades entering the room from a doorway on the opposite end, crossing to the other side of the reactor.

Now was her moment. Keeping low, Elise crept down the steps, pulling the baton from her waist. As the Red Blade walked into her line of sight, Elise shot out in front of him and struck with all the speed and power that Nezka had taught her. The baton hit the side of his neck, and the guard barely had time to let out a shout in surprise before he was crumbling to the ground with a hand around his throat. As he lifted his gun, Elise snapped her leg out, contacting the side of his head with a loud crack. The guard went limp as he fell to his side and remained still. Elise kicked his gun away just in time for another guard to come sauntering into the room.

"What the hell—"

Elise moved. The Red Blade lifted his gun and fired in her direction, barely missing her arm and thigh just as Elise leaped and brought the baton down on the top of his head. The Red Blade fell to his knees, and Elise made another blow to his face, splitting his mask. He, too, went down and didn't get back up, and Elise kicked his gun away just like the other.

She circled the men, watching and waiting to see if they would move, and was thankful when they didn't. She heard the steps of another coming down the passageway and quickly moved to the side of the doorway, ready for a surprise attack. As the third Red Blade entered the room, Elise cut low, thinking she'd hit his neck, only to find him taller than she anticipated and catching his chest instead. The Red Blade jumped back in surprise and fired his gun across the door's frame, sending sparks flying. Elise dodged, shielding herself against the wall as the Red Blade backed out into the passage, letting off a few more shots. When his firing ceased, Elise dared to look around the doorway and caught him tapping the Ulink on his wrist.

"She's in the reactor," he called into the device. Cursing, Elise rushed into the passage and swung out her arm. The Red Blade lifted his gun but wasn't fast enough. Elise struck the side of his wrist, sending red light across one wall then slammed her fist into the exposed part of his neck. Choking, the Red Blade stumbled back, dropping his weapon. Elise put all her weight into a kick to his stomach to send him flying. When his back hit the ground, she closed the distance between them and brought the baton down.

Elise stood for a few seconds, looking down at the unconscious man as she caught her breath. Her eyes turned upward to the end of the passage, and she backed away. Rushing back into the room, she found the pair still working on setting the bomb. "How much longer?" she asked.

"Not much," Meg said. "Lo is setting the charge now. Only another minute." Lo stood beside with her tablet device in hand while Meg made sure the bomb was secure and couldn't be ripped off the panel.

"We are about to have a whole lot of trouble," Elise said. "And I won't be able to take them all."

"We are nearly there. Stand your ground. Just one more minute!"

Elise nodded as her heart hammered in her chest, knowing they might not have even a minute before a whole group of Pyra's men came barreling into the room, guns locked. She stepped back to let them work, turning around to ready herself for the incoming fight, when she let out a sharp inhale of breath and froze.

She locked eyes with twin fires burning around a wicked storm.

Nezka stood as still as night before her. When he finally moved, Elise quickly stepped back, gripping her baton tight. "Don't," she hissed. "Don't come near me."

Nezka stilled once more. His body, as tense as hers, began to relax, his eyes never falling from hers. There was a sadness there, a sort of longing but she refused to believe it was real. "I can't make that promise," he said in a low voice.

"Just like you couldn't make any others. Not to me." Elise stood her ground, blocking the others.

"I know. I should have told you everything. I wanted to." Nezka slowly moved toward her, and Elise shifted away in response.

Elise clenched her jaw as her mouth trembled. "I don't believe you."

"I don't expect you to. Not yet." Nezka stopped. "I was assigned to take you. It was my sole mission to bring you and the others back. That is truth." His expression darkened. "But being with you...has changed things."

Elise shook her head, her face burning. "You're a liar."

"I have lied to you." He moved again and Elise with him. "But not about this, Starling—"

"Don't," Elise snapped. "My name is Stirling, and you are just trying to trick me again. But you can forget it. We are getting out of here, all of my people. We are getting out, and you can't stop us."

"I want that now too," Nezka said softly. "I won't let them take you. But I need you to trust me. Just this last time, Elise. I need you to come with me."

Elise shook her head as she raised her baton a little higher.

Nezka's eyes narrowed. "I won't fight you, Elise. If you come with me, I can get you and the others safely out. You just need to hold a little longer."

Elise let out a huff of bitter laughter. "You said yourself I was a fool to trust you. Well, I won't be fooled twice, Nezka. If you want to take me, you will have to fight me."

Elise caught a glint of some deeply unsettled emotion in Nezka's eyes before he bared his teeth in a hiss. He looked ready to lunge at her, his body tensing for a fight, and Elise prepared herself for his attack.

Then he dropped his stance, and he closed his eyes and took a deep breath. He opened his eyes, and for the first time, Elise saw in him a look of utter defeat.

"Do what you have to do to get out."

Elise lowered her arm. "What?"

"Go. I can give you some time but not much." His eyes flickered over to the women at the reactor. "I'm guessing you're going to blow the power. Once you do, make for the warehouse."

Elise didn't move, uncertain if it was a trick. But he didn't lunge forward to take her. Instead, he stepped away.

"Get to the ships," he said. "I will do what I can to keep them at bay."

Elise didn't know how to respond. The sounds of men were drawing closer, as they could be heard coming down the stairway. Elise stood in place, watching him in confusion.

"Done!" Meg called. "Elise, fight or flight, we have to go!"

Elise couldn't seem to turn her eyes away from his. She tried to find an inkling of falsehood in his expression but could find none. He was really letting her go.

"Why?" Elise said. "Why are you doing this?"

Nezka's stare went right through her as he bent his head. "You know why."

An awful, brilliant ache cut right across Elise's chest. She went to take a step toward him when the shouts of men brought her back.

"Elise!" Meg called.

She felt her throat tighten. Her vision blurred. She wanted to say something, but she had no time to find the right words, so, instead she turned from him. Meg and Lo were already inside the vent. She shot over and crawled inside after them just as the heavy sounds of the Red Blades' footsteps were coming down the passage. She wanted to look back and see Nezka, but Meg and Lo were already far into the vents, their light fading. Cursing, Elise followed.

They made good time crawling their way back up. Once they were past the central airway, Lo took a separate turn away from their hidden room. When she eventually stopped, she looked around and made gestures at Meg.

"She says just up ahead is an empty room leading out to the passage that will take us to where the others are being held. She's going to pop the bomb off from there. Once power is out, the doors should unlock. After that, though, we are on our own. Make like hell and get out."

"No," Elise said. "Make for the ships. That's what Nezka said."

"You trust his word?"

Elise thought for a moment then nodded her head slowly. "It's a sound plan. The warehouse also has weapons we might be able to use. Worse case, there is a secret entrance just beyond which can be used if in dire need. The warehouse is our best option."

Meg looked to Lo, who nodded her head in agreement and made a quick gesture with her hands.

"Your call then," Meg said.

They continued on down the ventway until Lo stopped at the end and kicked the grate. They each slid out into the empty room then crouched by the door. The voices of the Red Blades and their heavy steps running down the passage could be heard on the other side.

Lo took out her small tablet and looked to Elise and Meg.

"Here's hoping," Meg said.

Lo brought up the charge and tapped the screen.

There wasn't a bang. Just the slow whine of the reactor shutting off and the hiss and pop of whatever lights or machines just died. They heard the Red Blades shouting nearby along with the loud buzz of some alarm far away.

"Fuck me sideways, it worked!" Meg hissed.

Lo opened the door and beamed her light out into the passage. All was dark. Not even backup lights lit the way.

"Let's go," Elise said.

They raced down the passage. Elise tried to slow so that they could keep up, but all she could think of was her team. As she got closer to where they were being held, she began to fling doors open, first to see if they really were unlocked and to see if anyone was inside. They all lay empty until she got farther down and saw a small group of Red Blades near all the doors with lights and guns aimed at any who dared tried to open them.

"Don't try to escape, or we will shoot!" one yelled.

Elise clicked off her light. With baton still in hand, a surge of energy overtook her. She sprinted toward the men and leaped into one not expecting to be attacked from the passageway. She kicked him hard, sending him into another, making them fall to the ground. As they went down, she swung on another, his head hitting the wall. One man turned to fire on her when the door behind him flung open and a group of drogin leapt on him, bringing him down.

One by one, the doors flung open, and the drogin soldiers attacked with fists and teeth. Elise forced her way past them to the final room, only to be blocked by another set of guards coming from the other direction.

"She's human!" one shouted. "Immobilize!"

They shot toward her feet, and Elise stumbled back. They'd started for her when someone yelped in surprise, and the group of men swerved around, only to be attacked from behind. Elise saw Vijnn in the fray, cutting into each one. She shot forward and attacked, forcing the men back.

The door to the room ahead opened. Both Bruce and Reese came barreling out, tackling some of the last men standing. Behind them came the rest of Elise's team.

"Elise!" Helen shouted.

Elise jumped over a fallen guard and nearly knocked into Amy and Tom. They grabbed her shoulders to steady her. Helen closed the distance, and they quickly embraced.

"We have to get to the warehouse," Elise said, pulling away. The drogin soldiers were beginning to make their way down the passage to them, along with Meg and Lo. Out of the room where Elise and the others had been kept came the rest of the Grayhart team.

"Meg!" Vincent cried as the older woman approached. The group circled around her, patting her on the back and smiling, some even giving her a hug which she shrugged off. Elise looked around and saw Lo gesturing to the fellow soldiers, a few of which understood her sign language.

"What warehouse?" Helen asked. "Where?"

"The one with the ships," Elise said, not having the time to explain. "Follow me!" She'd started down the corridor that her memory told her went toward the warehouse when Vijnn stopped her.

"Not that way," he said. "Follow me."

They all hesitated, some looking at him still with suspicion.

"Can we trust him?" Tom asked.

Elise studied the shark-like man. She did witness him taking out some of the Red Blades which might be a good enough reason to trust him. But deep down, what she really wanted was to believe that Nezka was truly on her side. That, though he betrayed her, he was being true to his word, that he was going to help them escape. And his teammate was a part of that promise too.

"You have a lot of us against just you," Elise said to the corax. "So, if you betray us..."

"I won't. I gave my word to Nezka that I would help," he said. "And I've already called on the other hunters. They are attacking from outside as we speak which means they are distracting the other men and hopefully Pyra herself. We need to move quick if we wanna make it to the ships."

Her team looked to her, waiting for her response. Elise thought back to Nezka allowing her to leave the reactor.

She wanted to trust him again.

"Lead the way," she said.

Vijnn bowed his head then turned, not down the corridor to the control room but instead to the end of the passage where a stairway led downward. Elise looked to the Grayhart team and waved for them to follow.

"Are you sure it's safe?" Vincent said

"I'd say it's better to follow them than trying to find a way out on our own," Meg commented. No one seemed to argue this and so the Grayhart team began to join them.

"We will come too," said one of the drogin. "Better to stay together with larger numbers.

With that settled, Vijnn started down the stair and they all followed. The sounds of gunfire could be heard not far away. Elise assumed it must be the other hunters versus the rest of Pyra's men somewhere near the outside of the deposit. She wondered if Nezka was there and if he was taking Pyra and her Red Blades out. She hoped he was and a part of her wished she could be there with him. Instead, she ran beside Vijnn as they made their way down a different passage. No one met with them which reaffirmed the men were fighting somewhere else.

As they reached the end of the corridor, Vijnn took them up another flight of stairs then down another passage until he stopped at a large metal door. Once everyone had caught up, he started to plug in the code on the pad beside the door to unlock it—only to find it didn't work.

"Shit, what to do we do now?" Reese said.

As if to answer, Lo made her way out of the crowd and came over to the door. She looked up at Vijnn, the short cut hair along her skull standing on end. Vijnn tilted his head at her then moved aside. Lo crouched down then pointed to the ground, making a motion to lift up the door.

"We have to open it together," Elise realized aloud.

"Everyone start lifting. Come on!" Amy shouted.

Where they could make space, they all squeezed into a row along the wide door and, together, with all their strength, attempted to lift the heavy metal slab. The door groaned then slowly started to slide up into the ceiling as they pulled it open. To Elise's surprise, light broke from under the door, spilling onto their feet. But there was no way the lights inside could be on. Pushing concern aside for the moment, she continued to help in forcing the door open. Once there was enough space to pass through, they pushed their way inside.

The warehouse lights weren't on like Elise feared. It was natural light coming from above where the roof was partially opened by what looked to be a ship entrance. Below it sat the actual ships.

Vijnn started for one of them and everyone followed.

"I can't believe we're actually getting out," one of the women cried.

Vijnn ordered them to wait as he climbed his way up to the top of the large blue-gray ship, searching for a hatch. Everyone gathered tightly around, ready to get on board. The sounds of gunfire lessened, and other strange sounds took its place. Elise separated herself from the crowd to check on the door she and Nezka had attempted to enter through the first time. A sharp thud followed by voices could be heard on the other side. Heart dropping to her stomach, Elise turned and rushed back toward the group.

"They are trying to get in—"

Her shout was cut off by the deafening bang of the door being blasted open. Pieces of the metal door cut through the air, lodging themselves into crates and equipment. A few small pieces cut into Elise's arm and leg. She flattened herself on the ground, covering her head as a cloud of debris blew around her. She heard shouts and a few screams as her people, along with the drogin, took cover. As the debris settled, Elise lifted her head and looked around to see Pyra with a band of her troops.

Her eyes, cold with fury, glared down at her. She reminded Elise of the red queen from Alice in Wonderland with her blood red suit of armor and look of murder. Elise half expected her to scream, "off with their heads!" But instead, Pyra hissed down at her and said, "Pick her up and bring her to me."

Elise tried to shift away as two men grabbed her arms and dragged her up. Elise yelped in pain as one squeezed around one of the wounds on her arm. She was placed beside Pyra, who grabbed a fist of her hair and forced her head up.

"If you weren't such a precious resource to my brother, I would be slitting your throat this very instant," she spat. She turned back to her men. "Bring me the rest. Kill the soldiers."

The men started forward, guns aimed. From the corner of her eye, Elise could see the drogin soldiers falling back, taking shelter behind large crates. Her team and Grayhart's tried to take shelter near the back of the ship. Pyra tugged her back, forcing Elise to look at her.

"I might not be able to kill you, girl," she said. Her lips curled in a wicked smile. "But I can make you suffer. After all," she tilted her head and lifted her other hand, brushing her fingers along Elise's arm. "Where you are going, you won't need any arms or legs." She pressed hard into the cut on Elise's arm, and Elise screamed. Pyra released her without warning, making Elise stumble back into the men ordered to keep her still. Pyra took out a blade from her side and lifted it to Elise's face. "I'll try not to enjoy this too much," she said sweetly. "Hold her down," she ordered the men.

Elise fought as the men roughly brought her down to the ground, one grabbing her ankles and the other shoving her hands above her head. Pyra knelt down at her side and placed the knife against her thigh. She pressed the tip down, cutting her suit. Elise struggled and yelled, but everyone around her was too distracted by the Red Blades' assault, gunfire sweeping across the warehouse.

Pyra grinned and lifted her knife. She raised her arm up, ready to stab into Elise's thigh, when some dark object flashed by, hitting the side of her hand. Pyra shrieked with rage as blood gushed from her palm, the blade slipping, dropping to the ground along with a couple of her fingers. She drew back as another dark object hit one of her men and his mask split open. The men released her in a panic, and Elise rolled away. As she rose to her knees, she looked up and saw Nezka approaching from the other end of the warehouse, blades already returned to his hands. He started toward her, and Elise cried out as, from somewhere unseen, the vrisha dropped down, blocking his way.

Nezka bared his teeth, and the vrisha growled back. They circled one another; two powerful predators ready to tear each other apart. Elise watched, her heart pounding, realizing what she was feeling was fear. Fear that this was one enemy Nezka might not be able to defeat.

The vrisha whipped out his tail, cutting close to Nezka's throat as he dodged the attack. The alien was fast, if not faster than Nezka. And just as agile. But Nezka didn't falter. They would circle until one would attack and the other dodged. Like tigers or vipers, they struck violently, without mercy. Nezka swerved away from the vrisha's tail once more then lunged forward, catching the alien's leg, slicing apart his scales, leaving a dark gash. The alien shot back and hissed then returned to circling, undisturbed by the mark. The pointed end of the vrisha's tail was as sharp as Nezka's blade and could do just as much if not more damage. Elise struggled to her feet as their fight started to move from one side of the warehouse to the other, keeping back from the gunfire. Some of the drogin soldiers leapt out from their hiding spots to grapple with any of the Red Blades who chased them. Some were able to take a Red Blade down while others were not so lucky as the bursts of red light from the men's guns cut through the soldier's bodies.

Elise turned back to the ship in time to see Vijnn power it on and for her team to direct the others inside as the ship's ramp dropped to the ground. She looked back at Nezka as he brought the vrisha around, their fight continuing over to one wall near the blasted-in door. Elise, thinking her best chance was to help the others into the ship, started forward, but an arm wrapped tight around her throat and dragged her back.

Kicking and clawing at the arm, Elise twisted, trying to free herself, her feet slipping on puddles of blood.

"We're not finished," Pyra hissed in her ear. "When I'm done with you, you'll wish you were dead." Pyra's hold tightened around her, and Elise flung her arm back, trying to hit her face. Panic struck her as her vision began to blur. She was losing consciousness. She could feel her body beginning to slow.

A flash of brilliant light burst over her head, and for a moment, Elise thought something might have popped in her brain, until she caught the sparks of fire along the wall. Another burst of light shot down near the ground close to them, and Elise realized someone was firing off a large weapon. Pyra yelped in surprise as another shot fell close to her head. Her arm loosened for a mere second, but it was all Elise needed. She cut her elbow back, hitting Pyra in the stomach, then dropped down, freeing herself from her grip. Elise rolled forward and quickly jumped back up to her feet, twisting around to face Pyra head-on. The woman snarled at her and was about to charge when another flash of light followed by a spark of fire cut into the ground between them. Elise looked up and saw from the roof entrance above, one of the hunters—the lygin, Silfres—sporting a long, two-handed weapon. Beside him was another of the hunters— the golden woman, Jazlin. With incredible cat-like reflexes, she climbed down one side of the roof, dropping on a stack of equipment. As soon as she was back on her feet, she brought out one of her knives and jumped on a group of men firing at a pair of soldiers.

Elise turned back to Pyra, who glared at her from the wall of flames between them. Letting out a furious growl, she leapt over the flames toward Elise. Elise jumped back and dodged her first attack. Though the woman was missing part of her hand, she was relentless, striking fast and hard. She forced Elise back, trying to pin here against a wall, but Elise wasn't going to let the bitch get a hold of her again. She swerved to the side and made her movements fluid and quick, remembering what Nezka had taught her. As Pyra came at her again, Elise blocked her attempt at a blow to the head then slid to one side and struck the side of her face. Pyra took the hit and slammed her foot into Elise's stomach, making her fly back. Elise rolled on the ground, feeling the wind knock out of her. She lay on her side, feeling something sharp dig into her hip. When she sat up, she found a shard of metal from the broken door underneath her. She grasped it in hand just as Pyra came for her again. As the woman went to kick her down, Elise stabbed the sharp metal into the exposed underside of Pyra's leg.

Pyra fell to one knee with a yowl. She went to grab at Elise's throat but found she couldn't with her severed hand. Elise shoved her arm away and pushed off to tackle her to the ground. As Pyra's back hit the floor, Elise brought her fist down, smashing it into her face. Pyra went limp, her eyes rolling back, head dropping to the side.

Realizing Pyra wasn't going to get back up, Elise slid off her and rose to her feet. She looked down at the woman then lifted her head up in time to see the ship roaring to life. It floated up several feet then turned slowly toward the side of the warehouse where Nezka and the vrisha still fought. Nezka was bleeding now from several places, and the vrisha was attempting to back him into a corner. A burst of blue fire shot out from the ship's front, firing toward them.

"No!" Elise cried out.

Fire exploded along one side, causing stacks of shelves to come crashing down with Nezka and the vrisha between them. Elise cried out again and started forward, but Bruce and Reese blocked her way.

"Elise, we have to go!" Reese screamed in her ear over the roar of the engine. They tugged her toward the ship which still hovered close enough to the ground that they could climb onto the ramp. Pyra's men lay around them as did a few of the drogin soldiers. From back at the opposite end of the warehouse Elise caught Jazlin taking out the last group of Red Blades. As Elise made it around to the ship's backside she saw from the entrance the rest of her team helping the Grayhart men and women, along with Lo and the other surviving drogin, into seats. Elise halted beside the ramp as Bruce and Reese climbed aboard.

Heart dropping to her stomach, Elise turned back, searching frantically. She found herself stepping farther away from the ship as she searched the rubble of shelves and growing flames. Her eyes traveled downward, and she froze as she found Nezka freeing himself from underneath a collapsed shelf. Letting out a small breath of relief, she ran to him, making it over to him as he righted himself. She grasped his arm, and he tensed in surprise then quickly pulled her close.

"I believe you now," she said against him. Elise pulled back a little to look up at him. "Take us home."

Nezka dropped his forehead to hers then grabbed her firmly and led her back to the ship. Jazlin was there now. She gave Elise a tight frown before looking to Nezka.

"There are more coming. Me and Silfres saw them approaching from above," she said. "Someone must have called on reinforcements from the gates. Silfres has volunteered to stay behind to keep them at bay. We need to go."

Nezka signaled for her to get on the ship. Jazlin did so reluctantly. Elise tugged at Nezka's arm, pulling at him to follow her up the ramp. As he moved to enter the ship with her, he stopped suddenly and look back across to the pile of broken shelves. Elise followed his gaze and saw the vrisha climbing out from underneath. The alien freed himself and came at them, only to be tugged back suddenly, as if something still caught at him. He looked back and saw his tail caught under the rubble. The scene might have been amusing at some other time but now only brought on a wave of panic. Any second, he would tug himself loose and come for them.

Nezka looked back at Elise and, in a split moment, kissed her hard on the mouth then forced one of his blades into her hand.

"Be free," he said.

Before she could open her mouth, he took hold of her waist and threw her back into the ship entrance. Elise landed on her side, Nezka's blade nearly slipping from her hand as she slid against someone's feet. She let out a shout of surprise and climbed back to her feet, lunging forward. Before she could run down the ramp, someone had a hold of her.

"Nezka!" she screamed. She saw him outside the ship. The vrisha had freed himself and was now coming for him. She saw nothing more as the ship turned slightly to one side and began to rise. The ramp lifted up, and the door started to close. Elise struggled against whoever kept hold of her, calling out. But before she could rip herself free, the ship jolted upward and flew out of the warehouse. Whoever had her let her go, and she scrambled over to the front window of the pilot's seat.

Down below, the warehouse grew smaller as smoke billowed from the top and fire licked the sides. Elise turned to Vijnn. "We have to go back. Turn back," she snapped.

"No," Vijnn replied in a firm but sad tone. "We can't go back."

"We have to return for him, we have to—"

The ship shook as a loud boom followed by a blinding orange light hit them from below. Elise nearly fell as Vijnn swerved the ship to the side then continued to ascend past the bridges and trams of the high city. Elise turned back to the window and saw the warehouse roof was now engulfed in flames. Smoke and embers rose into the air.

The energy deposit was gone.

CHAPTER TWENTY-SIX

Elise wiped away the steam on the mirror. She stood still, watching her reflection with an acute interest. From the outer room, she could hear soft voices coming from the TV, a woman and a man talking. She took a towel from the rack and dried out her hair then combed it thoroughly as she listened to them. Another congressional debate about the outer systems and need for more military aid; faster ships, better weapons, more men. She'd heard it all many times. War seemed imminent. Especially now, with the discovery of hostile empires and new, untrustworthy races.

As she leaned forward, she stared hard at her face. She lifted her hand slowly to the tiniest scar across her cheek then dropped her hand with a sigh. The eyes that looked back seemed hardened. Sad.

Eleven months. Twenty-nine days. Twelve hours. Forty-three minutes.

Elise bent her head, letting her hair spill around her face. She tapped at the heating system on the wall, bathing the room in a warm orange light. Despite the heat filling the room, she still felt cold. She closed her eyes briefly, letting herself drift away just for a moment before a soft ring went off in the other room. Elise opened her eyes, put on a robe, and left the bathroom, walking out into the central common room. From a wide-open screen door, the distant roar of waves could be heard. Elise zipped over to the couch where her phone was ringing and looked down to see who was calling. Her lip curled up to one side, and she tapped on the screen.

"Elise, you still in your room? 'Cause I got a bottle of Jameson with your name on it."

Jerico.

Elise smirked. "I just took a shower. Just need to dress," she replied.

"All right. Mind if I come up in a bit? We can have a drink before the party starts."

"Of course, give me ten." Elise tapped the screen and left the common room for her bedroom. She took out a simple black sundress and de-robed. Pulling the dress on, she smoothed it out till it touched her ankles. The dress hugged her waist and hips and showed the curve of her breasts in a low v-neck. She never got many chances to wear dresses before or during her service as an operative, but now, it seemed she was wearing a new one every other month. With all the ceremonies and parties and even interviews, she'd become accustomed to them.

Thankfully, the sundress just might be her last for a while. One last celebration. Just her and the team before they parted.

Elise looked around the bedroom of her temporary quarters. Her eyes fell on the small drawer at the side of the bed. She crossed over and slowly opened it, reaching her hand in and taking out a leather sheath. She unclasped it then drew out the blade and gripped it firmly in hand. Nezka's blade shined a dark silvery black with a tinge of purple. It always took her breath away every time she held it. Its handle was smooth and warm while the sharp blade was almost rough, as if she could cut herself just by trailing her finger along the side. It had a weight to it, yet it was light at the same time, and its balance was near perfect. Most of the time, she just enjoyed holding it, but every so often, she would go by the water when no one was around and practice with it, throwing it at one of the 'low tide' signs. She couldn't bring it back to her like Nezka could, of course, but her aim was getting better.

She had the leather sheath made for the blade around month two, when she feared losing it. She kept it on her person, usually on her hip. Some would ask about it, and she would only say that it was given to her by a friend. Her team knew better. At least a couple of them had seen her and Nezka kiss by the entrance of the ship the day they escaped. The rest had witnessed her cry for him—the first time on the ship back to the city station and a second time when they landed back on a home base. They knew. And those who didn't were most definitely informed.

But she never said a word to them about it. She let her team talk, let them eye her with concern, but she never mentioned what happened; never said why she was so possessive of the blade, why she had to be alone sometimes. She just let them think what they liked.

Elise turned the blade in hand. It was the last piece of him she had left.

It was funny how things could change so quickly after one life-altering event. She felt different, even thought she looked different sometimes. She had somehow become calmer, less prone to anger, her features softened, though her eyes said the opposite. Maybe it was because she didn't clench her jaw so much anymore or tense up as if ready for a fight.

Even her dreams had changed. The dark memories she once had no longer seemed to weigh heavily on her mind. She no longer dreamt of the jungle or even of her sister much. Though she still thought of her from time to time, her sister was no longer the largest holder of her thoughts. That award now went to the original owner of the blade in her hand.

Elise sheathed the blade carefully and set it back in the drawer, shutting it closed. As she turned away, she heard a knock at her door.

Moving back into the common room, she slipped over to the door and opened it. Jerico's smiling face greeted her.

"You look great, Stirling," he said. He wore a dark blue suit and carried a bottle of whiskey and two glasses in his hands. Elise let him inside and closed the door.

They sat down on the couch as Jerico poured her a drink.

"Things are gonna get pretty major here soon," Jerico said, glancing up at the TV monitor on the wall. "Now that everything's out in the open. Just hope they don't plan to go to Xolis first to start anything. If we can avoid a war, we should."

"It would certainly be a bad idea," Elise said, taking the glass Jerico offered her. Jerico poured his drink then clinked his glass against hers.

"Here's to the team. Hope they find a little peace, wherever they go." Jerico took a drink, and Elise did the same. They sat for a moment in silence until Jerico gazed over at her. "So, I know what everyone else's got planned for their retirement. Some are going back to their families, some are returning to Earth, others are traveling to the next civilian world...but I still don't know what you have planned, Stirling."

Elise shrugged, taking another drink. Even she hadn't fully thought about it. She didn't want to go back to her father's ranch. Honestly, she didn't want to go back to Earth at all. She thought about just staying on the civilian world they were on now. Its ocean, though not as beautiful as Earth's, was at least something enjoyable to look at.

At one point, she had even thought about working for Grayhart. Becoming part of a security team. Now that they were more aware that the teams would need protection on their journeys, Sia and her sister agreed to start hiring soldiers to go on missions with the engineers and scientists. She could travel to outer worlds, maybe even find Nezka's kin if there were even any around. He had claimed to be the only one of his kind left, but Elise still couldn't believe it. They could be out there.

Of course, she didn't know what she would even do if she did find them, except maybe show them Nezka's blade and tell them how he had helped save her and the others. But even with that unlikely scenario, the chance to travel on a Grayhart ship at the moment was, in fact, not an option. Not with the danger of those still looking to trade humans to Xolis and the fear that empire presented. She learned all about the nillium and their want of human women. She'd learned about the girls that had escaped from Xolis and the men who hadn't. And of course, she knew about the bounty. There were likely other hunters out there searching for them.

So, as much as she would have liked to travel outside the governed systems, she had no way of doing so.

"I'm just going to take it one day at a time," Elise said. "What about you?"

Jerico reclined back. "Probably gonna start teaching self-defense and join a fighting league." He tapped on his leg, and it made a hard clinking noise. "Want to see what this bad boy can do."

"The new leg has been working well for you so far, huh?"

Jerico lifted his pant leg and revealed a thick metal calve. "The drogin have some impressive tech. Just glad they are still on our side."

"Me too," Elise said. She remembered when they had landed back on the station after leaving the energy deposit. There was some major concern at first, seeing as one of their head officials was working for Pyra. They had prepared to fight as soon as the ship grounded but, to their relief, were met with a crowd of drogin waiting to give their aid and support. It was there she learned that Councilman Qorey had disappeared, likely off the planet itself, when he learned the deposit had been compromised and that the new officials in charge were from a separate sector. After suspicions arose and investigations were under way after the attack on the gate, the drogin officials were looking to imprison any who were caught aiding the Red Blades. They had considered taking the remaining hunters into custody as well when Vijnn and Jazlin confessed they were in on the plot to trade the humans, but Elise convinced the officials to let them go and reward them their bounty for helping to take out the Red Blades and their leader. After that, the pair disappeared, never to be seen again.

The return to the station had also led to the discovery of Adrien and Jerico's survival. She remembered when they first reunited, seeing Jerico with his new leg and Adrien beside him had been the first real joy she had felt since their escape. Soldiers who had survived the attack had found them and brought them to the nearest medical center. They spent the whole of the mission recovering. Jerico claimed he was rather pissed about missing the whole thing, but Elise didn't believe him.

"I'm glad the drogin were there to help us. And I'm glad everyone got out, even if not entirely in one piece," he said, smiling. His smile faded as he took another sip of his drink and studied her. "You were real brave trying to save the others, Stirling. I know...I know it's hard for you to tell us what happened to you. Down in the undercity."

Elise drew her eyes away from his to look out the screen door across from them to the body of water beyond. Elise took one sip of her drink then stood, walking over to the open doorway. A soft breeze caught in her hair. There was no sense in not telling him, and if he wanted to judge her, so be it. Her feelings wouldn't change.

"I was with him the whole time... the head hunter, Nezka," she said. "He saved me from the gate collapse. He healed me. It was just him and me the whole way. I got to know him, and he taught me how to be a better fighter. I started to see him differently." Elise looked down at her glass. "He had been assigned to take us back to Xolis. I didn't find out until later. I thought he had betrayed us, but at the very end, he changed. He did that for me." Elise turned to Jerico, who was watching her carefully." And I wanted to be with him. I still do." Her throat tightened. "But all I have left is his blade. If he were here now, do you know what I would do?" She walked back over to stand in front of her friend and teammate and met his gaze. "I would go with him. Even if it meant never coming back here or returning to Earth. I would go with him and never leave his side."

Jerico stared up at her with a deep frown. He placed his glass beside him and reached out for her. Elise took his hands as he rose from his seat. He nodded slowly then pulled her to him. He hugged her tight, and Elise did the same.

* * *

The party consisted of her team sitting down by the outside bar in a central courtyard and drinking till sundown. Amy and Helen wore sundresses and hats, and the men wore suits. They drank and talked as the sun fell in the sky. Usually, a party at a bar would start later in the day, but half of the team's flights were in the early morning, and they wanted to have time to prepare. Elise sat by and watched them, smiling and laughing. She was there with them, but her mind wasn't. She would miss them, it was true, but she couldn't think of anything but what was going to happen after they left. She supposed she'd go down by the beach and just sit there watching the waves.

Adrien came to sit by her, placing his arm over the back of her chair. "I've decided that you're second in command of the team. Jerico has willingly stepped down."

Elise snorted, shaking her head. "A little late for that."

Adrien smiled. "Who knows, with a war possibly starting, they might need us again after all."

Elise knew he was half-joking, but she couldn't bring herself to even smile. "I think I've had enough fighting for a while."

Adrien nodded. "I can understand that." He placed a hand on her shoulder. "But you'd be the best. Just know that. I'm proud of you, Stirling."

Elise gave him a little smile. "I will miss everyone."

Adrien patted her on the back. They talked till the sun could no longer be seen over the top of the buildings, then everyone started to head away from the bar back into the complex.

"I'm beat," said Tom. "I'll see some of you tomorrow."

"I'm calling it too," said Amy. "Got a long flight in the morning."

The others agreed. As they went their separate ways back to their own rooms, Elise said goodnight to each before returning to her own.

As she slipped inside the now dark room, she noticed she had left the screen door open. She walked over to shut it but then stopped to watch the sun set over the water. Loneliness overtook her. Like a child needing her comfort toy, Elise went to the bedroom and over to the drawer to take out Nezka's blade one more time. As she opened the drawer, she found it empty.

Panic rose and she looked around the drawer and underneath, thinking it might have dropped out, but found nothing. She checked the bed then under it. She flung the drawer aside, spilling the contents, but still, there was nothing. Her panic grew worse, and she began to fling objects and furniture around the room in her desperate search. When she looked in every possible place within her bedroom, she went into the common room to search some more then froze to peer back at the screen door.

"No," she said softly.

She rushed for the door and flew out onto the deck, searching high and low, left and right, but didn't see a single person. Someone must have seen the open door and went inside. They must have found the blade.

She ran off the deck and went out onto the beach, the wind whipping her hair into her face. She swatted it away and searched again but found no sign of anyone walking along in any direction. She turned back to the complex and saw a set of cameras along the roof. If she called security, they could check the feed.

Elise started back for her room, determined to kill whoever took it. She had to get it back, she had to...

"Starling."

Elise froze, her heart skipping a beat. She was hallucinating. That was all. From the panic.

She turned. The sun, bright in her face, made her shield her eyes. She saw a shadow by the water but couldn't make out who it was. The shadow moved, coming toward her.

"Who is it?" She didn't move. The shadow blocked the light from her face, and she saw, instead, twin fires looking back at her. Yes, she must be hallucinating.

"You're not really here. I'm having a panic attack, and you're not really here," Elise said. as if it were a fact.

Nezka smiled. The skin on his face and arms showed swirls of purple and white, the scars no longer identifiable from one another. It reminded her of galaxies colliding in deep space. "Do you doubt me still?" he said.

Elise shook her head, and a sob escaped her lips. Hallucination or no, she went to him. When her body met with his, she let out a soft cry of shock and joy. He was as solid as the ground under her feet, as the trees swaying nearby. She clung to him and thought she'd never let go. When he gently released her, she shook her head again and smiled. "How? How are you here? How did you find me?"

"I've not been called the best hunter in all the systems for no reason." He lifted his hand, and in it, was her leather sheath with his blade still inside. "I feel its energy." He lowered his hand then lifted his other to brush his knuckles softly against her cheek. "What is a part of me can always be found."

Elise trembled. She wrapped her arms around his neck and brought him to her, touching her lips to his. He wrapped his arms around her waist and kissed her back. When he released her again, Elise touched the side of his face where the new scars melded together.

"How did you get out?" she asked. "How did you survive?"

"I barely did. But it's a long story."

"Tell me."

"It would be better to tell you while we are on my ship."

Elise gave him a confused looked. "Your ship?"

"How else do you think I got here?" He grinned.

Elise looked down one coast and then the other. "I see no ship."

"I hid it, obviously."

Elise looked back at him. "You want me to come with you?"

Nezka tilted his head. He drew a hand up to his ear and tapped it. "Obviously."

"Where?"

"I have a few places in mind." He looked over to the ocean before them. "Somewhere even better than here." He turned back to her. "What do you say, Starling? I taught you how to better fight. Care to teach me how to better swim?"

Elise smiled. "I think I can do that." She locked eyes with his and found the fires within to be more brilliant than before. Perhaps they weren't fires. More like twin suns. The color just like the setting sun before them.

And they were beautiful.

ABOUT THE AUTHOR

Olivia Riley loves the frightening possibilities of deep space, where dark heroes and brave heroines reside. She is also a gamer and film nut.

Instagram: oliviarileyauthor

Facebook: OlivaRileySFR